Your Friendly Neighborhood Criminal

Your Friendly Neighborhood Criminal

Michael Van Rooy

Minotaur Books

A Thomas Dunne Book
New York

A THOMAS DUNNE BOOK FOR MINOTAUR BOOKS.
An imprint of St. Martin's Publishing Group.

YOUR FRIENDLY NEIGHBORHOOD CRIMINAL. Copyright © 2008 by Michael Van Rooy. All rights reserved. Printed in the United States of America. For information, address St. Martin's Press, 175 Fifth Avenue, New York, N.Y. 10010.

www.thomasdunnebooks.com
www.minotaurbooks.com

Library of Congress Cataloging-in-Publication Data

Van Rooy, Michael, 1968–
    Your friendly neighborhood criminal / Michael Van Rooy.—
1st U.S. ed.
        p. cm.
    ISBN 978-0-312-60630-5
    1. Ex-convicts—Fiction. 2. Human smuggling—Fiction.
3. Refugees—Fiction. 4. Drug dealers—Fiction. I. Title.
    PR9199.4.V3656Y68 2011
    813'.6—dc22

                                                    2011008786

First published in Canada by Ravenstone, an imprint of Turnstone Press

First U.S. Edition: July 2011

10 9 8 7 6 5 4 3 2 1

In memory of Don Dewar, a gentle man and a gentleman.

And

To Laura, always.

Your Friendly Neighborhood Criminal

#1

It was not my fault. I swear to whatever God you want to name. It was not my fault. It was November in Winnipeg and I was not looking for trouble. I was limping around with a cane. I was in pretty rough shape overall with assorted ill-healed holes in my hide and the beginnings of the flu from hell.

I was not looking for trouble. I want to emphasize that.

I limped, hacking loudly, into the Entegra Credit Union on Selkirk Avenue in the North End about five minutes after it had opened, just in time to stand at the end of a long line of blue-collar retirees and middle-aged housewives. My wife, Claire, had stayed home from work to let me open my very own bank account and I was enjoying not babysitting, which was how I was currently earning my living. Not that the kids were that bad, they were just very, very, well ... bad.

After ten minutes I finally reached the teller. "I need a savings account, one that I can access through the automated tellers."

She stared at my bruised face and looked away. "Sure."

"I also need some deposit slips. There's nothing on the table over there."

The girl, whose name tag read EILEEN, was maybe twenty-five and pretty with black hair and dark blue eyes. She smiled with some condescension as she answered, "We haven't had those for five years at least, maybe longer."

She took the information form I'd filled out along with my social insurance card, my Manitoba Medical card and a piece of photo ID, in my case a Manitoba Liquor Control Commission card (cost $17, newly arrived), and $5,632 in cheques from the Manitoba Lotteries Corporation, and typed away on her computer. I'd phoned ahead of time and knew they'd run a credit check on me before I received the account, but I was sure I'd pass—ex-cons like me didn't generally have *any* credit rating, good or ill.

I was standing there with my cane hung on the counter when the robbers walked in.

Bang!

I turned around slowly to see two guys in the lobby behind me, one with a rifle and one with a pistol. They were both wearing rubber masks of Brian Mulroney, Canada's least loved prime minister. All of a sudden I was feeling every injury, bruise, and hole in my hide.

"NO ONE MOVE!"

Both robbers were painfully thin—drug thin—and wearing jean jackets and canvas gardening gloves. Both vibrated with adrenaline and, maybe, chemical speed. Not a good combination for anyone.

"THIS IS A ROBBERY!"

No shit.

A curl of smoke was coming from the barrel and breech of the rifle held by Mulroney Number One. It spiralled to the ceiling while he fumbled in his jacket to fish out a pillowcase with its mouth held open by a bent coat hanger. This meant he was the cash man, which meant that Mulroney Number Two was ...

"WHAT ARE YOU SMILING AT?"

... crowd control, and since the crowd consisted mostly of older people and me, he chose me. He took four fast steps and rammed the pistol barrel into my chest.

"I'm not smiling."

And I wasn't. These guys were amateurs, which made them dangerous. Amateurs are always worse than pros. Pros will kill you but they'll generally do it on purpose. Amateurs, however, can kill you by mistake as well as on purpose. Everything they did screamed that they were amateurs. Like the way that Mulroney Number Two was poking me with the pistol. You never, ever, touch someone with your gun. Touching someone with your gun makes it easy for whoever is being threatened to take the weapon away from you.

"WISE ASS!"

He screamed assorted obscenities at me and I could smell rye whiskey on his breath, which was a second mistake; never drink before work. Mulroney Number Two backed away and swung the pistol at the tellers. Mulroney Number One started to work the cashiers. Mulroney Number one was holding a lever-action rifle with the barrel cut right down to the top of the tubular magazine and the stock crudely shaped into a pistol grip. He waved the gun around and I saw the barrel width and guessed it was a .22 or a .32, a pretty small calibre. That was good and bad. Good because the hole it would make would be small. Bad because it meant that the magazine could carry a lot more rounds. Also bad because it meant the recoil would be lessened, which would mean Mulroney Number One could shoot more often and more accurately. I realized I hadn't heard or seen him work the action, which meant the hammer was sitting on a spent shell.

That would be the third mistake the Mulroneys made and *that* is another reason why none of it was my fault.

I shouldn't have been surprised. A bank robbery occurs every fifty-six minutes across North America, so the odds catch up with you eventually. That's like 9000 a year, each netting an average of two grand Canadian, which made for a lot of loot changing hands.

Of course generally I was the one doing the robbing. In the good old days when that was my business. Nowadays I don't do that.

Mulroney Number Two was standing there in the middle of the marble-floored lobby waving his gun around. It was a revolver, an old one with most of the bluing gone from the barrel and with the kind of forward-leaning lines that made me think it was single action. Single action meant that the hammer had to be pulled back to full cock before each shot. Double action meant pulling the trigger would cock the gun for you.

One teller had dumped handfuls of bills into the pillowcase and Mulroney number one bellowed, "THE COINS TOO! NOW!"

This was embarrassing. No one takes the coins—they're too heavy and too hard to dispose of, unless you own a pool hall. And, really, why make it any easier for the cops, who have a 70 percent clearance rate on bank robberies in the first place? Of course the clearance rate was little comfort for the banks because only 30 percent of the loot is ever recovered. The rest goes to broads, booze, and blow. And if the police captured the loot then some of it sometimes went for the occasional subsidized police vacation in Cancun.

"ARE YOU FUCKING SMILING AT ME? ARE YOU?"

It was Mulroney Number Two. The hammer was still down on his revolver and again he was pushing it into my chest and I was feeling pretty sore from assorted injuries.

"No sir." With all that pain I had no problem putting a quaver into my voice.

It didn't help and he slapped the barrel of the gun into my temple. Everything went dim and hazy and I barely stopped myself from falling. I reached up and touched the edges of the hole and it became wet. Blood welled down the side of my face and the pain blossomed and I just stood there.

The bright red blood and the open flower of a wound seemed to satisfy the robber and he walked away to yell at other people. A metre and a half away a plump white lady shook her head and muttered something in Ukrainian or Polish. Other than that the crowd was silent and I watched the robbers work. I tried not to think and my mind wandered. The most popular day to rob a bank is Friday and the second is Monday and the most popular time to do it is in the first two hours of opening. And more robberies occur in California and Florida in the States and Ontario and British Columbia in Canada. Vancouver is the bank-robbery capital of Canada. Go figure. The weather, I guess. In the States the robbery capital is Atlanta. I blame that on the Coca-Cola bottling plant and CNN.

Another teller was handing over her bills and coins. That left only one teller and then this would all be over. Then I could go home and find out how big the hole in my head actually was. Maybe it would earn me a little sympathy sex from my wife Claire. Maybe I could go back to healing from my own errors. Then I heard sirens and that made me flinch. These were amateurs in front of me and amateurs panicked when the cops showed up. And panicking amateurs might freak out, take hostages, or start shooting. All of those options would be bad.

To top it all off I knew Claire would never, ever, let me hear the end of it if I survived. All of which meant that I had no choice at all when I called out, "Hey, asshole, yeah, you."

Mulroney Number Two twitched like I'd slapped him and strode over to me. He paused and jammed the gun barrel into the centre of my chest. He still hadn't pulled the hammer to where it was supposed to be.

"WHAT DID YOU SAY?"

"I was just calling you an asshole, asshole."

I wondered if I was right. I wondered if the gun *was* single action. If not I was deeply and truly fucked.

Mulroney Number Two sputtered and pulled the trigger but I was right, the gun was single action. Nothing happened. While he was trying to figure out what was going wrong I grabbed the gun with my right hand and twisted it down with the barrel pointing towards his belly. The sound of his finger breaking was loud and his scream was louder. A few metres away Mulroney Number One dropped the pillowcase and raised the rifle with both hands.

I wasn't hurrying. Never rush these things. There's a rhythm to it all.

My left hand went to the centre of Mulroney Number Two's chest and pushed hard and I jammed my right foot down onto his to pin it in place. He was overbalanced and fell backwards slowly as I kept my weight on his foot. He fell and the weight of his own body tore the muscles and bones loose and turned his ankle into shredded meat. That made him scream even more and his voice filled the credit union like water pouring into a fishbowl.

Two metres away Mulroney Number One pulled the trigger

of his rifle but nothing happened and that gave me time to flip the pistol around and pull the hammer back through half-cock to full cock.

"Stop."

He did.

"Gun down."

The big question. The big chance. The thousand-dollar question. If he tried to work the lever I'd empty my gun into his narrow chest, but it was his choice.

The gun went down.

"Arms up."

His arms went up and the doorway filled with blue uniforms, black leather belts, anodized steel, white skin, and maybe a half metre of moustaches and about two square metres of bald skulls. I had the pistol pointed at the ceiling and I put it down on the ground. I did it all very slowly and I did it staring into the barrels of eight semi-automatic pistols held by eight stressed cops.

I sighed as I sank to my knees and said loudly, "This is not my fault."

#2

Early September, two months before.

Claire and I were walking up the front walkway of a tidy two-story brick house about six blocks from our place. "And why does your renter want to speak with me?" I asked my wife as I fiddled with the collar of my shirt. Finally I gave up and undid an extra button.

"No idea."

My wife is beautiful. She's a little shorter than me, 5'9" and about 140 pounds with long reddish hair and dark brown eyes that develop green tints when she is really angry. She also looked muy sexy in a dark blue sweater and skirt and the side of her breast rubbed pleasantly against my arm as we walked. Before we reached the front door it was opened by a middle-aged woman with greying-blond hair cut about an inch long and slightly slanted blue eyes. At a guess I put her height at 5'4" and her weight at around 100 pounds.

"Good afternoon, Claire, Mr. Haaviko."

She held her hand out and I shook it. "Call me Monty."

She smiled in a meaningless fashion and showed us both into a small room with no furniture. On the floor were heavy oblong carpets covered in brilliant, bright designs and piles of small round cushions. There was a woman in the corner of the room wearing a rich blue dress that covered her feet and pooled like water. She was sitting in front of a hibachi set out on a thick piece of grey-veined marble.

"I'm Marie Blue Duck. Please come in." Our host stepped aside.

"Thank you." Claire's murmur was polite and non-committal. Nothing else.

Marie went over to the figure by the hibachi. "This is my friend Eloise. She does not speak English so please do not be offended if she does not speak during our conversation."

Claire looked puzzled and we took cautious seats on the cushions. Marie sat down gracefully and looked at me. "You're wondering about my last name?"

"Not really." I was being polite. I wanted to scream 'Why do you want to talk to me?' but I didn't.

"I'll tell you anyway. My first husband was a Mohawk, a wonderful man. I kept his name after we parted ways, it's such a wonderful name, don't you think?"

I agreed and asked her what she did and she just smiled. After a second she quietly said, "I help people."

Her words made me pause and look at her more closely. She had the angled perversity of a hard-core believer and I started to become worried. I'd seen it before in the faces of social workers, white supremacists, parole officers, black supremacists, religious leaders, Jewish supremacists, drug dealers, and Muslim supremacists. I'd seen it before endlessly in the faces of people who wanted to convince me to do something or not to do something and it left me cold. With nothing to say I complimented her on the home. "You have a beautiful house."

"Your wife rented it to us. It's perfect for our needs, two storeys with finished basement and attached garage."

Her hands drummed briefly on her thighs and then she turned awkwardly and presented her profile to me while she talked to Claire. "I want to hire your husband."

Her vocabulary was educated and her tone was calm but it still startled me. "Me? Are you sure you're talking to the right person?"

"You are Monty Haaviko. Ex-thief, ex-burglar, ex-armed robber, ex-smuggler, ex-drug dealer ..." She sounded mostly amused and a brief smile ghosted across her face as I answered, "That's me."

Marie held up her hand politely. "Ahwah comes first. That's Turkish coffee. After that we can talk." Eloise at the brazier worked with small, brisk motions and dumped a handful of glossy brown beans into a small iron skillet, where they were quickly roasted. When they were done she used a blackened wooden dowel to crush them to a very coarse powder which she scooped into a brass pot with a long handle. That went back onto the brazier along with a little water from a plastic bottle and a piece of crystallized sugar.

When the brew came to a boil Eloise took it from the brazier using the long handle, unceremoniously dropped two green-ish-coloured things into the pot, and then put it back to heat. Claire looked at Marie and raised an eyebrow when she answered the implied question. "Cardamom pods for flavour."

When the pot boiled again Eloise picked it up carefully, took spoonfuls of froth from the pot, and placed them into three tiny steel cups. When the pot boiled a third time she picked it up, added more water, and then filled the cups with the thickened brew. Marie handed me and Claire cups and I drank the best coffee I'd ever had, sweet and strong and exquisite.

"Good?" She seemed genuinely concerned and interested.

"Very." Eloise tidied up and Marie faced me again. "I'll be direct. I bring people into Canada and the United States who cannot make it into the country any other way."

I put the cup down. "You smuggle them?"

"Yes. I help the hopeless and the dispossessed and I will pay you $5000 to help me. Five thousand dollars for one week's work."

Claire looked at me and squeezed my hand but I already had an answer. It wasn't the one Marie wanted but so it goes. "No."

"Why?" She was calm, very calm, and Eloise was looking down into her lap as I answered.

"Five thousand is too much money for you to pay me to do something even remotely legal. This means you want me to do something illegal. I do not want to do anything illegal. So the answer is no."

"Illegal? Does that bother you?"

That was a stupid question but I answered it anyway. "Illegal doesn't bother me. Being caught does. Prison bothers me, arrest bothers me."

"Even if it's for a good cause?"

"What is a good cause?"

"Let me put a face on what I deal with ... maybe that will help. Eloise was from Vietnam. She fled when she was twelve by boat, her family was Muslim." Behind the veil the woman kept her face averted.

"I see ..."

"Do you?" Marie's face was blank. "She had a brother, a

13

father, and two sisters when they left by boat. That first night they were attacked by Communists. They took everything of value and raped the women, the girls, and some of the boys. The next night fishermen found them and that happened the next night, and night after night. The fishermen would board, steal whatever they could find, rape whomever they chose, and leave. Within eighteen days the brother was eaten after a lottery, the father went mad and was drowned by the survivors, one sister hemorrhaged to death after being raped by Thai fishermen, the other vanished during a storm. They were rescued by the Red Cross and put into an internment camp in Thailand. And things became worse."

Eloise understood something and made a low noise in her throat and I looked at Claire and she looked at me. Marie cleared her throat and smiled serenely. "When my friends rescued her from the camp Eloise weighed seventy-three pounds and was dying of cholera. She was so weak she couldn't kill herself."

Marie looked at Eloise and her smile dipped and vanished. "No one should have to do any of that. Ever. Not just because they want to go somewhere else. Does her story help you change your mind?"

I smiled too and it was not a nice smile but Marie didn't know that. Claire did and frowned as I asked, "What exactly is it that you want me to do?"

"Help us set up the smuggling operation. Help us run it right. You can stay on the Canadian side and walk away at the end. I and my friend will be the only ones who know who you are. Simple enough, yes?"

"Next time, Tim Horton's or Starbucks will be fine. Because this ..." I gestured at the room. "This all makes me feel manipulated. Blackmailed."

Marie frowned and looked ten or twenty years older and I waited for her to say anything. When she didn't I went on. "And my response to blackmail is ingrained. And neither of us would like it. So I'm going to walk out and think for awhile. I'll talk it over with Claire and decide."

"I understand." She bit her lip hard and her brow furrowed. She was trying to understand. "I won't do it again."

When Claire and I were standing Marie spoke in a bantering tone: "Out of curiosity. Just what is your response to blackmail?"

I didn't smile. "I hurt you. I hurt you badly enough so you remember it forever. I burn down your house. I take an electric drill to your kneecaps. I blow up your workplace. Memorable shit like that." I gave her space and time to respond but she had nothing to say to that so I went on. "Claire and I are going to take a walk and when I'm not angry anymore we'll come back. Then we can talk and you can tell me what you want and I can answer."

We left.

#3

Outside Claire wrapped her fingers in mine and led me down the walk and towards the river. The night was warm but the wind was cool and every few minutes there would be a gust that made the drifts of leaves on the ground dance. After a few hundred metres I spoke up. "So we have to talk about this?"

"Yep."

"Right. We could use the money; it would make a difference in our lives. But I don't want to break the law."

"Bullshit, try again." Claire said it without turning.

"'Kay. I don't want to get caught."

"Better."

We walked down Cathedral Street and crossed Main. When we reached the Red River and the start of Scotia Street I stopped and Claire stopped with me. There were two houses that attracted me for some reason, one brightly lit and one dark. Beyond them was the river itself. The night was peaceful, serene, and I wished someone would try to rob us so I could beat the shit out of them. But nothing happened because shit like that never happens when you expect it to. If someone tried to rob me then I could take them apart and thereby make myself feel better.

So of course it didn't happen.

The truth was I did not want to think about helping Marie. I did not want to become involved. I did not want to risk anything. But the desire to work—to rob, to pillage, to move, to act—that was fucking powerful too. The urge to steal was strong in me.

The brightly lit house beckoned to me and I stood there and stared and thought dark thoughts. Equal chances. It could be a happy house with a fine father and upstanding mother, smart children, and happy pets. Or it could be a home of a pedophile father, alcoholic mother, abused and psychotic children, and vicious animals.

Black or white.

Right or wrong.

Pick one. Take your chances. Put your money down.

The rage at the attempted blackmail left along with the pain and only the two houses were left and beyond them, the river.

"Five grand is a lot of cash." When Claire spoke her voice was very thoughtful.

"It is." I agreed with her but kept my voice level.

"We're doing okay. But five grand would make things better. And it wouldn't be so bad if all you have to do is set the whole thing up and not break any laws on your own. Fifteen hundred and change would pay for a real estate licence. That would put me in the way of some serious cash further down the road. I could broker houses then and pull in a percentage instead of a salary."

"True?" I was listening carefully and my voice was still level and calm.

"True. And the rest could go into savings for when we can buy our own house." After a few seconds she added in an undertone, "Plus it's a good cause."

"Strong point."

I laced my arm into hers and we turned to go back to Marie's place. As we walked Claire leaned against my side and I whispered into her ear. "Tell you a secret; I'm starting to think that stealing is easier than being honest."

She giggled and I asked, "So what do you know about Marie?"

Claire shrugged and I watched her chest out of the corner of my eye. "Stop looking at my boobs."

"I thought you'd be flattered."

"I am. I don't know much about Marie. I think she is educated and determined and used to speaking to people and convincing them to do things. I'm starting to believe she rented the house from me because of you."

"So she's smart?"

"Yes. As opposed to you."

"Another strong point. What else do you know?"

Claire squeezed my arm. "Marie knew what kind of house she wanted and how much to pay. The account she uses to pay the rent belongs to an incorporated business and her references were from universities in Toronto and Prince George. The job she listed is as an executive secretary with the company that pays the rent. I can look all that up again if you want tomorrow, when I'm back at the office. Maybe there's more."

I looked at her and was impressed. "How did you find all that out?"

Claire smiled, "In business we call it 'due diligence,' making sure our client can pay their bills. I called the bank and her references."

I nodded. "Bad guys call it 'being nosy.'"

She squeezed my arm again and we kept walking.

When we were back at Marie's house the first thing I asked her was, "Why did you choose me?"

Marie thought about that question for quite a while before answering. "I'm dealing with people who are in the country illegally, that single truth overshadows everything else. I help them find jobs, arrange their papers, bring their families to them, I do whatever is necessary, but the people we help have their own special problems and are especially prone to abuse. They can't go to the police, can they? They become easy prey to everyone."

Claire was sipping more ahwah and answered. "Sure."

Marie gave her a wide smile. "Glad you agree. I thought it made sense. Then I thought that if I can't find a good guy to help me, maybe I could find a bad one."

She turned to me. "Which is you. You've smuggled."

It wasn't a question but I answered it like it had been one to give me time. "Sure I've smuggled. Jamaican marijuana from Montego Bay, Brazilian pistols from Imbituba, French paintings from Tokyo, Russian vodka from Vladivostok, North Carolina cigarettes through the Akwesasne reserve, classic cars from Cuba, Harley Davidson motorcycles from Pennsylvania, farm-grade gasoline off the farm, Canadian CFC's to Atlanta, Inuit sculpture to Reno, Turkish hashish via Marseilles, Aztec pottery from Brownsville. So on and on and on."

"Have you ever smuggled people?" Marie seemed genuinely interested.

"No ... yes. Twice; bad guys in the States I smuggled into

19

Canada and bad guys in Canada I smuggled into the States. One-time deals only though."

She held her hands out like she was balancing something. "Smuggling humans is maybe a $30-billion-a-year industry, mostly people for the sex trade but also ordinary economic refugees, mostly from poor countries to rich ones." She started to count off on her fingers. "Forgive the lecture here but this is the best way I know how to explain it. The key transshipment countries include Spain, the Ukraine, the Balkan nations, Malaysia, Mexico, and South Africa. The key target countries are America, Canada, and the European Union, the West mostly. Wherever the smuggled and displaced settle down they slip into those societies and vanish in a generation or so."

Marie kept eye contact with me. "Except when the shipper keeps a leash on them and makes them steal or pimp or whore or gamble or become slaves; in those cases anything can and does happen."

The woman in the corner brought more ahwah. I was unused to the personal service and it distracted me as Marie kept talking. "I've heard stories of migrants forced to become prostitutes to pay for the smuggling or forced to carry drugs. I've talked to migrants who had to steal and gamble to pay for the smuggling and I've met some who were raped and tortured for fun. There are other stories of migrants murdered or sold into slavery and even being chopped up for their organs."

Claire cleared her throat. "So who does it?"

Marie shrugged. "The smuggling? Everyone. Russian Mafiya moves Russian sex-trade workers and Chinese Triads move anyone looking for the good life. The Sicilian Mafia transships workers from Africa and Asia to Europe. Scandinavian human rights organizations move refugees when the red tape becomes too thick and South American drug organizations move anyone as long as they agree to carry a little something with them. The US military smuggle ex-Nazis and ex-Communists to fight whatever they call terrorism and Saudi Arabians smuggle the poor from anywhere into their country to fill menial jobs graduates of religious studies don't want to do. People smuggling has been going on for centuries."

Marie fiddled with her cup and looked off into the distance. "In the late 1800's Chinese men working on the railroads smuggled their wives to America to live the good life. In the early 1800's Americans smuggled black slaves past British blockades to sell in New Orleans. In ancient Egypt Ethiopians were considered to be the best slaves and were smuggled despite official prohibitions up into the Nile Valley."

I looked at Claire and she at me and then she asked Marie, "What kind of people do you smuggle?"

"Anyone who is refused entry to the US or Canada. I have friends and colleagues who refer them to me from all over the place. Baku, Kinshasa, Algiers, Asmara, Yangon, other places. I have friends who work in aid groups and they give me names and other information, scrape together funds, and send the people on. They fly to Toronto on tourist visas, then other friends pick them up and truck them to here and then I help them into the States or I help them stay in this country, whatever they want. Most of them want to be in the States though."

Great, me vs. the United States and Canada. *Semper fi*, do or die! In the back of my mind the only thing I could hear were the Crash Test Dummies playing the "Superman Song." And the only thing I could feel was a profound desire for a fix, which kind of took me my surprise. Drug addicts are never really free of their habits, it just becomes a long time between fixes, so I tried not to think about it. "What kind of cross-border route do you have?"

21

Marie smiled and stirred her coffee. "A good one. Are you in?"

Claire interrupted, "Let's be straight about this. Monty will be helping you set things up on this side of the border, right? Not crossing?"

"And helping me set up the safe houses here in Manitoba, making sure they're secure. Can you do that?" Marie looked at me expectantly.

"Sure." I asked about the route again and she thought it over before answering.

"There's a First Nations band on the border with Minnesota, right on the Lake of the Woods. We move the people there and then smuggle them across the bay in small boats and up a river to where they're off-loaded."

The ahwah was cold and I finished it anyway. "Who takes over from there?"

Marie smiled and intricate patterns of wrinkles showed up beside each eye. "Some Mennonite farmers and people take them from there; they're very reliable. And very close-mouthed."

Claire asked quietly, "What about out on the water?"

"What about it?" Marie was puzzled by the question.

I put the cup down. "I've smuggled before. In Canada there's the RCMP in Manitoba and sometimes the Ontario Provincial Police cross borders. Then there's the Federal Border Services and whoever is providing policing for the band itself."

Marie dismissed everything with a wave of the hand. "The band is clear. There's only a cop there on an as-needed basis and the band is small, 200 people, and we have friends there. We just don't bring people through if the police are awake. As for the rest of them, the RCMP are stationed twenty kilometres away in the town of Sprague and don't come on the band's land unless asked. As for the Border Services, they don't have a customs post nearer than Fort Frances, a long way away."

Sounded good. "Okay, what about on the US side? Their customs service is pretty good."

"It is. And they concentrate their attention on the posts in the eastern and western parts of the country. We've done research and, frankly, they don't have a lot of resources. There's also the anti-terrorism net and that is mostly holes, the middle of the country is wide open." She was being dismissive.

I probed a little. "And the crossing is in Lake of the Woods, so that means the US Coast Guard?"

"There's nothing. The Great Lakes are controlled by the 9th Coast Guard District, which has some Minnesota bases and some cutters stationed there but they're all in the Great Lakes, none in Lake of the Woods. They're never anywhere near where we are. As for the Canadian Coast Guard, they have a post in Kenora, which is over 100 kilometres away through some really complicated waterways."

She smiled again and shrugged. "Your best bet is to let me show you. Tomorrow?"

I looked at Claire and she at me. We both shrugged at the same time and I answered, "Might as well; can't dance."

#4

Marie showed Claire and me out and we started to walk hand in hand the six blocks back home. Out of curiosity I directed us along a different, slightly circuitous, route, along streets neither of us normally frequented. About halfway home we turned down a narrow, elm-lined street that was strangely dark. That didn't slow me down much; being an ex-bad guy thug means I'm fairly confident I'm the most dangerous thing standing—at least most of the time.

Halfway down the block there were no street lights at all and sitting on the boulevard was a torn and battered chintz sofa covered in yellow floral pattern cloth. On the sofa was a Caucasian man in his early twenties with a gaunt face and deeply sunken eyes. His hands trembled in the cold and despite the weather he wore a HARD ROCK CAFÉ HONOLULU T-shirt and a pair of unlaced leather work boots—nothing else. From the nearest house came hard rock and too-much bass and glimmers of light from heavily blocked windows.

When we were close I pushed Claire a little behind me and,

when I was two yards away, the man stood up with his hands out to his sides: "Hey man, how much for your ..."

He started to laugh somewhat hysterically and changed whatever it was he was going to say. "You got money? I need something real bad."

I stopped and looked him over. "What do you need?"

"Coke man, snap-CRACK-and fucking pop!" He smiled and I saw teeth rotted black in the almost non-existent light.

He gestured towards the house the music was coming from and I turned slightly to look at a dilapidated brick two-storey house with an expanse of garbage-littered grass in front.

"Hey man, never mind." His voice was shrill, but as I turned back to the half-naked man, he lowered his voice. Then he leaned towards me before saying something that made me blush: "I got a better idea. How much for ...?"

I let him finish the question before shifting weight and kicking him squarely in the testicles. His eyes bulged out and closed and he collapsed face down slowly onto the sidewalk.

Claire looked at me with horror and I gestured with my chin at the house. "... and that, my fine and lovely wife, I believe is a crack house."

She ignored me and started forward to kneel beside the man. "Why the hell did you kick him?"

I looked around the empty streets and saw no one running so I answered. "He said something very rude."

"That's no reason to ..."

I told Claire what he had said and she stood up briskly, brushing her hands. "Well. Fine. He deserved it."

"I felt so." I took her arm again as we started away, and Claire accidentally-on-purpose managed to kick the semi-conscious man hard in the top of the head.

About a hundred yards farther on Claire asked me why I thought it was a crack house.

When I answered I did it slowly, thinking my way through my opinion. "Actually we could more correctly call it a drug house, which is where one goes to buy drugs; crack or regular cocaine, crank or crystal meth, PCP or angel dust, OxyContin or hillbilly heroin and, of course, T's and R's, also know as Talwin and Ritalin. In other words, the heavy stuff as opposed to the lighter, fluffier drugs like ecstasy, GHB, cannabis, caffeine, and nicotine."

Claire made a snorting noise and I kissed her fairly hard and then went on. "Now drug houses are similar to marijuana grow operations in several ways and can be easily identified from the outside. Both suffer from short-term visits from pedestrians and cars, increased vandalism in the area, and increased noise from fights. Both also have untidy exteriors."

Claire leaned down to pick up a leaf which she idly examined. "I know about grow ops, the cops send us real estate workers warnings all the time to keep our eyes open."

I nodded. "Sure; however, grow ops generally have residents in attendance for only brief periods of time, they don't generally allow stoned assholes to hang around. Also, grow ops have garbage like plastic sheeting, bags, and piles of dirt thrown all about outside, none of which I saw back there."

I made an encouraging noise and Claire kept talking. "And they have garages attached because that's the best way to bring in the plants. And they cover the windows with paint to hide the lights because they are on all the time. And those windows end up covered with condensation, especially if they're growing the grass hydroponically. And, lastly, the air around a grow op frequently is redolent of a skunk-like aroma, the fine bouquet of ripening cannabis sativa."

I looked over at her and was impressed. She went on. "The cops tell us that there is even a nickname down in the lovely U S of A for the grass from Winnipeg. They call it Winnipeg Wheelchair Weed because after one hoot you can't walk."

"Bravo! I didn't know that. But that house isn't a grow op."

I stared out at the night and thought about how the building had looked. It was two stories high with blank brick walls covered in bold graffiti I could barely read. Graffiti that made me think of the warnings some poisonous snakes carried, black and red friend of Fred, or however it went for Coral snakes. 'Don't Tread on Me' is what all those messages across the way boiled down to.

"Grow ops are one thing, that place is something different."

Someone would have to do something about that place.

Claire respected my silence all the way home, by which point I was both sulking and jonesing. That was a nasty and extremely selfish combo every doper recognizes as being their main state of being.

Claire looked me over. "What are you thinking about?"

"Crime."

"You're sulking. Thinking about crime does not make you sulk; thinking about crime makes you wistful. So why are you sulking?"

"I'm being wistful about drugs."

"Drugs?"

"Drugs. Being a former user I think about them sometimes."

Claire didn't miss a beat. "And you are thinking what regarding drugs?"

I took a deep breath, "I'm thinking about need ... ready? Meth, crank, go, zip, cristy, black ice, ice, amp, blue belly, batak, batu kilat, bato, batu, billywhizz, blue funk, boo-ya, boorit cebuano, jib, cankinstein, chachacha, cricri, cube, debbie-tina and crissy, doo-my-lau, fetch, gear, gonzalles, jab, jenny crank program, chalk, jasmine, junk, magic, nazi dope, pieta, quick, quill, project propellant, scante, scooby snax, sha-bang, motivation, spinny, tadow, teena, tish, ugly dust, yaga, yama, and zoom."

"Are you finished?"

"Yep."

"Are you going to rationalize now that you're fixating?"

"What's to rationalize? Incans chewed coca leaves to survive at high altitudes, the German army used crystal meth to reduce hunger, the British passed out Benzedrine for soldiers on night watches, the Japanese gave their soldiers speed on their way to rape the shit out of Nanking, and the Americans pump up their pilots with dexamphetamines on their way to blow up Canadians in Afghanistan. It's all the rage; it's the relentless onslaught of civilization! No point in stopping or slowing. It's progress!"

"Uh-huh."

"It's only natural. Forget the brain damage, the psychosis, the weight loss, the panic attacks, the paranoia, the impotence, the facial sores, the bone rot, and the depression."

"Why forget it?"

"'Cause it feels so good when you're taking the shit. 'Cause you're immortal, invulnerable, unstoppable when it's in your bloodstream. 'Cause it's the best shit in the world, ever."

"Uh-huh. Want some?"

"Desperately."

"Too bad. You can't have any."

The words hung there and I started to laugh and everything was better and we headed home.

Inside my house Elena Ramirez, a Winnipeg cop, was sitting at the dining room table cleaning her service pistol on top of a thick pile of old newspapers. At her feet her son, Jacob, an angelic and evil baby, was wrestling with my son Fred, a slightly less angelic fifteen-month-old baby. I think Fred was winning and then Jacob bit him and Fred howled, "'Eater!" and clocked him in the side of the head.

In the back of the house our dog Renfield began to make a godawful racket from where he was locked in the kitchen.

Elena looked up when we came in and finished running the bore-cleaning brush through the disassembled barrel. "Glad to see you guys. Did you have a nice time?"

Elena is West Indian, fairly squat and pretty. She always smells of cinnamon and was the first person in Winnipeg to point a gun at me when Claire and I had arrived that spring. Don't get me wrong, Elena had every reason to point the gun at me, since I was in the process of being arrested for three murders, but that was then. Now I was her regular babysitter and she was just returning the favour.

Claire answered, "We had a great time, thanks."

I separated the babies. "And did you search the house and find anything incriminating?"

Elena smiled and it lit up her face. "Tsk-tsk. Of course."

I moved close to her. "Filthy pig!"

She smiled some more. Her hands flew and she finished reassembling her Smith & Wesson .40 calibre pistol before answering, "Felonious pervert!"

"Dirty, rotten copper!"

"Ne'er-do-well!"

That stopped me. "Ne'er-do-well?"

29

Elena picked up Jacob. "That's what my granny used to call people like you."

"Oh. You bringing over Jake tomorrow, same time?"

"You bet!"

"Claire will be handling them all tomorrow. I have a few things to do."

Elena bounced Jacob in her arms and he gurgled. "That's okay, he likes her more anyway."

With that she left. Claire let our idiot mutt Renfield out into the back yard to pee on things. While she was doing that I put Fred to bed with a sippy cup (which he hated and threw at me) and then I went down to feed our pet mouse who was sitting in his dry aquarium by the dining room table surveying everything with mousish contempt. When Claire let the dog back in he proceeded to race over and jam twenty-four kilos of nose into my ass while baying loudly. I swatted him away and looked at the mouse who looked back with his small black eyes.

Claire linked her arm in mine. "We should really name it."

"But what?"

The mouse was brown and white with a few small black patches and I considered him for a few seconds while I lowered a small chunk of carrot into his dish. Claire gave my arm a squeeze. "I know; we can call him Thor."

"Thor?"

Her eyes narrowed and the mouse took the carrot and vanished into the cedar shavings we had covering the bottom of the aquarium. "What's wrong with Thor?"

"Nothing. Just the other mice will make fun of him."

Claire shrugged. "I can live with that."

#5

Marie picked me up in a loaded Tacoma SUV battlestar masquerading as a car the next morning. Our first stop was at a Tim Horton's drive-thru for large coffees and six old-style sour cream doughnuts. She was getting her change and I spoke up.

"Do not introduce me to your friends by my real name."

"Why not?"

I ignored the question and explained that I wanted to be introduced as Seamus Fantomas. She stared at me until someone behind us in the line honked.

"Why?"

"I have no intention of letting anyone know my real name." I took a bite out of the doughnut and went on. "Also, I've never used that particular alias before."

She expressed outrage over my distrust. When she was finished talking I told her calmly and concisely that I didn't trust anyone, anytime, anyway. She complained some more and I told her the whole issue was covered in the thieves' mantra, which forced her to ask, "What's the thieves' mantra?"

"There is no honour amongst thieves and two can keep a secret if one is dead." We were headed south down Pembina Highway and I caught her looking at me out of the corner of her eye.

"That's kind of grim."

I went on, "Also no one can tell something to the cops, RCMP, CSIS, FBI, Mossad, the KGB, MI5, or Homeland Security if they don't know it in the first place."

She glanced at me and made an amused noise in her throat so I went on, "And you should always consider the abilities of your opponents, what they are capable of doing. Not what they can do."

She absorbed it silently with a slight smile and I looked at her with more respect. She could listen. After some doughnuts and coffee she asked me who Seamus Fantomas was. I told her that Seamus was Irish for James from the arch-enemy of Sherlock Holmes, James Mycroft. Fantomas was the name of a fictional surrealistic French terrorist from the early 1900's.

She looked at me oddly after that. "Okay. You're a strange man, you know that?"

"Yep to both."

By the time we reached highway 12 heading towards the eastern corner of Manitoba I was feeling more than a little travel sick. Eventually she turned to the right and we vanished into a wall of verdant green. Although it was fall, most of the trees were pines of various types and still a deep and potent green. Shining through the green, however, were chalk-white birch trees that became frames around the other trees. Outside the air was crystal clear and cold and the sky was a pure and unrelenting blue.

I turned to Marie and spoke up, "Tell me about the route again."

She drove badly and hit most of the bumps along the way, thinking of other things maybe. "What? Oh, the deliveries across the border. Actually ..." She turned to me despite driving at 110 kilometres per hour down a poorly graded road, "... we haven't made any deliveries yet. We've convinced the people on the other side set to do the pick up and we have ones on this side to make the deliveries. We just don't have them working together yet."

"Ah." She hadn't been completely honest with me. No big surprise. No one is ever honest with me; I'm working on getting used to it. I stopped thinking and stared at the trees and the granite rocks whipping by. After a little bit of time and considerable distance she turned again off the road. Now we were on a much narrower road with more of the skeletal poplar and birch trees reaching intertwining branches above the road. The idea of smuggling people didn't really bother me; they were just bodies shifting back across imaginary and arbitrary lines scratched in the dirt. Despite the propaganda it just wasn't such a big deal where people ended up. However, governments tended to take such things much more seriously, leading to things like arrest and imprisonment.

At the end of the road there was a sapphire expanse of water and two run-down shacks with split cedar shakes on the roofs. Past them was a wooden dock on floats stretching into the water. There was a tiny beach, but it was mostly grey rocks and pines, scrub oaks, and junipers growing up out of cracks in the rocks themselves. Scattered about on the rocks were eight or nine canoes of various sizes, some metal, some plastic, and even two of birch bark. Tied up to the dock itself were two heavy-duty dark green boats with big outboard engines. From where we were I could see that they were both full of nets and other crap.

The road went on for another twenty metres to a small parking lot between the buildings, but I asked Marie to stop. She did and asked, "Why?"

"Disguise time."

How to make a scar: take a large/small quantity of scar wax (can be bought at any novelty shop or makeup place; it's just wax and cotton for texture), mould it into a big, bejesus scar (the uglier the better). Can be stored in a baggie to keep it moist. Apply with spirit glue (also from a novelty shop). How to disguise yourself: apply scar on face (in my case from my right eye down to the corner of my mouth and then down my neck), now wear ugly baseball hat (from a team you don't like, in my case the Yokohama BayStars with their stupid mascots Hossy and Hossiena dancing), and lastly, glasses (non-corrective ones from a pharmacy). If you wear glasses, use contact lenses.

I'd had all the materials at home, the remainders of a life of crime.

I'd been going through boxes Claire and I had brought from Edmonton and I'd been amazed by what I'd accumulated over the years. Things I'd stored with one friend or another. Items the cops had seized and returned. Clothing that looked like one thing and was another. Things I'd hidden, booby traps of addiction and behaviour the old me had left for the new one.

Some of it I threw away and some I kept; I kept the leather jacket with the cop bullet hole below the shoulder (stopped by a Kevlar vest). That was a memento. And I kept unopened tins of makeup in a hollowed-out book. I threw away a package of syringes and a dried-out stash of magic mushrooms I must have hidden while stoned years before. As I winnowed through the crap I'd gathered over the years I became less and less the thief I had been.

When I was all made up, I turned to Marie and made sure the two paper-wrapped rolls of quarters (my only weapons) were handy in my jean pockets. "Ready."

"You don't look like anyone."

I answered patiently, "The essence of disguise is not to look like myself. Do I look like me?"

"No."

"There you are then."

I pulled on a pair of black leather racing gloves (I didn't want to leave fingerprints) and Marie started to ask me questions. "So where should we ..."

Before she could finish I interrupted, "Did you know that Manfred von Richthofen was murdered in Brazil? Beaten to death with iron rods by his daughter's boyfriends."

Marie glared at me suspiciously. "Who is ..."

"Manfred was a naturalized Brazilian and an engineer. The grandson of Manfred von Richthofen, the Red Baron, who shot down eighty Allied planes before being shot down by an Australian infantryman, a Canadian machine gunner, or a black and white beagle."

"What does that have to do with anything?"

"Nothing. Just something to think about." She stared at me. When we were both out of the car she looked me over and repeated, "What does that have to do with anything?"

"Nothing. I don't want to start this off with preconceived notions. Just show me who you're working with and what tools you have. Then show me the maps and by then I'll know what to do."

"Okay."

"And think about the Richthofen thing. It might be important."

She looked at me suspiciously and then led me towards the

nearest shack. It was on a sloping rock, so it was up on stilts to make it level. Leading to the door were three stairs, and then we were in a screened-in porch. Past that was the main room with three doors leading off of it. In the centre of the room were a new wooden table and six chairs. To one side of the table was a kitchenette with a wood-burning stove and an expensive double-door fridge in a dark brown colour. Up near the ceiling and circling the room were stuffed and mounted fish, birds, and small mammals. Around the table were three men drinking coffee and smoking a mixture of tailor-made and hand-rolled cigarettes in silence.

I took it all in.

The men looked up when Marie and I came in. As Marie introduced me I looked the men over and found myself unimpressed.

"Gentlemen, this is Seamus Fantomas. He will be helping us. I will let him introduce himself and describe his qualifications."

When I spoke I raised my voice slightly and spoke through my nose.

"Gentlemen, nice to meet you all. I am a professional smuggler. I have smuggled American machine guns in the Bere in County Cork for the Republicans, Bulgarian cigarettes across the Adriatic to Bari, South African diamonds across the Namibian border and French champagne and cognac on the champagne run in Belgium."

They looked at me uncomprehendingly as I went on, "I do not smuggle drugs, however; I disapprove of them; they're immoral and lead to degeneracy."

I smiled broadly and went on, "I look forward to working with you."

The men looked at me with open mouths and I sat down

and Marie brought me a cup of coffee with a slight smile play-ing on her lips. I went on, as prissy as I could be, "So. Tell me about yourselves. And your plans."

#6

The three men around the table looked vaguely at each other before talking. The guy nearest to me on my right was in his fifties, a very deeply tanned white man wearing khaki pants and a safari jacket that had seen better days. Although old, his clothes were ironed and showed signs of careful stitching and repair, repairs that in places crossed old blood and oil stains. His hair was some indeterminate colour between brown and nothing and his eyes were a light brown framed by many smile wrinkles. When he opened his mouth I could see that his teeth were immaculately white and even, and I wondered if they were fake. He held out his hand and I took it.

"I am Don Morris, and I own a farm northwest of here. I've fished and hunted the Aulneau peninsula since I was a kid." He spoke very quietly with a slight accent I didn't recognize.

The man beside him, younger, in his twenties, was aboriginal with lustrous black hair and dark skin. I couldn't see his pants but he was wearing a jean jacket with the sleeves ripped off over a black T-shirt. Above the neckline of his shirt I could see a tattoo of parallel tears in the skin with some kind of monstrous claw coming through. On his other arm an Apple iPod was attached with an elastic band and from it a thin cord led from the port to his breast pocket. He sat in his chair backwards and turned slightly away from me, which gave his right hand free access to his waist and hips. His left hand held a battered and chipped enamel mug full of whitish coffee. His eyes focused on my face and revealed nothing.

He looked vaguely familiar.

"I'm Greg Whitefox. I live on the rez south of here." He was much louder than Don and his voice had a cigarette-and-whiskey harshness to it that was also familiar.

The third man was also native, somewhere between thirty and eighty, with face and hands that had been seared by wind and sun. His hair was long and grey and gathered in a pony-tail, which was then gathered in a club and held with a pair of pink-and-sparkle scrunchies. His eyes were dark brown and very calm and I glanced down at his hands to find them crisscrossed with thin white scars and twisted. I'd seen hands like that before down in Florida and they'd belonged to old time net commercial fishermen who'd gotten the scars handling nets in surging waters. He wore blue jeans studded with copper rivets, rubber boots, and a thick black sweater with leather elbow patches on his thin body, and his voice was the softest of all. "I'm Al and I'm a fisherman."

I shook hands all around and drank some coffee (which was toxically strong) before starting, "So, Don, why are you involved with Marie?"

He shrugged. "God's will. Enough people have suffered all across this poor planet; here there is space for them all. Let them come."

"Even if it's against the law?"

He drew heavily on a filterless hand-rolled cigarette until it turned mostly to ash and then crushed it on a piece of rock on the table before dropping it in an empty can of Maxwell's coffee. "Fuck the law. God's law is to do good and it was first."

I turned to Greg, "And you?"

His left side went up an inch. "Money. Marie there promises me a hundred a head to take them across. I can use that."

Al spoke up then, "And I'm here because I like Marie."

I looked at her and to my surprise she blushed and he went on straight-faced, "And if I help her maybe she'll marry me and we can stop living this life of sin."

Everyone laughed and Marie said dryly, "In your dreams."

Al just nodded and everyone laughed again. I waited until they stopped and asked them their smuggling plans. Don had a series of aerial photographs which he dealt out on the table. As he did so the area started to take shape. When all nine pictures were out he took out a box of Redbird wooden matches and shook them into his hand.

"We're here …" A match went down and he went on, "And the delivery point …"

Marie interrupted him, "Seamus doesn't need to know more than where it is, Don."

Don nodded and moved his fingers before putting another match down. "Is about here."

More matches followed, a line to show the border and more to show the locations of towns and cabins. When he was done he stood back and looked at Al and Greg. "What am I forgetting?"

Al shook his head and Greg spoke up, "Nothing."

"What's your plan?"

Greg answered, "We load the Lunds; they each can carry about 600 kilos. Then we wait until there's no moon, use paddles to move us out onto the water, then buzz across, shut the engines down and land using the paddles again and zip back. We can use a GPS unit to make a perfect landing every time. It'll be simple and take maybe six hours; the round trip will be about eighty-four klicks."

I stood up. "Can I think about all this?"

Everyone looked at Al and he shrugged, "Sure."

Don and Greg pulled out a deck of cards and started to play something while Al went to start a fresh pot of coffee. Marie came with me outside and I walked over to the canoes. She waited a few minutes and then spoke up, "Why did you ask why they were involved?"

"I wanted to know. Cops worry about who and what. Good journalists are concerned with who, what, where, when, and why. Bad guys just care about why. 'Why' opens everything up."

"How do you mean?"

I stood there with my back to the cabin. "I'll give you an example. Back in the thirties Dillinger was betrayed by a woman in a red dress who was being pressured by the cops with threats of extradition to some country she didn't want to see again. Dillinger had paid her to provide a hideout and thought that was that; he didn't understand her real motive; he didn't understand her personal 'why.' If he had he could have dealt with the problem. So I like to know why people are doing what they do."

"What about me? What's my motivation?"

I looked at Marie and chose my words. "You're a fanatic. A do-gooder and a fanatic. You're scary."

"Scary?"

"Scary. You're capable of lots of things most people won't even think about. Most fanatics are like that."

"I see." She thought about it and then said confidently, "I prefer to think of myself as an altruist. Well? What about the plan?"

"It won't work. It'll work once or twice, sure, but not more than that."

"Why won't it work long-term? That's what we want."

The canoes were in good shape, especially the birchbark ones; someone had put those together with love and skill. As I ran my fingers down the gunwale I answered, "Anyone travelling at night without lights on a lake is going to stick out like a whore in an Anglican church. Noise travels five-six times as far over water as compared to land so everyone around will hear the engines; trust me, those suckers are loud. Also, if anyone has radar the boats are going to show up clear as day, slab-sided aluminum reflects radar like you wouldn't believe. Also the boats will leave a great big wake if anyone is taking pictures from above, like from a surveillance drone, a military helicopter, or a satellite. And a GPS signal can be backtracked easily if you have the technology, and guess who owns the tech? It's owned by the US military who own the satellites. And here you are crossing their border."

She swore and I answered, "Yeah. Who came up with the plan? It's kind of half-assed smart."

"Greg."

I scratched (carefully) around the edge of my fake scar and walked down to the dock to look at the two boats. Stencilled prominently on the side of both of them was "Lund 1660 Classic Tiller." The one on the right was pointed towards shore; the other was pointed towards the lake.

"Greg what?"

She seemed confused by my questions. "Greg Whitefox."

The boat on the right was full of a strange mixture of

things: bulging plastic bags, neatly tied sleeping bags (one in pink with a Barbie theme), a small-frame mountain bike, and about thirty fishing rods of various types, all of it jumbled together. I walked on and saw a scratched and dented butt stock of a rifle sticking out of a blanket on the right side of the boat near where the driver's leg would have been. For the moment I ignored it and kept walking. In the bow was a tiny rectangle where the serial number of the boat should have been, but there was nothing, it had been torn free and shards of brass still showed around the tiny bolts in the aluminum.

"Is this Greg's boat?"

"Yes."

I looked over the other boat and found it full of nylon dip and seine nets, neatly rolled and clean and ready for use. In the middle of the boat were two hand-made wooden tubs full of water and covered with hinged tops for minnows. All the normal stuff a man who fished for bait would carry.

"And this is Al's boat?"

"Yes. Don came with him."

"Is Greg at the window? I want to look around."

Out of the corner of my eye I saw her shift around and look. "No."

With a long reach I managed to grab the rifle from Greg's boat; it was a Ruger 10/22, a classic semi-auto rifle. The safety was not on so I clicked it into place before I pulled the rotary magazine out and emptied the small solid-headed rounds into my pocket. Then I worked the bolt and found an eleventh round which I also confiscated. With the gun completely safe I replaced it in the boat where it had been.

I had noticed a few other things. The serial number, which should have been on the side of the gun, had been filed off. There was rust where the bluing had been ground off and a few more spots showed up on the barrel as well. Marie waited until the rifle was back and then said, "What are you doing? It's just a gun; Don says lots of folks around here carry guns."

I grunted at Marie, "Well, it's a twenty-two rifle, a real light calibre, some people think it's a toy. But the serial numbers are burned off, which is majorly wrong, a felony I think, and I don't knock twenty-twos. More people are killed with twenty-two-calibre rounds than any others, and the Ruger there is a really good rifle; the Israelis use a silenced version of it to shoot Palestinian legs during riots."

I unhooked the gas line from the engine to the tank; five quick pumps pushed all the fuel into the big Yamaha outboard. I reattached the line, leaving a huge air bubble in place, and grinned up at Marie. "They also use that kind of rifle to shoot guard dogs during covert operations. Then it's called a hush-puppy or a dog-be-cool."

"Yes, but ..."

"You can kill a moose with a twenty-two, or a man. Just aim for the eye or the ear, it's not hard; the rifle is really accurate out to about fifty metres. A solid bullet like one of these goes in and doesn't have enough velocity to penetrate the skull on the other side, so it bounces around for awhile and turns the brain into hamburger. A hit that penetrates the ribs does the same thing to the heart and lungs." She was silent and I went on, "And the stuff in his boat makes me think Greg's been burglarizing cabins around here now that the tourist season is winding down."

She was stony-faced. "So."

"So indeed."

We walked back up to the cabin. Just outside the main door I pulled out the two rolls of quarters from my pocket and fitted them into my closed hands.

#7

Inside Greg and Don were still playing cards and Al was watching and drinking more coffee. The smoke in the room, the old and the new, made me gag a little but I covered it up. When Marie was inside and off to the side a little I said, "Hey, Greg!"

Greg looked up with his mouth half open and said absently, "Yeah?"

"How long have you been robbing cabins around here?"

"I'm not!" He sounded offended and Al and Don looked at him curiously.

"Sure you are. I just took a look at all the shit in your boat."

He shrugged and pushed back a little from the table. "What do you care? I need the money."

I looked him over and spoke slowly, less for him than for Al and Don and Marie. "You're robbing cabins and selling the stuff. The Ontario Provincial Police will become involved if you're stealing on their side of the border and the RCMP will become involved if you're stealing on the Manitoba side of the border."

"Fuck them."

"Fuck them yourself. And how will you be getting rid of the stuff? Through pawnshops? They keep records, by law they have to keep records of who sells what."

Greg sneered, "No, I'm not stupid." He looked uncomfortable but sounded belligerent. "Maybe. What the fuck do you care anyway?"

"I care because I am a pro. E-Bay keeps records and can be searched in half a second. Fences always have real tight relationships with the cops; it's the only way they ever stay in business."

"Fuck you!"

The quarters in my hands were getting heavy and the conversation was going nowhere good. I looked directly at Marie. "But the most important reason of all why I care is that you're ripping off cabins and that will attract attention."

He started to say something but I just talked right over his words. "It attracts attention from cabin owners. It attracts attention from any locals who might see you. It attracts attention from cops. And, when you sell the stuff, it attracts attention from them."

"Fuck you, I'll do what ..."

"Shut up, Greg, or I will hurt you. Last warning." I was calm but he wasn't backing down and I needed to be in charge if this was going to go right.

Greg's mouth opened again and I didn't want to hear his excuses anymore. Any restraint I might have had had vanished when I considered the filed-down serial numbers on the rifle. That one single fact meant he was a bad guy or a wannabe bad guy, and in both cases he was stupid. I wound up my right arm and threw the roll of quarters at his torso, the biggest target.

I used to pitch baseball in prison. Playing baseball was a good way to burn off stress (you are allowed to hit something), acquire an emergency weapon (the bat), and smuggle drugs (thrown over fences during games and retrieved by the outfielders). In Drumheller they had a laser speed tracker and my best throw was clocked at twenty-five metres per second, which is not bad. A baseball weighs 190 grams and a roll of quarters weighs around 230 grams, so they're close in weight at least. And the throw I made at Greg was pretty good. Power from the belly and hips, first with my elbow and wrist all loose and snapping. To my surprise I actually hit roughly where I was aiming at, which was Greg's upper stomach. I suppose it was the equivalent of getting hit with a pool cue at full swing. Something like that, anyway, because Greg said "OOOF" loudly at the same time as he farted.

"I'm tired of you interrupting me, asshole," I went on as though nothing had happened.

He leaned on the table gasping and Al said something that sounded like "stop," which I ignored. "You're doing penny-ante shit that might net you a year in the provincial jail and attracting attention to crimes that will net EVERYONE at this table ten to twenty years in a federal slam with a fair chance of doing time in an American pen. All that for a couple of hundred bucks."

There was silence and I said coldly, "Which means you are truly stupid and I do not work with stupid people."

Greg caught his breath and pushed himself away from the table and pulled a small framed pistol from the front of his pants at the same time.

I admit I was surprised. I was even shocked and amazed.

I was also moving, because in a fight you always keep moving. I was diving across the table with my right hand scrabbling for his gun and my left driving directly towards his face. The impact drove Greg back into the wall and a cascade of small, dead animals rained down upon us as his gun hand wriggled free. Before he could aim, my left fist hit him squarely in the top of his head, and the *bonk* noise would have been funny in any other circumstances.

The roll of coins in my hand split open and clattered to the ground, adding a note of psychotic merriment to the fight.

Behind us Al and Don were yelling while Marie was trying to take cover, but everyone shut up when the gun went off with a pathetic-sounding pop and a tiny jet of fire. Where the bullet went I have no idea, but everyone except for Greg stopped moving. Then he dropped the gun and shrugged me off to dive over the table. His landing was awkward but he was immediately on his feet and tearing through the screened-porch door. And then he was outside.

I followed and behind me by a few seconds were Don and Al and Marie.

At the base of the dock I slowed down, looked back, and saw that Al had an iron-headed hatchet with a long handle in his left hand and Don had a fifteen centimetre skinning knife with a blade about a centimetre wide in his right. They both stared at me and then past me to where Greg had reached his boat and was scrambling for something near the stern.

Before we could do anything Greg turned and we could all see the rifle in his hands. When he spoke his voice was hoarse, "You dumb fucks!"

No one moved.

"You guys think you are all so smart."

He gestured a little with the gun, there were maybe ten metres between us.

"This is what's going to happen: I'm in charge of your little charity now. You can still carry over the niggers and the Chinks but you'll be carrying my shit on the way back."

Marie's voice was cold and controlled. "Like what?"

"Like whatever the fuck I want."

I spoke up, "Like crack and guns. That about right?"

"You're so fucking smart ..."

He had taken a couple of steps forward on the dock and was holding the rifle at waist level, pointed in our general direction, as he repeated himself.

"Here's what's going to happen; I'm going to get in my boat and take off. Don't follow me. Tomorrow or the next day, Marie, you'll get a call telling you what happens next. Got it?"

Greg's eyes narrowed and I turned to Marie. "Heard enough?"

She nodded and I started to walk towards the gun which came up and went "click." Before the trigger was pulled again something flew by my ear and suddenly Greg had the iron hatchet buried deep in his right thigh.

His screaming went on and on and I turned to see Al recovering from the effort.

"Good throw."

He shrugged, "Thanks."

"His gun was empty."

Al shrugged again, "Didn't know that." His face was pensive. "Don't care."

"Yeah. Me either."

Don moved past us and behind him I saw that Marie's face was very pale indeed. He lumbered down the dock and asked in a conversational tone, "Shall I kill him?"

He sounded serious and I thought about the Christians during the Crusades and the words of the Papal Legate, the Abbot of Citeaux in 1209 during the taking of the city of Béziers: "Kill them all. God will know His own."

Fanatics, they were all fanatics.

It took two hours to straighten everything out. Two hours to shut Greg up, two hours to rock the hatchet out of his leg and to stop the bleeding.

And then it took another hour to carefully explain to Greg that he was being given a free pass. He would be dropped off in Kenora by Marie with $200 and an invitation to travel far, far away before finding a doctor to look at his injury.

It was an invitation I thought he would take.

While I was doing it I wondered about just killing the little shit but I knew that would freak them out—no matter how hard core they pretended to be, the truth was that they weren't. That meant that killing Greg was not an option.

Although it was the logical thing to do.

When everyone was off working I went to the kitchen, borrowed a tarnished stainless steel tablespoon that had seen better days, and approached Greg again. He was sitting on a cheap folding chair, holding his belt wound tightly around his thigh to control the bleeding. I knelt in front of him and looked at his pain-filled eyes that brimmed with tears and asked, "Who'd you tell?'

"What 'cha mean?"

His voice was rushed and sharp but I answered calmly, "Who did you tell about the smuggling plan? You told somebody, probably more than one person, who was it?"

"I didn't." He lowered his voice when he said it and narrowed his eyes.

"Do you know what I'm going to do with this?" I showed him the tablespoon.

"No." His throat convulsed and he repeated himself.

"Last chance, who did you tell?"

He started to speak and I put a finger on his lip and kept the spoon visible. "If you tell me you didn't tell anyone, I know you're lying, and I will take your eye out with this spoon."

Greg's face became green and pale and I went on, "I will slip it into your left eye under the eyeball and scoop it out."

He swallowed convulsively and couldn't stop looking at the stained utensil in my right hand. I leaned forward and told him lovingly, "The last thing you will see is the bowl of the spoon coming towards your eye and then it will be gone. Then your right eye will be able to see the left one, up close. If I do it right you'll still be able to see through the eye even after I've taken it out, won't that be interesting?"

Greg tried to slip away from me and I grabbed his injured leg with my left hand and squeezed.

He vomited off to the side and wiped his mouth. Then he spoke quickly and I ignored the sour smell of his breath. "I told a girl I know, Samantha, she deals meth and crack in the city. She told me she's always looking for new routes for her stuff."

I nodded and bounced the spoon on his knee. "You told no one else?"

"No."

He hesitated and I used the spoon to hit the hole in his leg, "Don't think about it, just answer."

"Fuck! I only told her, she's pretty tough. A guy ripped off one of her dealers and she fucked him up; shot him in the stomach with a load of twenty-gauge bird-shot. It took two surgeons eleven hours to pull 400 lead pellets out of his crotch

51

and belly." He swallowed loudly. "I just told her and she gave me two rocks on account."

"On account of what?"

"On account of me being stand up."

He was proud and there was no answer to that so I took the spoon back to the kitchen and left it in the drawer.

Marie drove Greg away with Don sitting on the rear seat and resting his feet on his prone body. While they were doing that it took Al and me a full hour to clean up any trace that Greg had ever been at the camp, wiping down the surfaces he might have touched and packing his boat. We used about 120 metres of twine, rope, and baling wire along with an old net of Al's to anchor everything in place.

"Where're you going to dump it all?"

Al thought about it and answered, "I know a seventy-metre-deep fishing hole out in the lake where the boat will go easy. I'll do it tonight."

"Don't."

Al looked at me while he tied the ropes down. "Why?"

"The boat will show up on depth finders and if people are looking for a fishing hole they'll have the depth finders going."

"So?"

"Dump it someplace where no one runs a depth finder. Someplace shallow with no fish."

"Ah."

Al talked about islands and channels and ice dams for a few minutes, musing out loud, and then he looked up. "Trust me."

I did.

When no one was around I looked over the wallet I had

taken from Greg. In it he had some ID along with $420 in cash; he also had four small scraps of paper with five phone numbers, two cell and the rest land lines, judging from the first three numbers. He also had a single-edged razor blade in a "secret" compartment that was really obvious.

While I was standing there Al brought me the gun Greg had pulled in the cabin and I looked it over gingerly. It was a real zip gun, a plastic starter pistol modified with duct tape and a file to fire one .22 short round. I added it to the boat load and waited for Marie to come back so she could give me a lift home.

In the Tacoma I told her, "This'll cost you more."

"So you're in?"

I looked out at the darkening night and the trees and fields racing by.

"Yeah. Yeah, I guess so. Might as well, still can't dance. Plus, Gods help me, I'm kind of enjoying this."

And it was true, I had missed the rush and bang of being a bad guy. I wondered what that meant?

#8

The next day I visited Marie and she gave me a thousand bucks in old tens and twenties for building supplies. I pocketed that and took her SUV and hit refit and second-hand stores. Those, along with a prolonged shopping spree at a big-box hardware store, allowed me to quickly and anonymously collect an assortment of tools and building supplies. When I had everything I thought I might need, I loaded it all into her garage and took the rest of the day off.

Up on Main Street I found a phone booth outside a dry cleaning store, far away from any cameras. There I made some phone calls using the numbers I'd taken off Greg's body; in each case I used the same line: "I'm looking for Sam."

I didn't bother blocking the number; if anyone had call display, all it would show was an MTS pay phone, which could be anything from anyone. No one answered the cell numbers, and the first land line found me talking to a young woman who told me to go fuck myself. The second number was for a downtown pawnshop which took a message for Sam while not admitting they'd ever heard of "him." The last number connected me to a young man who wheezed into the phone and told me Samantha wasn't there. In the background I heard music at a distance and someone laughing, so I asked another question: "Do you know when she'll be back? I'm holding something, something she wants."

The guy on the other end of the phone became excited, though he tried to be cool. "Yeah, well. She's my man, you can give me whatever and I'll hold it."

"Really? Okay. But you have to keep it cold, okay?"

"Oh. Sure."

"Yeah, a fridge is good, but don't freeze it ... so where are you?"

Suspicion crept into his voice. "You don't know?"

"No. I'm from Vancouver."

"Oh, sure."

He gave me an address in Saint Boniface and I filed it away.

Before I could deal with Sam I needed to think things through, so I decided to check out the drug house near our place. Twenty minutes later I was outside the address explaining the facts of life to my son. "... and that, my fine little sonny boy, well, that's a drug house."

Fred looked at me with bright eyes and very little comprehension, which was understandable, since he was fifteen months old, with a relatively simple vocabulary focused on food and the necessity for someone to clean his bum. He was in the red Flyer wagon with a pillow wedged in behind him and he struggled when I tucked his blanket around him.

"Can you say 'crack house'?"

"Cak-ouse!"

He was very tired and drooled a little. I wiped the corner of his mouth with my thumb and then dried it on Renfield, the dog, on the other side of me. The three of us were on the sidewalk looking across and down the street at the two-story brick building. In the evening light it looked in even worse shape than it had in moonlight. It looked battered and wicked and out of place amongst other, neater, cleaner, poorer houses that lined the street.

"Actually, though, we could more correctly call it a drug house." Fred said something that didn't make much sense to distract me while he tried to wriggle free of the wagon. While he was doing that the dog let his tongue hang out and tentatively wagged his tail.

It was past five in the afternoon; Claire had watched the kids all day and now had the chore of making dinner while I made my reconnaissance. She had argued that it was dangerous and I had explained that no one sees anyone if they have a baby and a dog. They're the most innocent combination of things imaginable.

I stared at the building and considered it from a professional, ex-bad-guy perspective. It was two stories high with blank brick walls and it had once been a big house, big enough maybe to have once had suites on the top floor and another in the basement. We walked around the block and then down the back alley and found that both front and rear yards were huge and open.

If I was going to guess I would say that the doors were solid steel and the windows were barred and covered in plywood. It had become a fortress of sorts. I had asked Claire, the budding real estate tycoon, to make an anonymous call to the real estate company that had sold the place. They'd said that the renters had intentions to do extensive renovations and then move in. That had been three months ago. According to Claire's partner, that translated into three long months of gradually increasing incidents in the neighbourhood and no police response worth mentioning.

"So, boys, I guess we're going to have to deal with it. If we're all agreed it's a drug house, that is?"

Fred pitched a rattle in disgust and said "Home!" while Renfield flopped down on his belly. I took that as mass agreement. "All right, then we're decided. They must go. And we're just the guys to do it."

I kept looking at the building and listened to the whisper of past experience that said fire always worked. I could use a little plastic squeeze bottle of gasoline and a length of plastic tubing to direct it through a window or under a door. Maybe a couple of cylinders of propane with some spark plugs and a car battery as a detonator to bring the walls down. There was always the tried and true diesel fuel and nitrate fertilizer packed into a stolen car for the Hertz special. Or I could steal some nice safe ANFO or Fragmax explosives from northern Manitoba. I was sure there were some hard rock mines up there waiting to be pillaged.

There must be fifty ways to leave your lover. And at least a hundred ways to take something out. Maybe that could be a new song, "A Hundred Ways to Tag a Target."

"... but really, all that would make a hell of a mess and what I want to do is clean the place up."

I said it out loud and the solution hit me all of a sudden and I started to laugh, which purely scared the crap out of both Fred and the dog.

#9

The next day I had all the kids to babysit and I took the whole menagerie on a long walk to try to wear them down a little. That also gave me a chance to think about Marie and Samantha and the drug house and smuggling in general. We did the walk with strict rules about holding hands, looking both ways, and with me pushing a heavy-duty double-baby buggy. I'd bought the damn thing from a pawnshop for $40 and it could hold two babies and about thirty kilos of snacks, water, blankets, and assorted baby-wrangling supplies. Downtown we reached the law courts building and we all stared at the seven-metre-high metal statue in front. It was a massive construction of metal beams, twisted and turned around like a giant knot.

"What is it?" I said wonderingly.

A hatchet-faced blond woman sitting on the edge of the pedestal smiled at the children and answered, "It's justice."

"Justice?"

"It's balanced, see?" She reached out one finger and touched the burnished aluminum side and it shifted slightly and squealed. She gestured at the building behind it. "Those are the courts back there so that's the statue they chose to represent themselves."

"Interesting." The babies were getting bored and starting to wander around. Rachel came over with two fingers in her mouth and removed them to say, "Tangle!"

The woman agreed, "Yes it is, honey, all tangled." She turned to me and said, "It's very strange."

I assumed she was talking about the statue or sculpture, whatever it actually was.

She turned back to it and lit a cigarette, then butted it out when Rachel coughed theatrically. "Sorry, babe. Anyhow, the statue's a big tangle, and if you try to go inside to the courtroom, well they run you through a metal detector and your bag through an x-ray machine."

"Nothing quite like a transparent, open system for fairness and responsibility." It made me smile and almost laugh.

"Yeah. I just wanted to see what went on in there. I'm from Miami and I thought it would be different up here."

She sounded sad and a haunted look came over face. Then she gathered herself together and shook my hand and introduced herself as Alice. Rachel invited her to eat snacks with me and the monsters and she agreed. We ate there under the big tangle and while I was cleaning up I pushed the statue myself a little and made it shake and squeal. "Not a tangle."

"No?" The woman was busy trying to make Rachel eat a carrot.

"Nope. It looks like an elephant. See—trunk, tusks, tail."

"Ah. But why?"

I lined the kids up go home. "Because elephants never forget. Hope you enjoy your stay."

She laughed. "Are there elephants in Manitoba?"

I thought about it. "No, not even in the zoo. But there used to be mammoths."

"In the zoo?" She looked at me like I was crazy.

"I wish. No, there used to be mammoths, or maybe it was mastodons, here in Manitoba a long time ago."

We both looked back at the tangle and she saluted it. "To the mammoths of justice."

She said it solemnly and we both laughed.

On the way back home I called Marie to find out if everything was still going fine. She sounded cheerful and told me she hadn't seen or heard anything suspicious at all.

That night Claire came home to find me sitting at the dining-room table with a pad of paper and a pencil, fully equipped with a deep, intense frown.

"Where's the baby?"

I didn't look up from my work. "I'm right here. See? Can't miss me."

"I meant the other baby. You know, the little one?" She kissed me and reached through the open-backed chair to pinch my ass.

"He's around somewhere ... he kept muttering something about how you were cramping his style and how he wanted to get away from it all. Mentioned how you were ruining his life. He talked about his greater goals and needs and yakked on endlessly about his desire to be free."

She put her purse down on the table and stretched. "So he's asleep?"

"Yep, or scoring chicks. Either or."

Claire leaned close and the smell of her personal fragrance filled my nose and throat. Her breast touched the back of my neck and I squirmed and stroked her hip.

"Does this mean I get a lap dance?"

She leaned on me, pulled off her shoes, and threw them toward the front entry. Renfield heard them land and began to trot in that direction until Claire spoke up. "Touch the shoes and die, dog. I mean dead. Dead-dead. Deceased. Mort. Muerte. Tot."

Renfield kept going until I said loudly, "No. Sit. Stay."

He did and Claire stretched again and kissed my cheek. She smelled slightly of sweat and slightly of soap and entirely good.

"A lap dance, is that what you want? Sure. Is it your birthday?"

"Eventually it will be. Plus think about all those birthdays you missed over the years. All those dozens of birthdays for which I am owed lap dances. Like the first and the second, and don't forget the tenth. That's a very significant birthday which should have been celebrated via lap-dance. As a matter of consideration I think it's a law in Quebec."

She ignored me, looked down at the pad of paper, and hummed loudly. "What you doing?"

"Math. What's 632 multiplied by 42?"

"No idea."

"Okay. Next question, when you figure out the square footage of a house you are renting or selling, do you include the basement?"

"No, sometimes, depends."

"You are a wealth of knowledge. You are an absolute wealth of untapped knowledge."

She touched my lips with her finger. "I know, I know. Ask me another one, tap away!" I turned and looked at her with love and affection. Her long, wavy hair made her look like she was always in motion and I felt it was appropriate— she was always moving, always doing something. Today she'd been working, so she was wearing a light blue skirt and jacket with a white blouse. She claimed it was confidence-inspiring costuming for prospective home-buyers and apartment-renters.

"Maybe later." I stood up from the table and took her by the hand and she resisted for a moment. "Hey, I thought you said later?"

"This is later. Now is later than the beginning of the sentence. Right now is even later than that. And now is later than that ..."

She laughed and we spent some time the best way there was, ever had been, or ever could be.

After supper we listened to music on the radio and read while Fred built sprawling cities out of small plain wooden blocks and the dog destroyed them.

"Bad OG! Ba-OG!"

The dog was nonplussed and kept wagging his tail and Fred went back to building. They both seemed happy with the game despite the emotion.

I was trying to read a very well-written mystery about a smart magistrate in ancient China. It was full of details and some realistically smart and stupid people.

"So, did you ever figure out your math problem?" Claire's sudden question pulled me out of that world and into the real one.

"Sort of."

"So what's the answer?"

"632 times 3 times 9. So a total of 17,064 feet. Divided by 3 equals 5688 metres."

"What's that?"

"The volume of a house. I think."

She put down her book, a brightly illustrated history of the Eaton's store that had graced downtown Winnipeg. I had never seen it, but the pictures in the book were spectacular. Greed had replaced it with a hockey rink and bandstand, which brought such notables as Hilary Duff and the Backstreet Boys. Greed and pop culture overcoming commercialism and greed; funny how that went.

Claire was alternating between that book and a real estate guidebook to help her study for her real estate licence, the Holy Grail of the house hunter-gatherer.

"I won't ask. Now, what are you going to do for Marie?"

I flipped the page on the book I was reading and found out that the body was under the bronze bell in the abandoned temple. I marked the point on the page with my finger and lifted my eyes while I marshalled my thoughts. I'd told Claire most of the problem with Marie and the smuggling and she was curious.

"I'm working on it."

"Working on it?"

"Yep. And that's not going well so I'm thinking about drug houses right now."

Claire nodded. "That's where the volume question comes in?"

"Yep. Although my math sucks."

"Tell me about the house."

"The doors are armoured and barricaded, ditto the windows. There are at least five, six people selling dope, probably cooking meth in the basement. And there will be hookers and johns and probably a nodding room inside."

"Nodding room?" I loved hearing her voice.

"A room where you can sleep off your high. Where you can crash."

She stared at me and then said accusingly, "You made that up."

I stuck out my tongue. "Be that as it may. Plus the guys in charge are probably—no, make that definitely—armed to deal with anyone ripping them off. And drug-fuelled psychosis plus greed plus guns means a gunfight if someone tries to go in through the front door."

"Why are you thinking about drug houses?"

I shrugged, "Because."

She brought her finger to her lips and kissed it. "Back to the nodding room—you have your very own language, you know that, right?"

I stuck my tongue out at her again. "Back to the subject, the whole space is undoubtedly booby-trapped as it's a place where paranoid drug users meet paranoid drug dealers." I picked the book up again and went on, "So there's nothing anyone can do. It's a job for the police. Or Batman. Period."

"Hmmmm. Let me rephrase the question: what are you going to do about the drug house near us? Hypothetically."

"Nothing. What drug house? And, do you really want to know?"

She smiled, somewhat amused. "No, not really."

"All right then, is tomorrow garbage day?"

"Yes."

I went back to my book and then looked up. "I love you."

She went back to her book and smiled to herself. After a minute she looked up, kissed the tip of her finger and pointed it at me. "I know."

#10

Before I went to bed I swallowed two litres of ice-cold water, so at midnight a full bladder forced me to wake up. Neither Claire nor the dog woke up and a few minutes later I was in the bathroom, where I dressed in the clothes I'd left there before I'd gone to sleep. First I pulled on a pair of white Adidas running shorts and a pale blue singlet, over them went black jeans and long-sleeved T-shirt, both large on me to break up my outline. Also cheap black runners and socks, all of it brand new and from a discount store far away from my home and paid for with cash. Last on was a black balaclava and leather gloves.

In my pockets were four heavy-gauge plastic ties from a plumbing store in case I had to tie anything and two quarters in case I had to phone someone. An important rule of thieves: never forget the quarters. I repeat, never forget the quarters. If worse comes to worse you can use them to bribe a cop.

Another rule of thieves is, if you can't fix one problem, fix another. There was nothing I could do with Marie's smuggling at the moment, but that didn't mean I had to sit there doing nothing.

That idea sort of explains what I did next.

No one saw me as I moved the two blocks towards the local fire station. I'd walked the route twice and knew where there were dogs and where there were bright lights and where there was open ground. I was almost caught when I was crawling by someone's backyard. They were taking advantage of the fairly warm early September night to get busy.

"Oh Wayne ..." I heard skin on skin slapping together. "... oh Wanda."

Oh God.

I ignored them and kept going. Beside the fire station I paused and listened but heard nothing. The front doors were wide open and the light spilled out onto the boulevard and attracted sluggishly flying moths and other small insects in great numbers. I stayed in the shadows and moved beside the entrance and kept listening, but all I could hear were the wings of the moths.

When I was sure I was alone I moved around the corner and directly to the big pump truck. I stepped along the side of the truck to right behind the drivers' cab. There I pulled the tool I wanted (a wrench with a long handle and weird head) off the brackets. Next I grabbed the rolled spare canvas hose from under the passenger side seat.

I'd taken a firehouse tour during the summer along with the kids and learned lots of interesting things, like that water comes out of a fire hose at seventy kilos of pressure and with a volume of six metres per second. I'd also learned that fire hydrants needed a special wrench to get the water moving. All useful information.

Huffing and puffing under the thirty-five-kilos hose, I went back the way I came and headed to the drug house. I started to work and, frankly, it was harder than I'd thought. After I'd barked my knuckles on the fire hydrant cap the second time I took a time out and felt sorry for myself until I realized it was wasted emotion.

With a fresh grip I managed to pull the cap off. Then I attached the female end of the stolen hose to the hydrant and admired my handiwork for maybe a tenth of a second. I was right behind the drug house on the boulevard and therefore in plain sight. Or I would have been if I hadn't piled all the garbage bags I could collect from the neighbourhood around the hydrant during the day when Fred had been sleeping nearby in the wagon. It also helped that the customers and staff of the drug house had systematically broken every street light they could find in the immediate area. This meant I had a nice bit of cover but could still hear the non-stop party in the house, and all around me the noise kept coming.

"... want to party?" Female voice. Frayed and coarsened and old. Listless.

"C'mon. I need some ..." Male voice. Young and desperate and frantic.

"Fuck you." Female voice but a younger one.

"Yeah, well, fuck you too." Male voice, sounding frantic and furious.

"... ha ... ha ... ha ... ha ..." Strange one that, didn't sound like either a man or a woman. It also didn't sound like whoever it was was having any fun at all. All mixed in with a radio blaring inside the house, so each time the door opened I absorbed a shock of white noise. Hip hop and rap and punk and heavy metal. Songs about fucking and fighting and hurting and being hurt and truth and lies and rage, but nothing about love at all.

Back at the hydrant I stayed low and duck-walked while I

dragged the hose towards the back wall of the house. When someone had done work on the house sometime before, they'd been sloppy and left a big pile of lumber in the back along with a fridge with the doors torn off and other junk. Using that as a boost I climbed until I could reach one of the second-floor windows. Up close the noise was a palpable thing through the plywood and heavy cast-iron bars that covered the windows. I pulled the hose up to the bars and hooked the nozzle into place touching the plywood. Then I took out the plastic ties and used them to secure the hose to the bars.

Each tie had a breaking strength of over 500 kilograms; cops used a minor variation as a handcuff during riots. This meant they should hold the hose steady and in place. I climbed down and went back to the hydrant. A little more grunting and I managed to turn the main valve all the way to on, and then I dropped the wrench and booked it.

Behind me the water surged through the hose, turning it as rigid as a bar of iron. Right after that the same water pounded the plywood aside on the second floor and blew it into the room. Then the water itself began to pour in. Seventy kilograms of pressure. A six-cubic-metre volume of water entering the building every second. So six goes into 5688 meant that the building would be filled in ... slightly less than 1000 seconds. Which was what? Sixteen minutes plus a bit?

This would definitely clean up the problem.

I went back home via a very roundabout route, along the way dumping my outer clothes in a big dust bin behind a shopping centre and finishing my trip as a very cold jogger in shorts and shirt. Claire greeted me at the back door holding the crowbar ready in her hand, the bayonet tucked down the front of her pants with the hilt on her right side. The sounds of sirens filled the air and a fire engine blew past the front of the house. The noise and light turned the whole neighbourhood into a carnival.

"Is that any way to greet your beloved husband?"

She adjusted her grip on the bar and spoke quietly. "What did you do?"

"Nothing."

She hefted the crowbar again and finally let me in. Upstairs we fought for a while and finally we made love and fell asleep, angry, sweaty, and both feeling like we had accomplished something.

The next morning Claire turned on the radio during breakfast. Over cereal we caught a very excited CBC voice describing the scene. Apparently the water had knocked all sorts of staff and clientele of the drug house about, then it had filled the basement and blown out the windows throughout. Apparently there were no windows on the main floor; they had been replaced with sheets of plywood supported with two-by-fours as well. Eventually even those went, and when they gave way, the water took the window frames with them and deposited the whole mess in the yards.

Included amongst the assorted trash were needles, condoms, loose cash, homemade crack pipes, a few sawed-down rifles, lots of no-name baggies, a bunch of stolen electronic equipment and CD's; even a couple of stained mattresses and cheap lawn chairs.

And people. Young people. Old people. Middle-aged people. Now broken and battered. Bruised from the water pressure. People scratched as they'd struggled against each other to find a door and escape. However, the main door had stayed locked. Pushed shut by the tons of water as the people were battered and smashed against it.

No one had drowned or otherwise died, although many were hospitalized.

"Probably not one of your better ideas." Claire had her arms crossed.

I looked her over and smiled while patting her hand. "I could have burned the place down. Or blown it up. Or, since the people inside are really the problem, I could have just gotten rid of them, I could have pumped carbon monoxide into a window. Or gone in with a shotgun and a bag of double-ought buck shells and cleared it out room by room." She flinched and I turned back to my generic corn and rye flakes. "At least this way no one died."

On the radio it described the cops on the scene gathering money and guns and drugs and knives and clubs.

Claire stared at me and I shrugged and turned off the radio. "The place was an eyesore and needed to be cleaned up. Water's clean."

That drew a smile from her.

#11

With the drug house out of the way I could focus on the smuggling. Which was what was paying the bills, so I spent the next three days with tools and an overactive imagination turning Marie's house into a fortress. I did nothing too obvious because there were limits to what I could and couldn't do. I couldn't tear the place apart and rebuild it; Marie was renting and Claire couldn't allow that. I also couldn't be too obvious about what I was doing because a variety of innocent people had access to the place, people like meter readers. If I was too obvious, someone would call the cops because Winnipeg, like most communities, had some fairly strict (and unenforceable laws) about defending your home and the cops would come down like a ton of bricks.

Marie might need a fortress to stash her cargo once her route was running and the route itself would be valuable and therefore worth protecting. Lots of people were always looking for a clean way across the border without having to deal with guards and other inconveniences. Some things were worth more on one side of the border than the other and that simple truth was behind all smuggling everywhere. Guns were cheaper and more available in the States than in Canada, so those came north. Hydroponic grass in Canada was cheaper and better than in the States, so that went south. Cocaine was cheaper in the States, so that came north. Methamphetamine precursors were more available in Canada, so those went south. Booze was cheaper in the States, so that went north.

There were lots of examples like that.

The route was valuable and Marie might need protection. I thought about that as I worked on Marie's house, installing motion alarms on the windows (battery powered in case the power was cut). I also put hanging bead curtains in all the doorways (to break up sight lines; no one, bad guy or good guy, moves into a place they can't see) and plastic horizontal shutters on all the windows, backed up by heavy black canvas drapes. I replaced the doors throughout with solid core ones (harder to break down) and each of the three exterior doors (front yard, back yard, garage) had six big bolts installed (four on the right side of the door, one on the jamb side of the door, one coming down from the ceiling).

When all that was done I went into the basement and knocked together some forms with two-by-fours and made shelves to cover the windows. Although they were lousy shelves they made excellent barricades and didn't look too obvious. Battery-powered smoke alarms went onto the ceiling of every room and in the corner went disposable flashlights, small first-aid kits and two medium-sized fire extinguishers, one set per room. While I was doing that I had Marie stock the basement with canned food (choosing stuff that wouldn't taste bad cold, like ravioli and fruit salad) and bottled water, just in case.

"What about protection?"

I dusted my hands off. "You have to make a decision now. Remember that anything you use as a defence can be taken away and used against you."

"I understand that."

"Okay. This is what I've brought."

I laid twenty-one cans out on the kitchen table while Eloise made regular coffee. Marie looked the items over with incomprehension. "What is this?"

"First. Air horns, one per room. Someone breaks in and you turn on the air horn. Bad guys don't like loud noises, it attracts attention. I've broken the latch so the horns can't be shut off."

I held up another can. "Cans of spray paint. This stuff is metallic neon green. Again, bad guys don't want the attention and if you spray someone with it they're going to stick out. Also, it can be sprayed in the face; it'll blind the person, permanently, I think."

Marie touched the last can. "And this?"

"Spray glue. Bonds almost instantly. Spray the target and whatever the target touches they stick to. It comes out fast; it's also mildly corrosive, unpleasant shit."

I went through the house and put three cans in each room. Then I came back. "There you go."

"And it's all legal?"

"Yeah. All of it. Until you use it on a person. Then it's assault with a dangerous weapon." Eloise gave me a cup of coffee and I sipped it and went on, "Just remember that there are no dangerous weapons, just dangerous people."

Two days later in the morning Claire took care of the kids and I caught a bus downtown to the Millennium Library which was right beside a big old church and the MTS Centre. Outside on the sidewalk I paused and looked the Centre over. I'd read Claire's book about the Eaton Building that had been there. The old building won hands down for style, but there was still a certain something about the new complex; a kind of modern, looming grandeur and artificial coolness.

Old habits made me walk the perimeter inside and outside and I sadly concluded that there would be no easy way to rob the place. Busy, one-way streets on all sides, tons of cameras, and easily secured loading zones.

That was too bad because the place would seat at least 16,000. And figuring an average ticket price of $30 (I picked the number out of the air), that meant a box office of maybe $480,000. That was if everyone paid in cash and bought the tickets when they arrived, which they never, ever did. And that sum of cash was a legitimately sized target, maybe thirty years' worth of work at a wage-slave job.

Those kinds of thoughts led inevitably to madness so, with difficulty, I turned my face away from temptation and the easy way.

Inside the library I admired the glassed-in rear which fronted on a small park; there was something divine and inspiring about the four floors of clean light and work space. Made me wish I was more, I don't know, academic with some great, important project to work on. Something like the complete history of the spoon. Instead I stayed on the first floor by the graphic novels and mysteries and picked up copies of the local papers, the *Free Press* and the *Sun*, for the past couple of days. No ID was needed to look so I picked them up and sat down at a table and scoured the news sections. I was looking for any reports about the drug house I'd wrecked, any references at all, but there was nothing. Just the normal byline that the police were expecting to make more arrests soon and that the guilty party (or parties) would face the full punishment of the law.

I really wasn't sure what I was looking for; just double-checking the cops didn't have a description of me listed along with a reward.

At the very tail end of the most recent *Free Press* article, though, the crime reporter gave the name of company that had rented the house out in the first place—Ultra Realty Rentals and Sales, which matched what Claire had told me. I wondered what kind of business would rent to a bunch of druggies; it could be an honest business fooled by the bad guys, or the realtor could be a front for the bad guys.

I wasn't positive either way, so I headed over to the free Express Internet service and dialed into Google, which directed me to a little web page that listed the address of Ultra Realty. I wrote that down on a little scrap of paper conveniently provided right next to the computer along with stupid little golf pencils. Knowing about the realtor would be a good thing and I stared into the distance and thought some more.

The Express Internet at the library was only usable for fifteen minutes at a time. Which was bad; however, again I didn't have to provide any ID to use them, which was good, privacy being hard to find and keep. And my search only took me five minutes, really.

Outside it was a beautifully warm fall day. The kind Claire's aunt would have called an Indian summer, which would have resulted in Claire's cousin giving her a lecture on political correctness. This would have resulted in a fight of some seriousness which I would have probably had to break up. Which would have meant someone would have called me a thieving so-and-so.

Sometimes I'm glad Claire and I don't live in the same city as her family.

Outside the library, on the sidewalk, I decided to burglarize Ultra Realty. That meant I'd need tools. I walked a few blocks to a small store that specialized in selling cheap junk at low prices; there a pinch-faced young Asian man greeted me with bustling cheer.

"Can I help you?"

"I'll just look around."

"Sure! Ask if you need anything."

For a moment I felt nostalgic and thought about going back to my favourite independent hardware store on Main where the owner hated me. I kept trying to make friends with him and it wasn't working. He couldn't forgive me for being an ex-con. A few months before he'd gone along with a Winnipeg detective named Walsh to try to force me out of town. After the dust had settled the cop had retired under psychiatric care and I was still coming into the hardware store whenever I could. And the old man kept snapping at me.

But this guy was worse, he was too damn happy.

Burglary requires thought and consideration and planning, all of which I was avoiding. Instead I picked up a couple of metres of different gauges of wire, some cheap screwdrivers, and a roll of wide, clear tape. Then a roll of paper towel, some lightweight canvas gloves, a glass cutter and a little pry bar forty-five centimetres long. When I went to pay, the owner kept smiling at me over the cash register. "Thank you for shopping!"

I nodded and he went on, "And have a nice day!"

It was barely 3:00 so I found a coffee shop to drink good coffee and wait. I figured the office of Ultra Realty probably closed at 5:00 or 5:30, so I'd wait until 6:00, early enough for people to be on the street so my presence wouldn't be as noticeable, because burglary is a profession best practised in peace and quiet.

#12

The office was west of downtown past the University of Winnipeg in a pretty battered neighbourhood. It was a region full of gangsters and hookers, drugged-out stoners and sniffers, determined panhandlers, stunned teenagers, and endemic poverty. And dozens of cops, walking in pairs down the sidewalks, driving in singletons in Crown Victorias, fingering their belts, saying please and thank you as long as the citizens were watching.

A blue blanket, thick and comforting.

Ultra Realty's office was on a tree-lined street, an older house turned into an office suite. I walked past it and saw the lights were out before heading down the alley behind it and checking that side out. There was a chain-link fence and a partially covered porch and small steel shed near the back of the house, not quite touching the wall. No dog that I could see and no piss marks on the lawn, which meant I was probably safe.

Without pausing I walked through the gate towards the

shed, ducked down between it and the house, and pulled on a pair of gloves. There was a small window so I took out the tape and glass cutter and went to work. Within seconds I had the tape over most of the window, leaving a big loop for a handle, and had scored around the outer edges with the cutter. Although there was a prominent security company sign promising instant alarm response on the front lawn and in the back window, there were no sensor wires on the window in front of me.

I wondered if that was an error or an omission.

With the glass on the grass beside me I took a deep breath and slid face first through into a dark basement. Standing on my tiptoes, I reached back and picked up the glass, held it by the tape loop, and put it back into the frame. Then I taped the glass back into place. My handiwork would be easily visible at close range but no one would probably notice from one or two metres away.

I went exploring. Fortunately there was enough light outside that I neither had to turn on the overheads nor use my flashlight. Because nothing attracts cops and nosy neighbours faster than lights suddenly going on in a supposedly empty business, except perhaps a flashlight beam bobbing along in a supposedly empty business.

Overall I gave the owners a grade of B for design and decor. Basement with an old furnace and water heater, walls stacked with file boxes, Rubbermaid tubs of smoke alarms and dead bolts, and a fairly complete set of decent quality hand tools in a kit under the stairs. The first floor had two offices, each with a desk and a couple of comfortable chairs, and a combo kitchen/dining room turned into a big meeting room with multiple coffee pots. The second floor had been turned into a single large room with many phones, assorted computers and towers, printers, fax machines, work tables, and a whole wall of filing cabinets. On top of the work table, under a lamp, was a metal cash box which rattled pleasantly, but I left it alone with just a little twitch of my larcenous soul.

First things first. I plugged in a big brand-name photocopier and let it warm up. Then I stood there and thought about the place. The purpose of any space defines its design, and this business rented houses. The offices downstairs were probably used by the realtors meeting with clients, so they had a casual and relaxed feel to them. The big meeting room was for the staff to have lunch and build morale and the upstairs was where the work was done, records were kept, properties tracked, and bad renters dunned.

I went to the filing cabinets and started at the one prominently labelled A. Ever wonder how a rental company organizes properties? They could do it by the street name of the property, which would be reasonable. Or they could do it by the owner of the property, which would make no sense because you'd have to know which property was owned by which owner. Of course, Ultra Realty did it by the owner, so it took me two hours to find the address I wanted. I also found one bottom filing drawer that was locked, which piqued my curiosity.

I stood there and read the files; the drug house belonged to a Mr. Jarrod Jarelski who lived in a house in the medium-rich River Heights district. He owned eleven other rental properties managed by Ultra. His wife, named Tho, also had cheque-signing privileges and other executive powers. I photocopied their contact information and put the papers back before returning to the file.

On the last page there were handwritten notes. Someone had written "Mr. J wants this property rented ASAP. Will take

$300.00/per. Maybe less." ASAP had been underlined twice. On another page the Jarelskis had waived the references normally required, which allowed Mr. and Mrs. Abernathy to rent the house. Their deposit had been $1000 cash, rental was paid in cash, dropped off on the first of each month by Mrs. Abernathy, and the contact numbers were cell phones, which raised warning flags. Most citizens have land lines AND cell phones but most bad guys ONLY have cell phones. Even a monkey can buy a cell phone, but a land line means a credit check.

When my two copied sheets were tucked away in my pockets, I unplugged the photocopier and went back to the locked cabinet. By locked, I mean seriously locked, with a steel Mastercraft padlock on a heavy-duty steel assembly spot welded onto the front frame of the cabinet.

A little voice inside me started to chirp about temptation and ego and challenge and I ignored it for a good ten seconds and then I gave in.

Curiosity plus ego plus a challenge is a nasty combination.

I studied the cabinet for two minutes and then pulled out the drawer above the locked one, but no luck; it was a model that wouldn't slide the drawer all the way out. No problem; I reached behind and walked the whole unit out into the middle of the room so I could see the back, which was cheap steel held in place by welded and folded edges.

I went to the basement and, after a brief search, picked up a hammer and flat-edged screwdriver. Upstairs, I went to the back of the file cabinet, sat down on the floor, and slipped the blade of the screwdriver into the welded edge at the bottom of the drawer. Then I covered the butt of the screwdriver with a rag before hitting it with the hammer, which made the weld open a little, enough for the fine edge of the pry to go in. Then I moved the screwdriver up and did it again and again and within a few minutes I had opened up a fold in the metal thirty centimetres square. Then I simply reached into the locked drawer.

Feeling around in the dark I felt familiar metal and leather. I pulled the gun out, put it on the carpet in front of me, and exhaled softly. There was dim twilight in the room brought by the street lights outside and the occasional parasitic light thrown up by cars cruising down the street, light that made the gun glow softly once out of its plain brown holster. It was an old piece, almost an antique, but in great condition, a Polish semi-automatic Radom pistol from before the Second World War. I looked it over and saw the five-digit serial number on the side along with the Polish imperial eagle stamp. It took 9-mm parabellum rounds and there was a loaded magazine in the gun and a second magazine in a pouch built into the holster along with a cleaning rod.

I had used a Radom before and had liked it, a good, reliable weapon, accurate as any other pistol I'd ever used. I left it alone and kept feeling around the drawer and found a plastic coin purse holding eleven more rounds and a hard canvas money belt with no money in it. It was empty. There was also a manila envelope with pictures of people, men, women, even children. On the back were dates and names and addresses. Bad renters' maybe?

Which meant what? The realtors carried the gun and the money belt when they went to pick up rent? Possibly. Very illegal and very American big city indeed. I couldn't even imagine the series of licences and rules you'd have to jump through in order to carry a concealed, loaded firearm. The federal government would be involved with their lame-duck gun registry. The provincial government would be involved, somehow, somewhere. And lastly, city hall and the cops both would be there like ... I couldn't come up with a simile. I put everything back into the drawer, pushed the edges back into place (sort of) and then pushed the unit back against the wall.

I started to think of the realtor as being at least semi-bent and then I fixed the gun in my memory in case I ever needed a cold piece with no links to me at all. Not that I'd ever need a gun again, but you never know.

When the screwdriver and hammer were back in place in the basement, I went to the rear door and peered out from the bottom to check if anyone was outside. Unfortunately, four guys in business suits were taking down a guy in track pants and expensive shoes just outside the chain fence and I had to wait until they'd tackled him, handcuffed him, wrestled him into the plastic back seat of their unmarked car (always identifiable by the lack of whitewall tires), and driven off. Since the guys in the business suits were white, except for one Asian, and the guy in the track suit had been black, I figured the whole scene was cops taking someone down.

When everyone was gone I opened the door, ignored the alarm system by the door that started to beep, and walked, never running, down towards the alley. Behind me I knew what was happening; the alarm would wait for thirty seconds for someone to punch in an override. Then the alarm would send a message to the alarm company, which would phone Ultra Realty's owner, who would decide that the alarm company, should respond. So they would phone the cops or security company who would send a patrol car down to look around.

But that would take time. And I was soon on a bus heading back home, ten blocks away and still moving. They'd check the place out from the outside, back door first; probably not even notice the window. Then they'd wait for the owner to show and they'd look around together.

And then they'd probably decide that the last person leaving hadn't locked the door.

Back at home Marie had left a message that said simply, "Problems, come quickly."

#13

Marie's message had sounded urgent so I went into over-drive, only taking time to look for the bayonet. I'd purchased it years before, a ninety-year-old wooden-handled Mauser bayonet with a thirty-centimetre blade that held edges perfectly and featured a blood groove down the centre. I'd intended for Claire to use it for self/home defence originally, but these days we mostly used it for cutting roasts; the rest of the time it stayed under the pillow in our bedroom. Finally I asked Claire, "Where's the bayonet?"

She looked at me coolly and started to rummage through kitchen drawers. "Problems?"

"Yeah."

She pulled the bayonet out of a drawer and drew the blade out of its metal sheath to show it to me. "We're having chicken tomorrow so I sharpened it. Be careful."

Claire's dad was a butcher and she had grown up sharpening knives and cleavers for him, so I took her at her word and took off my shirt. She helped me tape the sheath to my chest under my shirt with the handle pointing down. Then she repeated, "Be careful."

"I will."

"I'm not worried about you but I really like the knife."

I kissed her and left.

In front of Marie's house was a tricked-out black van and, sitting in the driver's seat, a fat kid reading a comic book. He didn't even notice me as I cut around behind the van and checked the licence plate. I was looking for any sign that the plate had been altered or replaced but there was nothing. No fresh screw marks, no clean spots, nothing, so I memorized the number and kept on walking.

Marie met me on the sidewalk with a smile that had drawn her skin tight and dry across her face.

"We have a problem." She licked her lips. "Inside. Her name is Samantha. Greg talked."

It made me pause and remember advice from long ago about how to deal with problems permanently the first time. I ignored it and went inside, where I found a strange tableau in the living room; three people I'd never seen before, two men and a woman standing in the farthest corner talking to each other while in the middle of the room Eloise was making ahwah.

"Seamus Fantomas?"

It was the woman, her voice calm and relaxed, and I looked her over carefully. She was Caucasian with light brown hair, in her early or mid thirties with a thin mouth. She had a blood-red bandanna wrapped around her head and was wearing expensive blue jeans and a black silk shirt with a white bull's-eye over her left nipple. She was also wearing a short black leather motorcycle jacket and a pair of fine-grained cowboy boots with chiselled silver tips on the toes.

Compared to her the two men with her weren't very impressive. One was in his early twenties, thin of build with long black hair and bright blue eyes. The other was in his late twenties, short and stocky with a face covered in scars under a shock of red hair. Both wore dark blue track suits, expensive runners and short black leather jackets that were opened up to the neck. Their hands were open and loose at their sides.

I answered the woman, "That's me."

She smiled a thin-lipped smile and walked towards me. When she was close she looked me over from my toes to the top of my head.

"You don't look so tough."

"Eat me and find out."

I said it blandly and the big, thin guy tensed up behind the woman. She shook her head and said, "I'm Sam. You chased one of my best customers right out of the fucking province."

"I chased who where?"

"A customer. His name was Greg. You stuck a hatchet in his leg and threatened to gouge his eye out. I had some associates catch up with him in Toronto. You did a good job; he was still heading east. Asked my boys where France was."

She reached into the pocket of her jacket and came out with small tape recorder, one of those that record directly into a hard drive of a computer. With a flourish she put it on the table and her finger hovered over the controls. "Wanna hear?"

"Sure."

The voice that came out of the machine was recognizably Greg's. "... okay. Yeah. This mean fucker was gonna crucify me, gouge my fucking eyes out with a spoon unless I gave him Sam's name ... I had no choice."

Sam reached down, pressed the "pause" button, and shook her head. "Once they start to rat people out it just keeps going, know what I mean? You really shouldn't have trusted him once he gave up my name. That's free advice."

I didn't say anything and she pressed the button again. "It's this chick called Marie and two old guys, Don and Al, they're gonna run wetbacks and Chinks across to the States. They've got a route down and help on the other side, just like I told Sam. Anyhow ..."

I turned the machine off and Sam pocketed the machine. "There's more, but your route sounds made to order."

She winked. "I want it."

I looked over at Marie, who was immobile by the entrance to the living room, before I answered. "No."

"No?"

Sam smiled with her mouth and the two guys behind her shifted their weight and moved their hands nervously.

I winked back at Sam. "No. You may not have the route."

Sam put her hands into the pockets of her jacket and leaned back on her heels before saying conversationally, "You gonna stop me?"

I looked at her and the two guys and then nodded thoughtfully. "You don't know me, right?"

The woman looked over at the two men and they both shook their heads before turning back to me and saying, "No, should I?"

"I could be connected. I could be laying something out for the Yamaguchi-gumi. Yakuza based in Tokyo's Shibuya district."

She shook her head. "I don't think so."

I let my voice harden. "Or I could be fronting for Mississippi Dixie Mafia hardasses looking for a new supplier of meth precursors now that the Mexico route is getting tight."

"Nooooo." She put her forefinger to her chin. "Probably not."

"Maybe I'm running an escape route for the Aryan Brotherhood who don't want to stay in Atwater or Lewisburg and, once they're out, don't want to spend their freedom eating beans and drinking mescal."

Sam bit her lower lip and I smiled, "Or I could be putting the final touches on a run for the Solntsevskaya out of Moscow to deliver Turkish hash to the Midwest."

There was silence in the room. I waited, but no one said anything. "Any of those could be true. Go find out who I am and then decide what you're going to do."

I stepped close to Sam and she recoiled as I snarled, "Because you should know that the route is mine and that's how it will stay."

When she spoke her voice was level. "So who are you really?"

"Montgomery Haaviko."

"Who should I ask?"

I walked to the door and the three followed me. When I opened the door they all stood there confused, the two men looking at Sam and Sam looking at me as she repeated, "Who should I ask?"

"Anyone."

They left and Marie came over to me. "That was scary."

"Yeah."

"Should I be worried?"

I looked her over and winked. "Definitely."

She exhaled through her nose and brought me a cup of ahwah and had one herself before going on, "What should we do? Start carrying guns?"

I drank the coffee before answering.

"Probably a good idea."

#14

In the middle of the night I couldn't sleep so I kissed my lovely wife awake. I'd debated lies to tell her and finally said, "I'm going to go find a loose woman."

"'Kay."

"Is that all you can say?"

She yawned. "Bring her home. We'll give her a spin. But if she's better than you then you'll be getting your walking papers."

It's very hard to shock my wife.

Outside it was cold and getting colder. I took a brisk walk and thought some fairly nasty thoughts. By 8:00 am I was tired and somewhat lost but in possession of a plan. Sam had struck me as being capable, smart, and with a potential for violence. She had also impressed me by having a team capable of picking up Greg quickly in a different city. All that information and impression made her scary and someone I should deal with fast.

Outside of a convenience store I made ten phone calls to

places that customized vans, figuring they'd open early like most garages. In each call I gave the same spiel: I had seen a van with the licence plate I'd seen outside Marie's house for sale and I wanted to buy it but the number on the "for sale" sign wasn't legible. On the fifth call I reached someone who knew something about the van and after three minutes of conversation they gave me a phone number. Ten minutes after that, with the help of the telephone operator, I had the address.

Then I went home and took a long nap while I was supposed to be watching the kids.

By six that night I was down at a big discount store on Portage Avenue by foot, Red Apple or Giant Tiger or Red Tiger or Giant Apple, I'm not sure which. For thirty-one dollars and a few cents I bought a dark blue cotton warm-up jacket, a black T-shirt, and a pair of black canvas pants with big pockets, along with three pairs of black sports socks and a pair of badly made runners from Taiwan. Further down the street there was a outdoor outfitter that sold me a big mountaineer's carabineer for eight dollars, a roll of black fabric tape, some cheap white gloves, and a dark blue balaclava.

I changed in the alley behind the place after checking for cameras, my own clothes going into the plastic bag, which I tucked behind a big garbage bag. Then I took ten minutes to arm myself. First I put three socks one inside the other and loaded it with a fistful of fine sand I picked up from a fancy outdoor ashtray outside a hotel. Then I taped the makeshift sap into relative stiffness and put it in my right jacket pocket. The carabineer I fitted over my left fist to make sure it fit and then I padded it with more tape, which also removed the metal glint, and that gave me a brass knuckle. That went into my left-hand pocket and I was ready to go to work.

An hour later I was on the corner of a street in Osborne Village watching the black van on a concrete pad behind a dilapidated house. I had stolen a bicycle from an Italian coffee bar on Corydon; the owner had used a padlock and a normal steel chain. The lock was good, but the chain itself had twisted and broken when I applied force using the carabineer for leverage, and I had a bike. If anyone noticed the theft no one said anything. I left the bike in a pile of garbage near the house and started my surveillance.

Standing on a residential street corner is not the best way to be unnoticeable so I walked up and down the alley where the van was parked. I needed a plausible reason to be in the area, so I clapped my hands repeatedly and whistled sharply. Every few minutes I called out gently, "Fido, here boy!" in a wheedling tone. When I was beside the van the first time, I saw it was freshly washed, giving a completely different impression from the slovenly house whose parking space it occupied.

The second time I went by a young, fattish woman came to the edge of a fenced-in yard and stared hard at me, saying, "What do you want?"

Her voice gave a different impression from her appearance; it was precise and the diction was excellent.

I answered cheerfully, "Just looking for my cat."

"Your cat is named Fido?"

"Yes."

She stared at me some more, "Fido means faithful."

"Yes. I almost named it Nemo."

She was standing on something on the other side of the fence and I could see the caption on her shirt, LA LUCHA CONTINUA.

"What does your shirt mean?"

The woman looked down as though surprised at her breasts and then back at me. She didn't smile, she never smiled during the whole conversation, and I began to wonder if she indeed could smile. She answered, "It means 'The Struggle Continues.'"

"Ah."

She turned abruptly and left and I kept walking back and forth trying to decide what to do. Finally the fat kid who'd been in Sam's van came out of the house and drove away. I followed on the bicycle.

The van outdistanced me quickly heading down Cockburn and I rode along slowly, ignoring stop signs and trying to keep it in sight. After three blocks it turned into a Tim Horton's parking lot and stopped.

Perfect.

I checked the restaurant from the lot of a tire store across the street. Inside were four people at four separate tables, none of them familiar except for the fat boy. I went in and bought a cup of coffee to go and checked the boy out more closely. He was about nineteen, dangerously overweight, eating chocolate donuts with chocolate frosting and drinking grape pop. On the table was a slim cell phone holding open a very thick, brightly coloured comic book. Possibly the same one he had been reading earlier, apparently titled *The League of Extraordinary Gentlemen*.

As he ate he wheezed and I snuck up close to see a paint-by-numbers picture of Dorian Gray. I vaguely remembered a lousy Hollywood movie of the same title with Dorian Gray as one of the villains. I also vaguely remembered Dorian Gray as a character in a horror movie and I wondered if it was the same person.

Outside I went to a phone booth by the nearest gas station and called the donut shop. When the counter clerk answered I told her I'd been driving through her lot and had scraped the side of a black van but that I was in hurry and couldn't stop. Then I asked her to tell the owner. As I was coming back to the shop I could see the clerk through the counter as she went directly to the fat boy and told him. He immediately gathered up his comic and phone and came out, almost running. By the time he reached the van in the corner of the lot I'd reached it as well, pulling the balaclava down as I went. He was swearing under his breath with his back to me as checked out the side panels when I made a final rush.

When I hit him, Fat Boy hissed loudly, lost control of his bladder and folded onto the ground, unconscious. Before he was all the way down I reached into his cheap leather jacket and retrieved his car keys. Two minutes later I had twisted him into the back of the van and I was driving serenely away. When I reached a big mall on the west end of town, I parked away from the doors and went into the back where Fat Boy was still out.

Ignoring the smell, I patted him down. He had the comic, two cell phones, a brass-handled Buck knife with a quick-release thumb switch soldered onto the blade, a wallet with a Visa card, and sixty-seven dollars in bills and coins. The van interior had been to turn it into a cargo carrier, but taped to one bare wall was an Easton Connexion aluminum bat spray-painted black. I pulled it free and used it as a lever to help me dislocate Fat Boy's right arm at the ball joint in his shoulder.

That woke him up and he screamed into his socks, which I'd knotted around his head to keep him quiet. When he stopped screaming I patted his cheek. "Hi! My name is Montgomery Uller Haaviko. Did your boss tell you about me?"

His eyes blinked repeatedly in the dim light from a nearby street.

"Can you understand me?"

He nodded.

"Do I have your undivided attention?"

He nodded again.

"Good."

I opened his knife one handed and cut the socks free so he could speak. The knife attracted his attention; knives are good for generating visceral fear. Fat Boy's first words were plaintive and whiny. "Jeeze, you didn't have to do that."

His face was grey-green and his eyes were pinpoints from the shock but I waved his comment away with the knife and said gently, "Let me tell you something about torture. If you are getting tortured, just give up the information as fast as you can. It's actually expected by professionals. Everyone breaks in time, so break quickly and keep your health intact."

"Why are you telling me this?"

"Because I'm torturing you. Right now."

"Oh." There was a long pause and then he added, "Oh."

"So are you going to tell me what I want to know?"

"I don't know …"

He shut up when I held his Buck knife before his eyes. Then I corrected him, "Wrong answer. The right answer is, yes. Or I'll cut off one testicle. I'll let you choose which one."

Fat Boy pissed his pants again and started to hyperventilate. When he calmed down I asked him again, "So are you going to tell me what I want to know?"

"Yes."

"That's a very, very good answer."

#15

Fat Boy was extremely helpful and for the next two hours he directed me around the city in the van and told me about the organization he worked for. To the best of his knowledge Sam owned two houses and he showed them both to me, one in the West End and one across the river in Saint Boniface. From there she ran eleven low-rent, tire-biter hookers (his term for a prostitute who worked in the back seats of cars only). She also dealt drugs to lower-level dealers and addicts and did a little bit of fencing. In total there were six guys employed as muscle, including Fat Boy. Samantha Ritchot was the boss but she did have a boyfriend who helped.

He told me all sorts of other stuff too, most of which I ignored.

The rest of the night sucked, mostly. I parked in another shopping mall lot and waited for the stores to open and every few hours Fat Boy would come out of shock and whine a little and then drift away again.

On the plus side, I got to read *The League of Extraordinary*

Gentlemen and found it to be very, very cool. Who knew comics could be smart?

At ten the next morning the stores opened and I tied Fat Boy up with his belt and shoe laces, stuffed his socks back in his mouth and covered his head with his jacket. When he complained I opened the knife again and he changed his mind. I made my first stop at the Fishing Hole tackle shop and bought a tan-coloured, multi-pocketed fish-killing vest. Then I went to the Cellar Dweller hobby shop for some radio-controlled car supplies and extra wire and finally to the European Sausage Experience, where I bought all the marzipan they had, two kilos of the sugar-and-almond paste.

In a parking lot for the Forks shopping centre in the middle of town, I cut the marzipan into slices about a centimetre thick, blotted them dry with napkins, and then stuffed lengths of wire into them, one to the other. When they were all done I tucked them into the pockets of the vest, closed the flaps, buttons, and zippers, and made a few more adjustments here and there before pulling my jacket on to cover the vest. The smell was very strong but that was okay, I wanted it strong.

Next I stopped at a Canadian Tire store off St. James and bought ten full tanks of propane using Fat Boy's Visa. A couple of blocks away from that I stopped at a Wal-Mart and used the same card to buy twenty plastic containers for gasoline, some highway flares, a mechanical alarm clock, some heavy-gauge wire, and a car battery. Then I went down Portage Avenue and filled two gas cans at each station I found until they were all full, and parked near a McDonald's to assemble the fuse and detonator from the clock and battery.

I set it for one hour and drove to the house in Saint Boniface where Fat Boy had said Sam would probably be. I parked beside the house with the nose of the van touching the garage itself. Then I went into the back and checked the restraints on Fat Boy. They were good and I opened his hand. He stared at me wild-eyed and tried to talk around the gag as I reassured him.

"I'm not going to hurt you. Not unless you make me. I'm going to duct tape your cell phone so you can reach it, 'kay?"

He nodded and I gestured with my head while working. "Look around. See the gas cans? I've turned the van into a bomb."

His eyes bulged. "Now, someone's going to call you on the cell. Just tell them there's a bomb. Understand?"

He nodded. "Good. Now if you do anything else—like call the cops or whatever—then I'll blow you into little bits. 'Kay?"

He nodded and I put the jacket back over his head with the cell phone tied right in front of his nose and went back to the driver's seat and sat down. It was a nice neighbourhood and the house looked in good repair, not like a drug house at all. I waited ten minutes to let them notice me and then locked the van, walked to the door, and knocked.

Immediately the door opened an inch and a big guy looked me over dispassionately from under a heavy chain. "Where's Tony?"

"Who's Tony?"

"The driver."

I shrugged. "In the van. It's booby-trapped though. Let me in."

He undid some bolts and let me into a narrow entryway, where the air smelled of burnt chemicals, flint, ozone, battery acid, tobacco, marijuana, sweat, fried food, pepper spray, unflushed toilets, and mould. The big guy was white, maybe six foot six and made up of terrace upon terrace of muscle, all stuffed into a greyish leather vest, Doc Marten boots, and a pair of spandex shorts. In his right hand he casually held a mountaineer's ice axe with rust spots showing on both pick and axe end. He stared at me with lustrous brown eyes under a shaggy mop of black hair and I showed him my empty right hand.

"Klaatu-barada-nicto."

"What?"

A voice from behind him said, "It's a joke. From an old movie about the end of the world. It's a code to deactivate a robot."

I couldn't see who was speaking and the guy's eyes narrowed, "'zat so?"

"It's a compliment." I spoke quickly; my options were relatively few. "I'm comparing you to a kick-ass robot with the power to destroy the world."

His eyes opened a little more. "Cool." And then he let me pass. Behind him Samantha was wearing a dark-blue track suit. "Montgomery Uller Haaviko."

"Yep."

"I talked to some people who talked to some people. You did the racetrack in Surrey three years ago."

The hair on the back of my neck went up; I'd never been convicted, connected, or even arrested about that one. "Maybe."

She smiled. "Yeah. And you did a Texas hold 'em game at the Blue Goose lodge on the little Sou-west about eight years ago. And a getaway man named Ron in Banff, him you knee-capped; he's still around but moving slowly. He talks about you with a lot of hate but seems to be unwilling to do much about the whole thing."

"You've done your homework."

"I did."

"I'm just checking to make sure you understood me before. I don't want any trouble, I just want you to leave me and what's mine alone."

My smile was false and she said, "No." Her smile was genuine and she went on, "You like movies?"

"What do you mean, no?"

Her face lit up. "No means no. Me, I love movies. But I hate the latest version of the first *Star Wars*. Where Lucas gives Greedo the first shot at Han Solo under the table in the Cantina scene. You know what I mean? In the original, Han has balls, he's a drug smuggler, someone braces him and he pulls his piece under the table and BOOM. Bye-bye Greedo. Know what I mean?"

She leaned forward and kept talking. "Guess what's pointed at you right now? Through the plaster wall right beside you."

"A gun?"

"That was too easy, what kind of gun?"

I kept my voice level. "No idea. So you're not going to make nice?"

Samantha's face tightened and her voice dropped. "There's a boy with a twenty-gauge sawed-off pump shotgun pointed at your head right now. It's loaded with slugs. Listen, hear that?"

The ratcheting sound of the pump being worked somewhere to the right of me through the thin wall was loud.

Very slowly I held up my hand. "I came here in good faith …"

She shrugged and her eyes sparkled. "That's your problem. Not mine."

"… but I'm not an idiot. You know what this is?"

I held up the yellow plastic handgrip in front of her and she stared at it. "No."

"It's a remote off a set of toy race cars. A short-range radio, hooked up to four kilos of Semtex, which are rolled thin around my chest right now in this stupid vest. If your boy pulls the trigger, that might set the detonators off, or I might drop the remote as I die and that might do it."

She chewed her bottom lip and I watched her eyes absorb what I was saying. When her eyes started to narrow I waited and counted my own heartbeats.

One.

You gotta make bad guys fear and their capacity for violence is truly amazing, so their capacity for fear is awesome indeed. That's because they can imagine bad things happening.

Two.

In other words the bad ones can do really bad things and therefore believe the same in others.

Three, and I went on, "Smell, that's not air you're breathing. That's the sweet chemical tang of Slovakian plastique, a mixture of cyclonite and pentaerythrite tetranitrate. Shipped from the Synthesia Pardubice factory to Odessa in Ukraine and from there by freighter to Churchill, Manitoba, where it is exchanged for Levi jeans, Viagra, and Colombian cocaine. And from there to me."

"Bullshit."

I nodded. "Sure. I'm lying. I walked into this place with my dick in my hand and no plan. And maybe the van outside is loaded with gasoline and propane tanks to blow this house into orbit. And maybe it has a timer, just in case the vest fails."

"Bullshit. Why are you so willing to die for this kind of shit?"

"I'm not fucking around; I want to show you that, so here are all the cards on the table. I'm showing you some respect here; I'm laying it on the line with no bargaining. I'm telling you that I'm connected, honey, that I'm wired, pardon the expression. And I do not lie and I do not play games. My past will hopefully have shown you that."

"Bullshit."

"There's enough bang here to make a hole twenty metres across and six deep. Enough to kill every person within thirty metres of here, guaranteed."

"Bullshit."

"Why don't you call Fat Boy? He's taped up in the van but I taped his cell phone into his hand. He should be able to text you something."

Sam pulled out a cell phone and tapped away quickly for a few seconds and then read the message out loud. "He says the van is wired. That's the van right outside?"

"That's the one. That's my back-up with anti-tampering fuzes, a timer, and it's linked to the same controller as this one. Breathe heavy on it and BOOM!"

"Sure …"

She sounded less positive and I nodded again. "Instant urban renewal. So I'm gonna walk one way and you walk the other and if I see you anywhere near Marie's route or around me then I pull my gloves off and take you out."

Samantha wasn't moving. "You're bluffing."

"Trust your nose."

It wrinkled slowly and deliberately, and about a minute later I walked out, went to the van, and shut the timer attached to the propane and gas off with twenty-eight minutes to go.

Two blocks away I took the bus home. When I arrived

I was A) smacked by Claire, B) kissed by Claire and told to behave better, and C) mobbed by many small children. After Claire had left, the kids helped me make 142 chocolate brownies with marzipan frosting. When the parents came to redeem their kids, each received a dozen brownies decorated by their kids.

I hate to let things go to waste.

#16

I spent the next week growing ears and eyes in strange places and double- and triple-checking everything around me. But no Sam, no nothing at all, and at the end of the week I had enough confidence to take the monsters with me on a long walk that touched three separate playgrounds in our neighbourhood. While we played, wreaked havoc, and played some more, I had time to think about tracking down the original owners of the drug house I'd flooded and dealing with them.

Just for practice, just to keep busy.

I sat there and watched the kids play and wondered why I had wrecked the drug house in the first place. The best thing I could come up with was that wrecking the place had been reflex; it had offended my sense of something or other.

A union guy I'd worked with once had said that every employee should keep a hammer handy at all times. Not for work. Just to tap the foreman every now and then to get their attention. Later I found out the union guy had stolen the line from a science fiction novel, but the principle was still sound.

On the way back home with very tired children I passed by the drug house. It was quickly turning grey. The lawn was still littered with garbage and the whole building was plastered with sheets of cardboard and plywood and sealed with bright yellow police caution tape. Already all the surfaces were starting to accumulate a new crop of graffiti and obscenities, some of it beautifully done in curlicues and ornate lettering. I walked around back and saw that one of the boards on the rear door had already been moved, and I figured squatters and runaways had begun moving in.

My nose wrinkled in memory. I'd been in a lot of places like that over the years and the smell was memorable, even unforgettable. With no toilet the inhabitants would piss and shit in dark corners and leave it. With no stove they'd cook over piles of twigs and broken furniture, generally in the sinks or in the basement on concrete. Garbage would be left everywhere, untended. The filth would accumulate and attract small creatures, disease bearing, stealthy and biting. Colonial ants with their workers and queens and larvae, fighting and scavenging and fucking, while in the corners and cracks would be the bedbugs laying four eggs a day, every day. Cockroaches born carrying their eggs already fertilized and waiting, capable of producing 4500 young a year and each female infant being capable of doing the same. Fleas, biting and leaping, incontinent mice darting everywhere, rats, where the conditions were right, nightmarish silverfish, organized termites chewing in the walls, vampiric ticks.

Rabies and hantavirus possible from mammals. Bubonic plague and Lyme disease from their parasites. Hookworms and tapeworms and other parasites from other parasites. A brand new ecosystem, all starting six blocks from my home.

While I was standing there a very thin lady came over and shoved a clipboard in my face: "Sign!"

I signed a false name with my left hand and then asked, "What am I signing?"

"It's a petition to force the owners of this place to clean it up or tear it down. It's an eyesore."

"It is that. So who owns it?"

"We're not sure, the management company isn't returning our calls but we're looking into it."

"Good for you."

Me and the monsters went home, had a snack, and then a brisk nap.

Later on, the phone did the double, long-distance ring. The voice on the other end was polite, precise, and very professional. There was nothing in the background to give his location away.

"Am I speaking to Mr. Haaviko?"

"Yep."

"Mr. Montgomery Haaviko? I have to be positive so please forgive me. Montgomery Haaviko, formerly a federal prisoner?"

I didn't say anything and he added, "Number … "

He repeated six digits and a letter that I was unlikely to forget but I just waited. The voice repeated it accurately again and I felt myself getting cold and angry. "Who are you?"

"I am Lawrence McQuaid of Chang and McQuaid. I'm a lawyer based out of Vancouver and I have a client who wants to speak with you."

"Your client is?"

"He is very cautious. He will introduce himself."

"I see."

I thought about what the man had said. Then I thought about how far a lawyer would stick his neck out? Perhaps it depended on the fee, perhaps I was being cynical. Probably a lawyer would not break the law, which meant they would not be setting someone up for a murder. Probably but not guaranteed.

The voice repeated the federal prisoner number that had been mine. "Is that you?"

"It was. Have your client call me before he comes anywhere near."

"That's up to him."

"No. Make sure he calls me first. I'm making it your responsibility."

"I'll do my best."

"Just as long as it happens. He calls me first. First."

"And if not?"

I left the question hang and he repeated himself twice more before I hung up. When the phone rang again I let it alone but he kept calling. After sixty-two tries during the evening he finally gave up and Claire and I went to bed.

Upstairs I lay in the dark and thought about the next day, about the final touches on the route. No point in doing it early because Marie had to be ready and she wasn't yet.

Finally I drifted off to sleep.

#17

The doorbell rang at half-past two in the morning and I rolled out of bed and jogged downstairs in a pair of boxers and a T-shirt. Outside the door was someone I had never expected to see again and when I opened it his face lit up. "Hey, Monty. You scared the piss out of my liar."

Smiley's hands were open at his sides and he wore a black canvas windbreaker down to mid-thigh and the dark green oversized shirt and pants the screws give you in prison. You weren't supposed to take them with you when you left but everyone did because guys who wanted to be bad wore them on the street to advertise. And guys like me sold them to rappers who wrote songs about shooting niggers, stabbing fags in the head, and beating up their bitches.

Smiley wore the clothes when he was out because he liked how they fit.

He was a bad man. As a bad man myself I can say with confidence that he was worse than I had ever been. He was a little shorter than six feet and maybe 180 pounds, solidly built and covered with tattoos that were hidden from every-day viewers. His hair was short and black and his eyes were pale brown, washed out, and emotionless, except for the smile that constantly played around his lips.

He was always a happy man.

I'd met him three or four times in different prisons over two decades and had worked with him twice in the outside world. Both jobs had gone perfectly, which translated into cash and no heat.

He was very bad and very skilled and he enjoyed it all a lot.

"What do you want?"

"To come in."

"Sure."

He came in sideways through the door and his expensive camouflage backpack brushed the frame heavily. He put it down on the floor and looked around the living room.

"Nice place. No television?"

"Can't afford one and we don't want one so that works out. Here, we can sit in the dining room."

I took him back through to the dining table and sat him down with his back to the living room. Then I sat across from him with my back to the wall. "How'd you find me?"

He shrugged. "Easy. Cops tell lawyers all sorts of shit and lawyers talk, you just have to ask 'em nice. My lawyer's bent as they come and always willing to help someone out for a little extra."

"What do you want to talk about?"

He chewed on his upper lip and stared at me with his pale eyes that had seen too much. They had seen as much as mine had and maybe more and for the first time I realized how old and tired he looked. There were lines across his forehead and grey in the stubble on his cheeks, signs of aging that hadn't been there when I'd last seen him two years before.

Out of the corner of my eye I saw Claire ghost down the stairs in her bathrobe and move silently to the umbrella stand by the front door. With impeccable silence she pulled the crowbar out and started to move towards Smiley.

"Someone told me you went straight. That true?"

I shrugged. "You mean flaming or so-so?"

He didn't understand and elaborated for me, "Off the job. No longer a crook. No longer working. No longer stealing. Honest. A citizen."

He said it without contempt and I nodded. "Yep. That's me, a productive member of society. A citizen of the republic."

"Serial?" He leaned forward in his chair and it creaked. His hands were on the table and his knuckles were bright white with tension.

"I'm straight, serial. Serious as can be."

He nodded and before I could move he pulled a gun out from under his right arm and put it on the table between us. I swallowed. "Well, you've acquired my undivided attention."

"I wanted to show you I'm serious about what I'm saying. I want to go straight too. I just need a little help. I also need a place to stay and I can pay. But I really need help going straight. I'm serious about that."

"I believe you."

He touched the gun with a forefinger. "It's a Norinco Coach double-barrelled shotgun in twelve gauge. Stock rasped down to a pistol grip, barrel filed down to eighteen centimetres. Remember? Just like Doc Holliday."

We had discussed Doc in Drumheller prison while jogging on the track and watching out for the baby rattlesnakes that were supposed to be there but I never saw. Doc Holliday had carried a sawn-down shotgun under his arm attached by a rubber cord, a gun like the one Smiley had put on the table. The point of balance on the concealed piece was kept over the triggers so it always wanted to swing up, but if you wore a coat it kept the barrels pointed down. Open the coat and the piece swings into place, as sweet as pie.

I wondered why I hadn't seen the gun under his coat. I wondered how rusty I was getting.

He touched the gun again with affection. "Makes for a quick draw. External hammers. KISS."

Keep it simple, stupid. An external hammer meant you could tell it was cocked just by feel. It was also the safest kind of gun, it was either cocked or ready to fire or uncocked and you couldn't fire it by accident. My breathing was shallow and the hair on my arms was raised and my bladder wanted to empty. The adrenaline surged through me and sped up my blood flow and gave me the start of a wicked headache. It was flight or fight time and behind him Claire was moving very slowly and very quietly indeed and I tried not to look at her.

"Double-ought pellets in the left barrel for soft targets." Like people. "A rifled lead slug in the right barrel for hard targets." Like cops wearing body armour. In both cases the barrel was so short that half the unfired powder would be blown out still burning, which would make a huge mess. That would be all on top of the holes being blown into the target's body.

"A quality piece of work."

Smiley licked his lips and flexed his hand. For a moment he stared at it like it belonged to a stranger. Claire was about three feet behind him with the crowbar held to the side and back like a baseball bat.

"Do you know what Doc Holliday's last words were?"

"No."

"He was dying from tuberculosis and woke up in pain and alone. He asked for, and drank, a glass of whiskey. Then he said, 'This is funny.' And then he died."

"Uh-huh."

"Did you know that his shotgun sold for fifty grand down in Fort Worth about six years ago? The guy who owned it said that his kids had no idea what it was so it wasn't worth anything to them."

I nodded. "So?"

"So lots of shit. So I want to go straight and I want you to help me. Like I said, I can pay, but I need a place to stay."

Claire lowered the crowbar until the end touched the ground, then she spoke. "Monty? Why don't you find Smiley some coffee?"

He very slowly turned his head until he could see her. The smile didn't start again until he saw the crowbar. "Claire."

Claire was speaking with more calm than I felt. "Smiley. You want to stay? You want to go straight?"

"Yes. Honest." He turned back to me and let the smile flower. "You still have the prettiest girl in the free world."

Claire nodded. "I'm a woman. And that is true. And if you don't dump the gun far, far away from here right now, then I'll beat you to death with this crowbar and bury you in the basement."

If anything the smile became bigger and he stood up and hooked the shotgun back up under his arm. "And the meanest, prettiest and meanest, bar none."

He started to leave and Claire stopped him. "Do not ever come into my home with any weapons or drugs or anything even mildly illegal."

I spoke up, "I'll come with you and then you can come back."

Claire looked at me strangely and then followed me upstairs while I dressed—one of our rules is never to fight in front of other people. Upstairs she whispered in my ear, "What are you doing? I do not like Smiley, I do not trust Smiley. Why are we helping him?"

She glared at me and waited for an answer, which I gave after sorting it out in my mind. "I don't trust him either."

"So why are we inviting him into our home?"

That made me think. Finally I answered slowly, "I want him close. He's the only person I've ever met who's meaner than me."

"That doesn't make sense!"

"True. I have no idea why he's suddenly shown up and I need to know, that means keeping him very close."

Claire blew air through her nose. "This is dangerous for me and you and for Fred."

"Low blow. Having him here is dangerous and having him out there is dangerous too."

Claire thought about it and nodded reluctantly. I went on, "If there's a rabid, man-eating tiger with hemorrhoids and a hard-on in my neighbourhood then I want to know where he is all the time. And that means keeping Smiley close while we find out what the fuck is going on."

"Oh." She thought about it and then said slowly, "Well then. I want to repeat: you're putting your family in harm's way."

I felt very old. "If Smiley's here then my family is already in trouble. I just need to know where the trouble is coming from."

She thought about that and then reluctantly kissed me and

I went with Smiley towards the river. As we left the house Smiley turned back to Claire and did a kind of half-assed bow. "Prettiest and meanest. And smartest. Bar none."

She smiled herself and then closed the door.

#18

The shotgun went *plop* in the cold, muddy waters of the Red River, and following it were the multiple splashes of a double handful of shells. We were on the northern edge of St. John's Park, where there were trees and dirt-bike monkey trails that ended suddenly. That fact was what made riding them fun-fun-fun, according to some of the neighbourhood kids. There were also small bushes growing up between the trees so we had cover, unless someone was looking at us from across the river with night vision glasses, which was doubtful.

"There you are."

I looked over at Smiley and waited. Then I turned back to the river and tossed a pebble in. "Holliday carried a shotgun, true. He also carried a revolver on his hip. And one in a holster he wore under his arm. And he packed a knife on his other hip."

He looked over at me and reached behind him at waist level and pulled out a short-barrelled automatic which he unhesitatingly tossed into the water. It was followed by a wood-handled and cork-tipped ice pick out of his front pocket.

"That it?"

"Almost."

A plastic film container full of pills spilled into the water and, finally, he pulled a Korean-made switchblade knife taped to his calf under his pants and pitched that.

"Clean."

I patted his back.

"Feels weird."

"Yeah. Well. Yeah, it does."

I didn't look at him. "You're pretty heavy for someone who wants to go straight."

He slapped me on the back. "Yeah. Well. Old habits. There are bad people out here in the real world. You know how it is."

"Right." We started home. "Smiley, I'm going to give you some rules for life on the outside. Just so we're both on the same page, since I'm going to be helping you."

He brightened at that. "Rules? Like …"

I held up my hand. "Yeah. Like those."

"Say 'em again, man."

His enthusiasm made me smile. "Rules for bad guys: remember, anything you say that the cops can hear can be used in a court and the cops can always listen. Micro-miniature bugs and lasers bouncing off windowpanes. They even have some computer that can listen to you type on a keyboard and extrapolate what you say. So don't ever say, write, or think anything. Ever. 'Bout my past or yours. You start being a citizen now."

He nodded.

"In the real world, rule one is appearance. In the real world

116

you have to appear honest. You have to look like you belong where you're standing."

"Got it."

"Rule two is to follow your dream. Whatever it is and wherever it goes."

"Makes sense."

"Now I'm gonna tell you a secret about the real world. Ready? It is probably the biggest, baddest secret there is. So listen real careful."

He nodded and listened.

"No one ever made a million dollars honestly."

"Huh?"

"The citizens out there, they all want to make a million dollars and they are not honest because no one ever made a million dollars honestly. Citizens underpay their taxes. They buy grass and untaxed booze and cigarettes. They buy unregistered guns if they feel they are in danger. They run unsafe work environments. They accept bribes. They pocket money from their work places. They shortchange each other. They lie and bear false witness and fill out documents with intent to defraud. Unions run cozy arrangements with management or steal from the dues-payers without restraint or balance. Banks overcharge, stack their boards, and arrange for their own oversight. The taxman never gives you back exactly what you owe. And drive-thru restaurants never give you what you ordered. Etcetera and so on and ad infinitum."

Smiley was following every word.

"But, and this is a big but, the citizens and the citizen world always appears honest, and if you told any of them any of this, they would be deeply, deeply shocked and offended. And they would be righteously furious at your ideas and opinions."

I let it sink in and then continued.

"So that is the first and most important lesson: appear honest and be aware that everyone out here isn't."

Smiley grinned and finished, "And thus endeth the lesson."

I slapped him on the back. "And now we get you a real job. Maybe dishwasher or carpark attendant."

He told me to do something physically impossible. At home I put Smiley in the spare room and Claire and I went to bed and fought quietly for a long time before finally calling a ceasefire and making love.

There are worse ways to end arguments and, to be honest, sometimes I thought that I picked fights just for the making up.

#19

Sunday was a quiet day. Not a religious day, not a holy day; neither Claire nor I was religious. But it was a day to rest and recoup, rethink and plot and plan for the next week. Sundays were normally lazy days—normally, but then most Sundays we didn't have Smiley living with us.

"Hey man, up and at 'em!"

It was way too early in the morning and Smiley was yelling up from downstairs. Claire rolled over on her elbow and stared blankly at me and I shrugged. "I can still kill him."

"It's an option."

"I wouldn't mind, really."

I pulled on a pair of sweatpants and a tattered T-shirt.

"Just keep thinking you're doing a good deed."

"It's not helping."

We kissed and Smiley began to sing.

"… So get out of here with your bump-bump-bump …"

Fred started to howl in happiness and I went downstairs to find Smiley bouncing him up and down in his arms. Which froze me for a moment: Smiley had to have come upstairs without awakening me or Claire, gotten Fred up, dressed him, and brought him down. And as I watched them both I realized what was bothering me. It was that Smiley looked as though he was acting. It didn't matter what he was doing, even if he loved it, he always looked like he was acting a role off a script only he could see. Nothing outside could impact that armour he wore, at least nothing I had ever seen.

"I'm here."

Smiley cupped his hand around his mouth and did a credible bugle call and Fred yelled, "Unca 'Miley!"

I ignored him and asked, "What the hell was that?"

He looked at his hands as though the answer was there. "Taps, I think. Or wake up, reveille I think it's called. No idea really. Pretty good though, huh?"

"Just perfect."

He kept bouncing Fred. "So, you ready to run?"

Last night he had mentioned the two of us going jogging but I'd forgotten. I'd agreed because running might help me recover some of the strength I'd lost over the years. As I grew older I found my body was not behaving the way I remembered and wanted it to.

Hopefully the running would help.

Claire came down the stairs in her bathrobe and gathered Fred up and stomped on Smiley's foot. He swore and she smiled, showing all her teeth. "Never wake me up on a Sunday before ten, ten or eleven. Make it eleven. And don't touch my son, not ever, without my permission or that of my idiot husband. And never swear in front of my son either."

Fred looked at both of them and said, "FUCK!" loudly and Claire smiled seraphically and I knew what Mona Lisa was thinking and what Jesus really meant when he said, "Love thy neighbour."

Then she asked him, "So, do you have a job yet?"

He looked at me and then at her. "Time to run?"

I answered, "You bet. A quick retreat is probably our best option."

Running with Smiley was an experience, a time warp backwards and not a good one. We'd done it inside frequently, running around a track with screws on the walls and towers tracking us with rifles for practice. We'd jogged away from demons at Drumheller Medium/Minimum Federal Pen and Millhaven Maximum Fed Pen, or maybe we'd jogged towards them. Moving around in circles that never ended, wherever and whenever we could find space and time. This was the first time we'd done it in the outside world and I picked a direction at random and started.

"Always meant to ask you, man, why did you start to run on the inside?"

His voice brought me back to the now and I thought about it before answering. "To get away from the cell, the block, the rest of the prisoners, all that shit. And to make myself a moving target. What about you?"

We dodged a little girl pushing an old pram full of stuffed animals down the sidewalk as he answered, "I did it for the quiet to work on the next gig. I did it to think about my crew. But mostly I did it to become stronger."

We turned on Mountain Avenue and ran west past the little businesses and churches, repair shops and diners.

"Nice neighbourhood. Lot of crime?" He was looking through criminal's eyes. Bars on the windows, heavy steel doors, and thick wires on the windows linked to alarm companies and cops. There were even bars on the church windows and garbage in the gutters and filling the dumpsters.

"A bit."

I could see what he saw but I could also see other things. I could see the yards someone had spent hours on. I could see fences in good repair. I saw walls with fresh paint jobs and paint-bombed obscenities scrubbed out. And I could see an absence of panhandlers and bums sucking back on paper bags of Canadian Club sherry and Lysol or flaming rocks of crack.

"There are opportunities here."

He sounded like he was thinking as his feet easily kept the rhythm, hammering away at the sidewalk, darting effortlessly around the occasional pedestrian. And as we went we kept dodging bikes and skateboarders. Pain was starting in my back, so I changed the subject to distract us both.

"You remember Stan?"

Smiley glanced at me. "Stanley? Drum-Stan?"

"Yeah. Remember what he could do?"

There was silence for a block while he thought. "What do you mean? I never worked with him."

"Not what I meant. Remember the sit-ups he did in prison?"

"Yeah, he did sit-ups, I remember that now. He was up to what ...?"

A little old lady pushed another little old lady in a wheelchair out from a church. Both were tiny and frail and moved like clockwork dolls, determined to make it wherever they were going. Without thinking I broke left over a fire hydrant and took three steps in the street before making the sidewalk again. Smiley broke right and took two steps on the tops of steel newspaper boxes and then joined me.

"Sorry, ma'ams!" He apologized at the two women as he

ran by. Despite that they still called him several somethings I didn't quite catch.

"Anyhow, I was asking how many he was up too?"

"One thousand eight hundred sit-ups a day. Every day. Every single, stinking day."

"Really?"

We turned right down Arlington and found fewer obstacles, so we pushed it up a notch. By the time we reached Cathedral we were exhausted and slowed to a more sedate pace.

Smiley's voice was starting to get ragged. "Too bad he was such a goof."

"Who?"

"Stan."

"True." I thought about Stan and about what a bad thief he had been. He had been a comically bad thief, an epically bad one. He had robbed a Police Credit Union in Waterloo. He had robbed a car ferry on its way to Isle Royale on Lake Superior and then had been stuck on the island for two days while the cops locked down access and looked for him. And he had once stolen a panel truck full of autographed hockey jerseys and tried to sell them at a flea market in the same town two days later.

He had given thieves a bad name and I was glad he was in prison where he could hurt very few people.

We crossed McGregor against the lights and received a severe honking from a big suburban assault vehicle heavily loaded with one fat woman talking on a cell phone. Since she had been a good fifteen metres from the stop-line when we'd crossed, I felt somewhat aggrieved.

"'Scuse me."

Smiley paused while I turned back towards the woman. She was gesturing with one hand towards me and still talking on the phone. When her eyes caught mine I showed all my teeth and held my hand to my ear and then gestured with the other for her to roll down her window. She floored it and I went back to talking with Smiley.

"I do hate rude people. Like I said, it's true he's a goof but now Stan's a goof with the stomach muscles of a Greek god."

We ran some more in silence.

"Monty?"

We turned left on the final lap home.

"Yeah?"

"Why 'Greek god'?"

I thought about it and couldn't come up with an answer. "No idea. Maybe because the Greeks thought their gods were pretty."

He stretched his legs and we finished in a sprint which he won easily.

After I'd showered Smiley cleaned himself up and then we sat down with Claire at the table. To keep Fred and Renfield happy we rolled a bright red plastic ball into the living room. Half the time the baby brought it back, the rest of the time the dog did. When the grown-up humans all had coffee in front of them and I was eating some rye toast, Claire started.

"All right, I've been thinking about Smiley's problem." She left it there, hanging.

"And …?"

"He has one." She sipped her coffee and looked cheerful, for lack of a better word, but Smiley wanted more information.

"Actually I have many problems. Which one are we currently discussing?"

"Pay attention. We are discussing the possibilities of finding you gainful employment. We tried this with Monty in the spring and it was ... difficult."

I interjected. "Actually it blew chunks."

Smiley looked doubtful. "That bad?"

Claire made a small gesture. "It was difficult ..."

" ... difficult? Difficult? Circumcising a weasel is difficult, this was ..."

Claire cut me off, " ... but not impossible. In Monty's case we found him a job babysitting."

Smiley couldn't help himself. "BULLSHIT!"

I winced, "No. Serious."

He started to laugh. I threw the ball for the dog and the baby and said something under my breath and my wife kicked me under the table. Smiley finally calmed down and his face swivelled back and forth between us as he chewed on his lower lip. "'Kay. Okay. I'm fine." He took a deep breath. "So I need a job. So what do I do?"

"As an ex-con you have some disadvantages, so you should create your own job. And it should be something new and unique. It should be something that will force people to judge you, and not your past."

This was news to me and I finished my toast and coffee while Smiley thought it through. "Such as ...?"

We were all silent and then I offered, "What can you do?"

He didn't even have to think about that. "Take things that aren't mine. Go through locked doors. Force people to do things. Set fires for profit. Torture people."

"Fight?"

"Yeah. But I cheat."

Claire nodded and absorbed all that he'd said. "What about bouncing?"

"In a bar?"

We all thought about it and Smiley said slowly, "I guess I could do that. Sure. Spot troublemakers before they make trouble. Deal with them quietly. Also, drunks aren't that dangerous, all things considered. Do you need a certificate? Some places I think you need a certificate."

He thought about it some more and I went into the kitchen for more coffee, Claire following. When the cup was half full she put her hand over it and stopped me. "The doctor's orders are to reduce caffeine."

"My doctor is an idiot." I'd taken a first-class beating from some Winnipeg cops six months before that had almost destroyed my kidneys and that, combined with decades of amphetamine and narcotic abuse, made me hyper sensitive to caffeine. Claire just stared at me and then she screwed her face up and her eyes filled with tears and became bigger and bigger while her mouth started to tremble. "Still ... you don't want me to be an unhappy widow, do you?"

It was an unfair argument, but one I lost. I dumped the coffee and we went into the dining room where our guest was still sitting, staring out over his cup of coffee which had grown tepid. When we came in he snapped his head around and shook his head. "I don't know."

"About bouncing, what's to know? A little psychology and a little intimidation with a little mayhem equal easy money."

"All right, it's worth a try."

He sounded doubtful and Claire slapped a deck of cards in front of him along with a crudely carved crib board she'd brought into our marriage from some earlier relationship.

"That's decided. Let's play."

I stood there and finally shook my head and headed upstairs to change, "Not me. I have to go to work, Marie's expecting me."

Smiley didn't say anything at all and I found that very interesting indeed. He should have asked questions, he should have wondered, but he didn't, he just nodded and went along with the crib game.

#20

Marie and I were back in the SUV heading east again and drinking coffee and I, personally, was feeling pretty damn guilty indeed. I had almost, almost, asked for decaf but what's the point in that? So I dealt with my guilt by ignoring it and spent the time thinking about the tools and equipment in the back of the car and what I could do with them. After about a 100 klicks she spoke up. "So what happens next?"

"I set up protection around your camp and we finalize the delivery arrangements. Should take us maybe two days, maybe a little longer."

"Do you have a plan?"

"I do. Not a great one, but I do have a plan."

"So tell me."

"Let's wait until Don and Al are there as well, that way I can tell everybody at once."

At the campsite both men were waiting, drinking cans of Olympia Ale beer and sitting in the screened-in porch while contemplating the afternoon. We drove up and I shook hands with both of them before asking Al, "Shouldn't you be fishing?"

"I am. I have two nets out right now."

"Isn't that cheating?"

"Sure, but rods are for losers. Dynamite works even better. So does cranking, but those hand-powered generators are hard to find these days."

He squinted. "And didn't you used to look different?"

He said it straight and I smiled. "I'm wearing my own face today."

"That's good."

Don came over wearing a plain black three-piece suit with a painfully starched shirt and pencil-thin string tie done up tight around his neck. His handshake was hearty, and up close he smelled of mothballs and beer and very faintly of cows. I shook his hand and he looked closely at my face. "Are you a Mennonite?"

"No. I'm kind of a mutt, really. A little of this and a little of that."

He nodded and went on, "I'm a Mennonite. Glad you're not one of us though."

"Why?"

He just shrugged. "Because then we'd argue about God."

He turned and led me inside and kept talking. "And I hate that."

We all sat around the table to talk, and at my request Don laid the aerial photographs out again.

"The original plan was to head out in the outboards at night and make landings using a pre-programmed GPS system. Right?"

The two men nodded, Marie was listening carefully, and I shook my head. "That's not really going to work. Boats travelling at night make a lot of noise and attract a lot of attention. There's also the chance that Greg talked to other people besides Sam about your original plans, so we're going to change things around. Mess things up a little."

Al spoke, "So what's your idea?"

"It's about eighty-four klicks round trip, right?" Don nodded agreement. "So that's a long way. What's this?"

I tapped a spot on the map and Al answered, "An island, tiny, maybe ten, twelve metres across with a few pines and bushes. If the water's really high most of it's under water except for a big clump of pines and scrub oak on top. It's nothing special."

"It's also ten klicks from your destination?"

Both men agreed.

"So. One of you leaves in the morning with your cargo, four people plus you both and Marie. You reach the island and Marie drops you all off. Then you and the travellers just wait there until evening. At around midnight you put the travellers in two birch canoes that are already there. We equip with electric engines and you whisper in the last ten klicks, drop them off and come back to the island. The next morning Marie picks you up."

Al and Don didn't say a word but Marie finally asked, "Why is that plan better?"

"The illegality of the whole thing is concentrated in the last ten-kilometre rush. There's nothing illegal about taking people on a boat ride and there's nothing illegal about Al and Don getting lost out on the lake."

Don asked, "What about the radar?"

I shook my head. "Radar doesn't work so well against wood, shouldn't work very well against birchbark either, plus canoes are so low to the surface of the water that the waves will interfere with the pick-up. And no fast engine means no wake to track from above."

Al traced lines with his fingertip. "Where are we going to get electric engines?"

I handed him a flyer from my back pocket that I had folded in two. "Any sporting goods store. We'll use trolling engines; they run off a twelve-volt battery and they're about $300 or so."

Don shook his head. "That won't work, not over that kind of distance; those things just barely push your boat along."

"In a big boat they push you along, true, but in a canoe, you'll fly. And you can carry a couple of extra batteries in case."

He kept looking at the pictures. "Okay, how do we find the drop-off point? And how do we find the way back once we've dropped off the travellers?"

I shrugged. "Use compass headings and dead reckoning. So many minutes southwest, then reverse it on the way back. It'll take some practice but it should work fine. Have the pick-up crew carry a flashlight with a coloured lens to signal you in the final stretch. We can make a couple of practice runs."

Marie spoke up, "It'll be cold out there."

I nodded and handed over another flyer. "Yep. So everyone dresses warm. We can buy full-body Ski-doo suits for the travellers, wrap them in Mylar space blankets and give them hand warmers. When we drop them off we have them strip down to their normal clothes. As for Al and Don, they can do the same thing; there is extra-heavy-duty, heavy-weather stuff we can buy for them. We have them pull on Mylar ponchos and everything should be fine."

"Why the Mylar?"

"Blocks radiant heat. That way no one shows up on infrared sensors."

Marie said dryly, "I suppose you have …" Before she could finish I handed her some more flyers and then left them alone to think while I went to work on the outside of the cabins. It had been awhile since the contract with Marie had started and I was way behind in prepping the camp and making it secure.

Outside the birds and small animals were starting to become agitated as the seasons changed, going into overdrive looking for food and a warm place to sleep/hibernate/whatever. And they seemed to be everywhere; small red squirrels moving purposefully in the trees, blue and grey jays darting past on unknown errands, and chipmunks darting through the leaf litter with bulging cheeks. I wondered about deer and other animals and realized they were probably asleep. The problem with the campsite was not to provide security but to provide a warning if anyone approached from land or water. Fortunately, since the camp was on the end of a narrow peninsula sticking out into the lake, it wouldn't be as hard as it could have been.

I started with vibration sensors, little plastic security devices I'd spray-painted black and mottled green that ran off a nine-volt battery. I put eight of those thirty metres from the cabin, screwed securely to the sides of trees. Running from each unit was a strand of Spiderwire, unbreakable fishing line stretching out four to six metres to another tree. Touch the line and the sensor goes off, touch the sensor and the sensor goes off, breathe and the sensor goes off. Each line was set about sixty centimetres above ground level, out of the way of squirrels and chipmunks but right at knee height for most two-legged folks.

Next came twelve little passive infrared motion sensors with a fifteen-metre range; six at the thirty-metre limit pointing out, and six at the three-metre mark, also pointing out.

Those I put three metres up because most people never look up, just forward and at ground level.

All those sensors were hooked into a central receiving unit which I put in the main cabin. If any of the sensors were disturbed, the system would light up and a siren would start blowing. In case anyone cut the power, I hooked the panel up to an emergency battery pack that was supposed to be used for computers, and would give three hours of juice.

To back those up I also set up ten portable units with built-in alarms. They were motion sensors as well, with a ten metre range and would chirp in an alarming fashion if anything came near them. They went on metre-high sticks that could be planted anywhere, and moved in seconds.

Four hours later Al and Don and Marie were still talking as I unpacked two home monitoring systems which fed data along cables (harder to jam) to television units. Each system could handle three cameras, which I installed outside the cabins. In addition, each camera was hooked to a motion sensor alarm that would give a nice warning and start filming anytime anyone moved too close.

It would have been quicker to let Marie and friends help, but I needed the quiet to work and they would have asked questions. I also had a desire to keep my own secrets. The last layer of defence was distinctly non-technological and consisted of sixty of my very own homemade trip wires, each attached to fifteen-millimetre white flares, the kind campers are supposed to carry in case they become lost. The traps were made out of mouse traps and lengths of PVC pipe, and if the wire was cut or disturbed, the mouse trap would snap down on a blank .22 cartridge, which would provide an audible warning. These I bought at a sports supply store; they were supposed to be used in starter pistols. The cartridge would trigger a 14,000-candlepower white flare which would go straight up seventy metres and burn for about five seconds. Those suckers I scattered everywhere, each attached to metre lengths of fishing line.

By the time I was done it was dark and Marie drove me home, but not after I told everyone what I'd done to the camp. I didn't want them taking a walk and wrecking their day.

On the way home I fondled some unused alarm component units I'd pocketed. I'd feel better when they were installed at home.

It wasn't that I didn't trust Smiley.

It was just that I didn't trust Smiley.

#21

Claire let me sleep in the next day while she took care of the kids. One of the nice things about her real estate job was that her hours were flexible. It meant she could help with the kids when I had things to do.

If I could only learn how to sell houses, we'd have some equality in our lives.

When I'd gotten dressed I came down and found Smiley sitting in the living room at the coffee table shuffling a deck of cards. He looked at me and cheated brazenly, dealing seconds, and flicking the cards across the table to Claire. She sat with a small pile of wooden matches in front of her and looked up when I came in. The kids were playing, colouring, and reading at their feet.

"We're playing poker. She thinks she's good. She also keeps telling me to get a job. Which I am working on."

I watched him work and commented. "Pretty smooth."

"Yes, I am."

His fingers flickered again and the top card stayed in place and the second flickered out. Claire watched him and folded her hand. "Could we do this without the cheating?"

"Sure. I think I remember how."

Claire took the cards he offered next and slid them over face down and took his in return. Then she spoke without looking up. "Have fun."

"At the library?"

"Well, you're weird that way ..."

"If I'm not back in three hours ..." My wife and Smiley looked up at me from the cards. "... just wait longer."

At the library I headed to the reference desk, picked up copies of the papers for the week, and went through them looking for anything odd. Anything that might indicate Smiley was conning me, which translated into anything violent and/or profitable. But there was nothing abnormal. The cops seized two stun guns and a few grams of crack cocaine during a street sweep and claimed it showed the gangs were on the run. A fire alarm revealed a hidden room in a postal worker's home where over a million pieces of undelivered mail were stored. A confidential informant in a stolen identity scam refused to testify despite having been paid over $80,000 by the police. The party not in power complained about the increased crime rate across Canada while the party in power defended their actions.

But there was nothing that pointed to Smiley being active in the city.

I used the Internet access to run a search and found nothing new, so then I checked out the Government of Manitoba site to find some answers for Smiley. When my time was up I headed back home where the game was still going on. I sat down and held out my hand for the deck.

"Bad news, Smiley."

"How bad?"

The cards were in my hands and I shuffled backwards and forwards and dealt out five cards each. Smiley looked confused. "No Texas Hold 'em?"

"That's for wimps. Five card. Two draw. Two card. Table stakes. Each of you suckers gives me five matches." I gave them my best wolf grin.

They passed the matches and I anted up. "As for the bad, it's fairly bad but not 'You've got the clap' bad."

Claire took two cards, Smiley one, and me two and then Claire folded and Smiley bet a lot. I matched him and took the pot.

Smiley frowned and asked, "So that kind of bad is okay, give me two."

The cards flew over, Fred came over to look, yelled, "'ARDS!" and wandered away while I took one. I'd played with Smiley before; he had a considerable talent to change plans in midstream if they weren't going well or if he thought he had a new, better plan. He was flexible, whereas I was stubborn.

His face twitched. "Shitfuck."

Claire smacked him hard and told him, "No swearing. Not in my house."

"You swear, so does Monty."

"True. But that doesn't mean you can."

He shook his head in admiration and I went on, "Nice poker face."

He lost with a queen of hearts and a queen of spades along with three other spades. I held three eights and garbage.

I handed the deck to Claire and five matches back to Smiley.

"What are these for?"

"I borrowed those to raise. They're yours; the ones I won are mine. Anyhow, the bad news is that the law here in Manitoba is fucked up. You can't be a bouncer if you have a criminal record ..."

We were playing Texas Hold 'em now, with Claire dealing and ignoring my profanity. Smiley took his cards and smiled. "Which would be me."

I agreed with him. "Also you'd need to meet ..." The matches flicked into the pile and I played expansively, quickly forcing Smiley to fold while Claire met my poker face with one of her own. "... and I quote, 'minimum competency standards.'"

"Which means?"

Claire answered. "Whatever they want it to mean. So that won't work."

She raised me and I raised her and I won and Smiley gathered the cards and dealt. "Wait a minute. There have to be some places hiring under the table ... stuff like that."

"True, but you don't want that." Claire shrugged and motioned for me to ante up.

"Why not?"

I answered that one. "You don't want that because you want to be above board now, completely above board. Honest. Pay your taxes. Walk in the light of the day. Shit like that."

He'd forgotten. "Right, I want to go straight."

She won that hand and Smiley won the next two as I folded fast and thought about how to bring up the issue of money. Finally I realized there was no nice way to bring up the subject of money. "I'll take one card. Smiley, what about the money?"

"Huh? Oh."

Smiley had mentioned money the night before, money he could contribute to pay his way, and now I was bringing it up.

The hand fell to me. Claire took back the initial five matches I'd borrowed and it was my turn to deal, I went on, "Yeah, that. I want to make sure this deal is fair all around. Claire and I want to do this but there are costs that need to be covered. Living costs money, rent is expensive, food is expensive, electricity and water cost money, and so forth."

"Of course! That's cool, so let's treat this like a real contract between all of us. So what do you want?"

Smiley and I folded, so Claire took the pot and the deal moved on. Smiley kept talking. "Me, I want a real job and a straight life. No crime and no punishment and none of the rest of it."

He said it deadpan. My wife and I looked at each other and she answered, "Fine, you live in this house. We help you until you're ready to stand on your own. We help with the apartment, the job, the clothes ..."

He was offended. "What's wrong with my clothes?"

"You look like a cheap hood." Claire made it sound okay.

"Well. Shit."

I defended Smiley. "But it's true though; Smiley *is* a cheap hood."

"You're not helping." She blew hair out of her eyes and stuck her tongue out.

I won the next hand and raked in the matches while phrasing what I wanted to say to our guest. "That's what you were. As of now, you're not."

The cards flew and bets were made before Smiley spoke again. "So what the fuck am I?"

Claire answered. "You're in limbo. Consider it a Zen exercise."

"Zen? Like *And the Art of Motorcycle Maintenance*?"

"Yes."

"Never read it."

She ignored him. "Right now you just exist, drifting in the void that is this world."

He looked at me. "Sounds deep."

The cards loved me and I took another hand. "Think of it like this: you're waiting for the bank to open."

"Oh."

Claire brought us back to the main subject. "Now, what do we get out of it?"

He exhaled. "Let me make some calls. I've got some cash coming to me."

Claire asked sweetly, "How much?"

"About ten."

"Good. Room and board is three hundred a month."

"That works." He was silent for awhile and then asked, "Monty, you ever miss it?"

"No."

"Never."

"Remember the last one we did?"

"No."

He wanted to tell the story but I kept saying no and ten minutes later I had cleaned everyone out and the game folded.

That night Claire poked me hard in the ribs while we were in bed. "Do you miss it, and be honest."

"No."

She looked directly in my eyes before doing certain things. When she was done she purred low in her throat. "Tell me now."

My voice was hoarse as I answered, "No."

She began to move. "Now I believe you."

When she was asleep I crept out of the house and went out a few blocks until I found a pay phone I'd never used before. There I phoned Marie's cell and found out that everything was going well and that Don and Al were practising with the canoes and cursing me and my stupid ideas.

I found out no one was sniffing around the route that she could tell and that didn't make sense at all. Sam should at least be looking around. Quietly, probably, but she should still be looking.

When I made it back home, Smiley met me in the doorway with the crowbar. When he realized who it was he gave me a thumbs up and I went back up to my wife, who was lying serenely in bed with her right hand under the pillow touching the bayonet.

#22

The next day over an early breakfast Smiley looked at me wearing black pants and T-shirt and then over at Claire.

"Why's he all whored up?"

"He has to go work at the local archery shop today. He helps out there and Frank, the owner, has an appointment, so Monty gets to play at being a responsible-type businessman."

"Oh. Should I go with …?"

She interrupted him. "No, you are staying here with me while we watch over assorted monsters masquerading as children. We can talk some more over what you're going to need. Sound good?"

Fred was in his high chair and he took the opportunity to fling a handful of generic, round, oat-based cereal at me. Mostly he missed and the rest the dog ate, and when I threw some back at him, Claire took the opportunity to steal a piece of toast off my plate.

"Hey!"

"Serves you right." She said it through a mouthful of crumbs and I ignored her and turned back to Smiley, who was drinking coffee. There were big bags under both eyes. Going straight apparently didn't agree with him. Going from despotism to anarchy was a hard step for anyone. Plus (and this is a secret) many crooks *like* prison, I don't know why, nor do I want too.

"I've been thinking; what about a pawnshop? What about running one of those? I could do that." He stretched.

"Really?"

"Sure. I've been a fence and it's pretty much the same thing. And I could set up with stock pretty fast by visiting a few swap shops and flea markets. All I have to do is put some cash together."

Claire looked interested. "Maybe."

"Maybe nothing."

She made a face. "Maybe. It's heavily regulated, maybe not what you want to do. The cops visit all the time. Not a low-stress thing at all. I still think carpark attendant is the way to go, or maybe towel boy in a men's bathhouse. They make lots of tips."

Smiley stared at her bemusedly and Claire finished feeding Fred and then released him onto the floor. When I had finished my coffee I stood up and went to work.

Frank Wyzik was waiting for me, impatiently, just inside his shop, which was called The Buttes.

"Where the hell were you?"

Frank was maybe five feet nothing, 100 pounds soaking wet, with white hair he'd recently cut short and beautiful brown eyes set in skin tanned into a kind of leather. Like always, he was wearing clothes that didn't match, this time a short-sleeved T-shirt advertising an opera called *Nosferatu* along with black rubber boots and plaid pants.

"I was rushing here, *Mein Führer.*"

"Good, respect is good."

He rubbed his hands together. I put my windbreaker behind the counter and stood there in front of him.

"Do you know what to do?"

"I have absolutely no idea."

"Good. I like that. No bad habits to unlearn. Cash box is under the till. Lane rental is $2 an hour. Bows for rent are the ones on the upper rack, they cost $3 per hour, and arrow rental is $1 per hour per arrow."

I turned on the lights using the master switches under the counter and tapped the keys on the register.

"Don't bother. It's broken, it's always been broken, and it always will be broken. Use the cash box, and if anyone buys anything make sure you charge the taxes, which are 14 percent."

"It's 12 percent."

"You sure?"

"Yep. Seven percent provincial, 5 percent federal. Twelve percent."

"Shit. Okay, 12 percent then. And write down the sales in the book under the counter."

"*Jawohl.*"

He was nervous, fingering the racks of camouflage clothes, accessories, and bags that filled the store. Drumming his fingers on the Plexiglas countertops, staring down the two lanes at the back of the room that ended in walls made up of pressboard held together with clamps. As he wandered he talked. "The doctor shouldn't take me long. Not long at all."

"Everything will be fine."

"Sure. Sure! Hey, do you want to go hunting wild boar with me?"

"Frank? I'm an ex-con. How can I go hunting?"

"The boars don't care. You live in Manitoba, so you're a resident. That's fine. Also, no licence needed to shoot boar."

He kept moving and ticking things off on his fingers, making a godawful squeaking noise with his boots. "No training for archers is required. You're already better than most of the morons I've shot with. You do need a Hunter Safety course, one day, $35, and at the end you answer a multiple choice test. Then off we go."

Frank rubbed his hands together. "It'll be great. We can take as many grey squirrels, rabbits, and wild boar we want …"

His words were finally sinking in. "Wild boar?"

"Yessir."

"You mean, big pigs, covered in fur? Big pigs with big tusks and sharp hooves?"

"Oh yeah, that's the beastie we'll be trying for, there's no limit on those. Bout eighty or ninety escaped a few years ago from wild game farms and have adapted real well. And it's not fur on them: they have hair."

"Is there a difference?"

"No, not really …"

"We're talking about wild boars? We're talking about shooting wild boars with little-bitty arrows?"

"Yeah, some ecologists thought they'd die off real fast during the first winter but they're smart. Mean, too. And big. They're survivors, big time. They've become the alpha predators in some places."

I counted the money in the cash box twice, did it again; finally I reached the same number twice in a row.

"I just want to make sure I have this idea straight: you want to hunt wild boar?"

He ignored me. "Now I've seen the spoor where they've killed black bears and a friend of mine, well, not really a friend, said that he's heard of them killing wolves, but I think he's full of shit. Pardon the French."

"Wild boar? Frank, tell me you're kidding?"

"Nope. Latin name *sus scrofa*, they can reach 400 kilograms. One in Georgia, one of the tusks was forty-five centimetres long! Another one from Alabama topped out at over 500 kilograms, three metres from snout to tail! But they don't end up that big here. And I know a great place south of the city where there are a couple of sounders, packs of pigs, plus everything else. It's a deserted little chunk of abandoned farmstead owned by someone who died years ago. One of the neighbours is a friend of mine and he tells me the pigs come out and tear up his gardens every now and then. He'd love it if some were dealt with. It'll be great!"

He had me speechless and he continued to gush, "Yeah. Imagine it. Imagine the food! Lapereau aux champignons, lapereau de garenne a la braconniere, civet de lievre a l'ardennaise, noisettes de chevreuil aux avocats, selle de marcassin a la bordelaise ..."

"Gesundheit."

He waved his arms triumphantly and intoned, " ... and squirrel mesquite jambalaya!"

"You made that last one up."

"Nope. It'll be great! Trust me."

"You're a very strange man, Frank."

He was distracted and repeated, "Yeah, it'll be great."

He wasn't paying attention which allowed me to slide the next question across his plate. "Why only grey squirrels, why not red?"

"Oh. Red? They're fur bearing, you need a trapper's licence

for those." He scratched his nose and looked at his finger in surprise and changed the subject. "In Russia a long time ago they used to hunt sables for the fur, but it was so valuable they couldn't use traps; 'soft gold' they called it."

"What did they do if they couldn't use traps?"

"They shot them in the nose with crossbows."

Before I could figure out whether he was bullshitting or not, he saw the time and dashed out. Carefully I picked up the phone and called Claire, who answered abruptly, "Joe's Pool Hall, rack your balls and shoot 'em."

"Is my wife there?"

"Sure. What do you need?"

"Assurance. Frank wants me to go hunting with him."

"No problems."

"It'll cost $35."

"Doable."

There was silence on the line as I racked my brain.

"You don't understand—we'll be hunting squirrels …"

"Great." She sounded distracted.

"And rabbits …"

"Those are delicious if cooked right, I have some good recipes. What's the problem? Rachel, let go of that man's nose! Sorry about that."

The conversation was going nowhere, so I pulled my last card. "And wild boar."

"Wild boar?"

She started to laugh and finally put the phone down to tell Smiley. When she'd stopped laughing I asked if she was all right. "Yes. We are talking about wild boar here? Those are big pigs with tusks and hair?"

"Exactly. It's either hair or fur, I don't know which. Claire, I don't want to do this."

"Coward. Frank's a friend, Monty. You really don't have very many friends, I'm not really sure you have any, you're still new in town, and your reputation is not the best. If he wants you to go hunt squirrels and rabbits and wild boar, you should go."

A headache started to pound behind my eyes. "I'm hanging up now."

She was laughing again, breathlessly. "You do that."

#23

It turned out to be a slow morning, business-wise, that is. I dusted everything behind the counter, wiped down, the Plexiglas and started to clean the front window. While I was doing that a young man in his early twenties came in. He was wearing black jeans and T-shirt, and cowboy boots, and his hair was ash blond and cut down to about a millimetre in length. When he came over to the counter I could see that his eyes were dark brown, almost black, under the longest lashes I'd ever seen, and he carried a plastic bow case in one hand. He stared at me blankly.

"Hi." His voice was very remote.

"Hi."

He waited and then asked, "Can I shoot?"

"Yep. Costs two dollars an hour, plus more if you need to rent a bow or arrows."

His hand dipped into a pocket and put a twenty on the counter between us. "I brought my own."

He took the lane farthest away from me, opened the case,

and pulled out the bow. Frank supplied a wooden stand and the man put his bow on it while he fumbled around in the case for more equipment. I tried not to watch but I had to; there were little boxes and clip-ons and grips and a weight set and other shit I couldn't identify. Some ended up attached to the bow string; more went onto the bow itself; some he Velcroed onto his hands and wrists. And it just kept going on. By the time his bow was ready it didn't look like anything I'd ever seen before. But when he started to shoot he missed the blue and the yellow and the red of the target over and over again. Sometimes he hit the white, but not often.

About an hour and two sales later Frank came back behind the counter with me and whispered, "How's he doing?"

"Not well."

"He's been coming in for years now."

"What's he put on his bow?"

Frank shrugged. "Limb tamer to reduce vibrations and improve accuracy, a glide slide to smooth the string action, arrow trapper rest for a steady release off the handle, stabilizer to control the bow during the release, sharpshooter release for a cleaner string release, and ..., well, that sneaky bastard, now he's hooked up a laser site."

He kept shooting and I found I was still whispering. "But he can't hit anything."

Frank shrugged. "I know. As a matter of fact, now that I think of it, he's the one who sold me the bow I sold you. He traded it for something or other four years ago."

I glanced over at my bow. Frank let me keep it in the shop because that was the only place I used it. It sat on a shelf beside a tool bench full of vises and such that Frank used for repairs. When I looked back at Frank, he was rifling the cash box. "What did you sell?"

"A used quiver and a new tree stand rest. It's been slow. How are you doing?"

"Fine. The doctor says I'm okay, if you can trust your doctor. What do I owe you?"

"Three hours. Call it twenty bucks. Let me shoot, though, and pay me the difference."

"Sure ... hey, you cleaned!" He made it sound like an accusation.

"Yep." I gathered up my bow and the three arrows I had in the holder attached to the handle and went quietly to the second lane. Leaving the bow at the top, I walked down to the target wall and taped three 3x5-inch cards I'd stolen from Claire's real estate briefcase to the wall. I made sure the cards were at least two feet apart and then walked back to the bow and adjusted my feet.

Left foot first, just in front of the line on the floor, right foot at shoulder width and a little forward on a line drawn from the left foot through my hips. Left arm holding the bow, right arm putting the nock onto the string and resting the shaft on the holder. Draw back. Release and repeat.

When all three arrows were gone, I walked down and gathered them. I'd spaced the targets to avoid spoiling arrows—frequently my eye would be drawn to the arrow at the target when I released. That generally meant the next arrow would hit it, which looked cool if you were Robin Hood, but I didn't think he had to pay eight dollars per arrow.

Compared to the guy in the next lane, the sound of my arrow leaving the string was deafening. But at least I was hitting the target, over and over. Gradually my mind emptied of fear and worry and the arrows flew and I retrieved them and shot again, and again, and again. When I was done, two hours had passed and I went to Frank to collect my pay.

"How'd you do?"

"Fine. You owe me sixteen dollars."

He paid and then said, "What about the hunting?"

"Sure."

He became enthusiastic. "That's great; I'll arrange the training and the ticket for next week. Is there any day that doesn't work for you?"

"Sunday. Can I phone Claire?"

"Sure, sure."

I called her and told her I'd be back later and not to wait dinner. She growled at me for awhile; then I turned back to Frank, who was looking concerned. "Problems?"

"None. See ya on Wednesday?"

That was the next day deliveries were scheduled for the shop, when I'd come down and help Frank out for a few bucks under the table. He agreed that was fine and I left. Behind me the guy with the expensive bow kept shooting and missing.

I went to Marie's and started to quarter the neighbourhood looking for anything out of place, but there was nothing. Finally I made it home long past dark, where I found Smiley drunk and Claire asleep upstairs. Smiley was sitting at the dining room table with his hands curled palm up on the table in front of him. To his right side was a bottle of toxic Golden Wedding rye whiskey sitting beside a water glass. "Hi."

I sat down across from him and noticed the bottle was down by two-thirds. "Hello. Having fun?"

"Loads." After a moment he went on, "It's been a shit-filled day." His hands trembled and he sipped at the glass and went on. "I went out there to talk to some people, to see what kind of thieves you have in Winnipeg. I found skinners and rats and con men of all sizes. Not a solid con anywhere to be seen."

His eyes were focused somewhere far away. "You ever think how unfair it is?"

"What, specifically, are we talking about?"

He drank most of the glass neat and turned it around in his fingers before finishing it.

"Cops and robbers."

I was gentle. "You're not doing that anymore, remember?"

"Yeah. But I was. So were you. We were both in the life and did you ever wonder why? I mean it's not like it was ever a fair fight."

"What's that? Never had me a fair fight. Neither have you."

He stared at me, almost blind drunk, and I started listing stuff. "Cops have computers and cell phone scanners. They have laser-sighted semi-automatic pistols loaded with explosive bullets it would be illegal to use in war, but legal to use on us. They've got spare guns on their ankles and the back of their belts and underarms and everywhere else."

Smiley filled his glass and drained it.

"They have shotguns loaded with slugs and buckshot. Submachine guns and assault rifles kicking out 1000 rounds, 1000 fucking rounds a minute. Which is like sixteen a second. They're trained on rifles that'll dump a round into your brain stem at 200 metres, 400 metres, 600 metres, each and every time."

He interrupted me. "Well, yes, all that's true ..."

I kept talking. "They've developed sonic devices to pick up your voice a block away. Tear gas and pepper spray to blind and disable. Tape and video recorders. They wear Kevlar body armour with steel and ceramic inserts and they carry flashlights that double as clubs. Motorcycles and dirt bikes, horses and boats and even goddamned bicycles! Steel push-bar bumpers on their cars so they can ram on the highways."

The whiskey level kept dropping; it was fascinating watching him get drunk, and I started to want to drink. And that want was bad, it was really most extremely bad, so I just kept talking.

"Helicopters and planes, scuba gear, anti-bomb suits, armoured cars, tanks. Robots. Chase cars with nitro injectors so they can go fast, fast, fast. Plastic clubs and collapsible clubs, electric guns and prods. Plastic zipper handcuffs they can hide in the lining of their hat and steel ones they can use like brass knuckles, spring-loaded saps, and lead-lined gloves. Flash-bang grenades, smoke grenades, concussion grenades, tear gas grenades."

The rye was almost gone and it took a conscious effort not to move my hands. They wanted to reach for it even if I didn't, and I kept talking instead. "The cops carry shields you'd need cannon to penetrate. Grappling hooks, grenade launchers, oxyacetylene torches. Dogs that'll rip you from balls to throat in a half second, dogs they even wrap in armour from snout to tail, dogs smarter than most cops."

He finished the dregs of the rye and I could relax. I kept talking, trying to relax him. Smiley nodded like he was listening and I kept talking about the future and the past and people we knew and people we'd never met and people who'd never existed. I kept talking about good music and cold beer, women and roller coasters, steaks and fried potatoes, ice cream and good coffee. He kept nodding and eventually he fell asleep and I picked him up and put him to bed.

I wasn't sure if I had reached him but I had tried.

#24

The kids were in the front of the house at 10:00 am, playing some intricate game, and Claire was off hustling real estate commissions with her partner. I made fresh coffee and knocked on the door to Smiley's room.

"Come in."

He was lying naked on the sofa bed and staring up at the ceiling, wearing mirrored sunglasses.

"Coffee?"

His head turned slowly while the rest of his body stayed absolutely motionless. "Yes it is."

I handed it over and he sat up to drink it and then he dressed. As he did so I found myself staring. His skin looked like mine and I never really had a chance to look at mine from the outside. A fairly apt talker, a con artist and smuggler I'd known in Halifax, had called his body his blooded passport. And looking at Smiley I could appreciate the term; he had made his body into his own.

Tiny seed pearls inserted under his foreskin, a Turkish

crook thing saying, *this is how tough I am*. Tattoos of flames on his knees and a razor-clawed eagle on his chest, a Russian crook thing stating *I do not kneel* and *I will avenge myself*. Tattoo of a tiger on his back in three colours, a Chinese crook thing so nothing could attack him from behind. But nothing tattooed on his hands, arms, or face; nothing that could be used to identify him when he was working.

Scars from knives on his face and forearms, defensive wounds sewn up with fishing line or dental floss or whatever was handy and allowed to heal badly. Scars from fists on his face. Scars from fire on his ankles and lower back, from stories I'd never heard. Two puckered scars on his front, little dimples from twenty-two hollow points in the shaky hands of a South Korean jade dealer who decided to play instead of pay. Three big scars on his back from police buckshot and glass chunks, because glass becomes shrapnel when force is applied. When he was dressed he looked at me and all I could see was my reflection in his sunglasses. He said hoarsely, "I'm going out for awhile, okay?"

"Sure."

"Any more job ideas for me?"

"Claire left a list. There's a copy for you so you can think about them."

"Sure, I'll take it with me."

He took it and left and I went back to the kids.

When they were napping I went and used the extra alarm components I'd borrowed from Marie. I wired Smiley's door, tucking the machinery into the panelling of the door itself. When it was all in place I checked the receiver. If the door was closed, the receiver was green; when it opened, it turned red and stayed that way. I marked that one and its receiver as number one with a black marker and then marked the rest of the alarms.

The kids were still asleep, so I wired the other doors in the front and back of the house and then the ones to the main bedroom and Fred's room as well. I had three units left, so I pulled the carpeting from the stairs and put them under the risers there. Then I put all the receivers in the pocket of Claire's winter coat in the upstairs closet.

With them in place I would have a rough idea of everything that went on in the house, even when I wasn't there. It wasn't perfect, but it was a start.

When Claire arrived home for lunch I kissed her, fed her, and then showed her how to read the sensors.

"If Smiley's door indicator turns red it means someone has opened it. If the ones on the stairs go red it means someone has used the stairs."

When I'd shown her everything she looked at me sadly. "So that's how it's going to be?"

"Yes." Then I kissed her and fled into the early afternoon. The first thing I did was visit Marie. She told me no one had been around either the camp or the house. I nodded, "Okay. By the way, find an extra vehicle and don't keep using the same one. The cops might start noticing."

"Sure."

"You can rent one or borrow it. If you rent it, pay cash. Keep your trail cold. Tell them you're using it meet your lover and use a smaller rental place, not a national one—they're more likely to go for that."

I rechecked the house and went to work with some of the tools and equipment I'd left in the garage making adjustments to the front door. By the time I was done, I'd reinforced the whole inside door frame with bar steel scavenged from an abandoned pawnshop and I'd attached extra sets of quarter-inch steel chain to hold it open at fifteen centimetres. You could break in by chopping the centre panels into kindling or by taking the whole front of the house off. You could not, however, knock the door off the hinges. Not without an arc welder, Jaws of Life, or maybe a shaped explosive charge (God bless you Major Munroe, inventor of the shaped charge; the world is a better place for your contributions.)

When I was done, Marie gave me a bottle of designer water. "Where are you off to now?"

"Wreaking more havoc."

"Ah. Should I ask?"

"No. Keep your head down."

Outside I thought about what to do next. While I thought I walked, finally stopping at the end of my block where an Anglican church sat on a lot surrounded by tall, well-tended trees. The wind picked up and I sat on a bench in a dark corner beside a thick elm. While I rested two boys, maybe eleven, walked past. There was no way they could see me, so I eavesdropped.

"She let me put it in her mouth."

"Bullshit!" A pause. "She did?"

"Yeah. I gave her ten dollars but she did. She said I could do it again, too."

The second boy whistled. "So where's she at?"

"Her and her cousin got kicked out by their stepdad. They're living in that old house."

"Yeah?"

They were both standing on the sidewalk with their hands in their pockets and the second boy said, "Betcha I can get ten bucks from home."

"Yeah?"

"Yeah. I'll tell Auntie it's for school books."

They took off and I followed them at a distance. I watched them run into a bungalow and then out again. With idle curiosity I followed them the rest of the way until they entered the drug house I'd destroyed.

I made a list: I was helping Marie, that was what I was being paid for. I was helping Smiley and keeping an eye on him, and that was going fine. And I had warned Samantha in a serious way to back off, and she seemed to be doing just that. Lastly, I had dealt with the drug house, permanently, I hoped.

However, the house itself was still there, albeit falling apart.

There were consequences to my actions there, something I'd never considered.

The house was a wreck and no one seemed to be cleaning it up, which meant that the lost and forgotten would continue to use the building. I could do something about that which would keep me busy and that was a good thing. As my uncle Sal used to say, "Idle hands are the devil's tools." Or something like that.

And I couldn't fix any other problem, so I might as well focus on the one I could fix.

I had two names, the Abernathys, who had rented the house, and Jarrod and Tho Jarelski, who owned the house. Abernathy was probably an alias or they were in jail. In any case, the address they had was fake, so finding them would be difficult. I took the path of least resistance via a quick bus ride and a nice walk through River Heights, the Jarelskis' neighbourhood, just to check things out.

Big, well-kept houses in a clean neighbourhood. Lots of carefully trimmed trees, well-maintained sidewalks, good walls between the properties, grass all shorn at roughly the same height. People walking dogs and barbecuing things.

Frankly, too many people.

The absolute best time to burglarize a place is in the mid-morning when most honest, law-abiding folk are at work. Best time to perform a home invasion is in the early evening when you can be sure most people are going to be at the home you want to invade. Unfortunately, my rule didn't work here because there were too many people around, so I'd have to do it the hard way, at night.

I went home, plotting all the way.

#25

The next evening I was back in the Jarelskis' neighbourhood, only this time wearing a suit of second-hand clothes I'd bought at a Salvation Army thrift store. The jeans, parka (to make me look truly homeless and decrepit) and T-shirt fit fine but the boots were a bit too wide and I'd pulled on three pairs of socks to make sure of a fit. A few blocks down from the thrift store I stopped in a Wal-Mart. In the hardware section I grabbed a short-handled pry bar and two rolls of duct tape. In the men's wear section I found a dark red jogging suit, pants and jacket just slightly too big for me. In the sporting goods I picked up a black wool ski hat and a Bionic Ear, an audio amplification device favoured by bird watchers, amateur spies, and bad guys like myself.

The device was powered by two triple A batteries and looked like a set of fairly fancy ear phones for a CD player, a radio or an MP3 player. It would amplify sounds out to a range of thirty metres using a three-band equalizer that included safety shut offs, so really loud noises wouldn't deafen the user.

With my shopping basket almost full I stopped at the pharmacy and bought a small pack of rubber gloves and a set of triangular-bladed Exacto knives. At the cash register an older female clerk slowed me down by asking me, "Did you find everything you needed?"

"I did."

"And was everyone kind to you?"

"They were."

"And is there anything else we can do for you today?"

I was getting annoyed. "You could unionize."

"What?"

"Unionize. Join a union. Earn a living wage. Fight the power. Take a stand."

Her hands were flashing as she bagged my purchases. Nodding at me and smiling brightly, "Uh-huh. Yes. Of course."

I recalled what the fattish woman's T-shirt had read, LA LUCHA CONTINUA! Strike while the iron is hot! Struggle to overcome imperialism!

The woman was starting to sweat. I took pity on her as she accepted my money and gave me back my change. She'd remember me if the cops asked but she'd remember me as nuts, which I'm not.

Sometimes, if you can't be invisible, it's best to be an asshole.

Six blocks away I changed clothes in the restroom of a coffee shop attached to a non-chain hotel (less chance of security cameras) and then crossed the St. James Bridge into River Heights. I found a small park near a high school where I sat in the pale autumn sunshine and folded my original clothes small and packed them in several layers of plastic bags for later disposal. With that out of the way, I fiddled with the

Bionic Ear and entertained myself by listening in to the angry and abusive and pitying conversations of high school students when the classes let out. It was one way to wait for the right time to work.

Twenty metres away, dressed as I was, I was invisible. Neither the kids nor the teachers so much as looked at me as I watched them all and I raised a silent toast of welcome to the real world in commiseration.

I waited two more hours and then started walking slowly, shuffling actually, towards the Jarelskis' house, fiddling with the ear pieces as I went, mumbling to myself. Everyone I met gave me a wide berth; pretty young housewives walking their dogs, grumpy-looking middle-aged men coming home from their work, and clean white children dressed in the latest gangster fashion.

I kept walking, turning my head slowly from side to side and listening to what people were saying in their cars and on their yards and even in their homes. At the Jarelskis' house, I heard nothing in the front, so I circled around in the beginnings of the twilight and listened from the back lane. From there I could hear the clattering of metal and glass along with a single female voice speaking in a language I didn't recognize.

At a guess I'd say it was Ms. Tho Jarelski talking on a phone while cooking. Maybe waiting for Mr. Jarelski to come home from wherever. I'd also guess they didn't have a dog; there was no shit in the backyard and there was no hint of barking or scrabbling inside.

With that in mind I headed two blocks over to where a big Catholic church occupied a whole block. In the back was a dumpster pulled away from the wall. I curled up to wait until eleven. It was a long time but the early approach had allowed me to scope out the whole area for cops and crooks.

No one had paid any attention to me. It was always like that when I disguised myself as a derelict—no one notices or really pays attention to the lost ones who wander the streets. Indeed, most of the time no one even looks them in the eyes, because to do that would be to acknowledge their humanity.

I have a theory about that fear. I suspect that most people don't want to acknowledge the humanity of the street people because then they'd have to acknowledge that maybe there wasn't that much difference between them.

And that would maybe make them start wondering about what exactly the difference was.

And that might make them start believing in luck and divine fate.

And that might make them start wondering about why other people had more than they did.

And that might make them realize that the whole world was billionaires laughing at millionaires.

#26

At slightly past eleven I woke up and pulled on the jogging suit, not the easiest thing to do while lying in the dirt and grime, but doable. I then pulled on a pair of rubber surgical gloves (hard to recognize at a distance) and padded the straight edge of the pry bar with about ten layers of duct tape, to muffle the sound in case I had to use it to break glass. It would also make it a lot harder to lift a fingerprint. The padded pry bar went down the front of my pants, the Exacto knives (still in their plastic) went into my right-hand jacket pocket, and I put a roll of duct tape over each fist. With luck anyone who saw me would assume that I was carrying hand weights of some new and unusual design.

I cut the top off the ski hat and pulled it over my head to cover my neck and mouth like a muffler and then put the Bionic Ear back on with the gain turned to full. All my regular clothes along with my wallet (always bring your wallet; if you ever get stopped by the cops, for whatever reason, not having ID is like waving a red flag at a bull, so bring your wallet until you are actually doing something bad, then leave it behind) were already carefully wrapped up in three plastic bags and those went under the dumpster. The parka and the clothes I'd bought from the Salvation Army went into the dumpster. Once I was sure no one was watching I walked out onto the sidewalk, stretched, and started to jog slowly down back lanes, spiralling slowly towards the Jarelski house with the pry bar tapping my dick every few feet.

I reached the Jarelskis' near midnight. I could hear vague strains of television coming through from the back of the house but no one seemed to be in the kitchen. Without pausing I opened the gate and ran softly up the rear walk. Just before I reached the cedar stairs I wrenched my boots off and put them neatly on the top step.

While I was doing all that my ears were growing points listening for any dangerous sounds, but there was nothing: no neighbours saying, who's that, Martha? No bystanders calling the cops, no sirens in the distance, no dogs barking. Nothing but sounds of televisions playing shows with titles like *Who Wants to Marry a Million Bears*, *24/7: The Torture Show* and *American Idiot*.

At the top of the steps I slowly twisted the door handle. It turned easily. Almost no one locks their doors until they're going to sleep. Two seconds later, silent on stocking feet, I was inside.

As far as kitchens went, it was pretty nice. Dark but nice: black granite counters, a high end gas stove, coffee pod system, microwave, bagel guillotine; all in blacks and fine lines of chrome. Also a black fridge and built-in dishwasher with a black-and-white-checkered floor and black-and-grey-tiled walls.

Expensive.

The Bionic Ear worked perfectly. I could hear a television in the front room and two people talking quietly during the commercials. I pulled my hood up, put the duct tape on top of the fridge, drew out the pry bar, and waited.

After twenty minutes I heard someone padding towards the kitchen from the front room. I stood to the left of the entrance in front of a door and held my breath.

It was the wife; small boned with fine hair, about five foot nothing and wearing a lavender pantsuit and leather moccasins. She turned towards the microwave and yawned and didn't expect a thing as I surged forward and scooped her up.

She went rigid and her back arced, but she was already off the ground with my left arm around her throat and my right arm holding her arms to her sides.

Her scream was more a whisper and she kicked my shins, which didn't hurt much, and her hands scrabbled for my nuts.

I ignored it all and did something a Los Angeles cop showed me once, a Los Angeles Police bar choke hold, outlawed back in the nineties. It was called a blood choke. I felt with my hand until I found the right spot and applied steady, relentless pressure.

She spasmed and stopped moving. In general the person choked out will stay unconscious for two or three times the length of time the hold is applied. That gave me time to very slowly strip lengths of tape off the spool and bind her hands and feet together. Duct tape is never quiet but I did my best. Then I flipped her over and hogtied her feet to her hands before putting a couple of loops around her mouth but leaving her nose free so she could breathe.

She was still breathing and that was good, because the

downside of the blood hold is death by asphyxiation, which is why the Lost Angels Police Department had been forced to abandon it. A large number of black men had been killed or turned into vegetables by a large number of white men. Eventually the public had become aware that the hold had some inherent problems and it had been outlawed.

When I was sure her breathing was okay I picked up a glass jar of spaghetti noodles and stepped back into my corner. I took a deep breath and tossed the jar to shatter in the sink.

Smash.

"Honey?"

It was a man's voice. I stood still and waited for him to do something.

"Honey, are you okay?"

Sound of him getting to his feet and rushing toward the kitchen. I'd put her on the floor in the far corner so he had to turn his head when he came in to see her. His back was to me and he was quite big; over ninety kilos, short and squat; so I cheated a bit and used the pry bar to apply the same blood hold. Ten seconds later he was out too.

Once Mr. Jarelski was hogtied I locked the front, back, and garage doors, checked the house from top to bottom, and found no one. When that was done I dragged them both down to a carpenter's workshop they had in the basement. Each of them struggled a little but I choked them out again and propped them in two lawn chairs I found in a storage closet. I duct-taped the chairs together, side by side, and then I duct-taped the Jarelskis into immobility, securing their forearms to the arms of the chairs and their calves to the legs of the chairs. Their mouths were still taped shut, and I put an extra roll across their eyes as well.

By the time I was done I had used one roll of tape and most of the second.

Then I searched the place, not tearing it apart but not leaving much undone either. In the master bedroom I found her purse and his wallet and confiscated the sixty-some odd bucks therein, along with eight credit cards. It all went into a royal blue silk pillowcase along with the good jewelry from her mahogany jewel box and the hardened leather case in the top drawer of his dresser. Then I went through the kitchen and found $430 in tens in a baggie at the bottom of the flour bowl.

In the very masculine study I found a gun safe built into a closet. Ten seconds with the pry bar pulled the lock out. Inside were two over and under twelve-gauge Weatherby shotguns (about $3500 each) and a Sako model 85 bolt-action rifle in .338 calibre (about $2000). The ammunition was in a separate locked box on the floor of the closet. Beside it was an antique teak case with brass fittings that held thirty-nine small gold coins sealed in plastic coin condoms and marked 1726 CHRS REGN VING IMPER. On the other side of each coin was the date 2007 and an engraving of Queen Elizabeth II.

I took the guns, the ammunition, and the pillowcase full of loot, and laid it all out on the workbench in front of the Jarelskis who were now conscious and stirring. I placed the Exacto knives in a neat row, parallel to the edge of the table, and loaded one shotgun with two shells full of #6 buckshot. Then I loaded the rifle.

The noise of me loading the weapons made the Jarelskis freeze in place.

While they were immobile and blind, I searched through the tools in the shop and found a set of clamps, a hacksaw with a fresh blade, and some unused sandpaper. Those I laid beside the unloaded shotgun. Then I pulled the balaclava down over my face and turned back to my prisoners to tear the tape off their eyes. As they adjusted to the light I spoke in the coldest, roughest voice I could manage:

"Is there any reason why I shouldn't kill you now?"

#27

The Jarelskis both went into spasms of motion, threatening to overturn the chairs, and I just waited. The choke hold produced a horrible headache, almost migraine level, combined with nausea, exhaustion, and a sense of dislocation. Neither would be feeling good and their fear was heightened because I'd tied them together. They had no hope; neither could possibly believe the other would be saving them.

They were alone. Together but alone.

And they were in their own house, trussed up and trapped. They were surrounded by power tools with dire cultural values attached: the chainsaw, machete, and car battery with jumper cables. In the minds of most North Americans those translated into *The Texas Chain Saw Massacre*, *Friday the 13th* and *American Psycho*. And facing them was a guy in a bright red jogging suit with a balaclava over his face making him look like the generic terrorist.

I would be surprised if they weren't scared.

Eventually they stopped struggling. "My brother got a

hotshot in your crack house," I said. "An armload of pure crystal when he was used to stepped-on-shit. It blew his heart out like a candle."

I didn't have a brother; frankly, I didn't have much of any family but the Jarelskis didn't know that. While I talked I clamped the unloaded shotgun to the table and went to work with the hacksaw, cruelly and viciously ruining the beautiful lines of the weapon by cutting the fifty-five-centimetre barrels down to an easily concealable twenty.

"I already talked to the fuckwad you had running the place. I eventually found him and he talked. The cops'll find the body by the smell …"

The cut-off barrels rang like bells on the concrete floor. I flipped the weapon around and started on the fine-grained walnut stock, cutting it into a pistol grip. In my peripheral vision I could see them staring at each other and shifting their eyes frantically from side to side.

"You hired a tough little prick there. It took him an hour before he gave you up. Blunted two razors before he gave in."

I raised my head and admired the shotgun.

"Pretty good."

One shotgun was finished. I pulled the rounds from the first one, loaded the sawed-down gun, put the first one in the clamps, and repeated my handiwork. When I was finished I loaded it and then poked through the contents of the pillow-case and discarded two fake pearl earrings, a watch I wasn't sure about, and the box the coins had come in. I found a leather backpack under the workbench and loaded it with the shotguns, ammo, and loot, and then I turned back to my prisoners.

"Any last words before I send you screaming to hell?"

Their eyes were pleading and I reached over with the tip of one of the Exacto knives and carefully cut the gag off the man, who sputtered out, "You're making a mistake."

I sat back against the workbench. "People always say that. What are you going to do, offer me money? Offer me your wife? Offer me everything?"

He begged and I felt disgusted as he whispered, "I'll give you anything!"

I took a deep breath and screamed into his face. "I WANT MY BROTHER BACK!"

There was silence in the room. I stood back and said, "What the fuck is the point."

I flicked the Exacto knife into the air, caught it easily by the handle, and said cheerily, "Time to die."

The man was shaking his head and beside him his wife was shaking hers. His voice was earnest: "You've got the wrong people ... we don't know anything about no crack house. You gotta believe me!"

"Fuck this! Your name is Jarelski, your wife is Tho. You own a house in the North End. It was destroyed by flooding a little while ago. The house was run by a real beauty that I caught and who gave you up. Right?"

Mr. Jarelski was shaking his head so hard he almost dislocated his neck. "NO! We own the house, yes. But we rented it out. We had no idea what was going on. When the cops told us we were completely surprised."

I stared at them both for a long time and tapped my chin with the knife.

"No. The guy you hired to run the place gave you up. You're insulting me."

Tho was grunting rhythmically and I cut her gag free as well. "No. We never knew anything about any of that! We just rented the place out. We didn't know anything about nothing else."

I stood there and shrugged. "Shit. I believe you. I really do. I guess the other guy just gave your names up so I'd cut him slack."

Relief showed in their eyes but it vanished when I went on, "On the other hand, I also know about the rest of the homes you two own."

They both got quiet.

The addresses of the rest of the properties had been listed in Ultra Realty files and the newspaper records had been helpful. The police had also helped; they kept a public list of raided houses, including pictures posted on their website. Of the eleven properties owned by the Jarelskis, four had been shut down as marijuana grow operations and one other had been raided on prostitution charges.

Five out of eleven were a significant number and the Jarelskis realized it as the blood drained from their faces. Five out of eleven meant they weren't being very good landlords at all. I waited until the tension was as high as I could bear and then I went on, "Which means I've still got to kill you."

They were both talking so fast that nothing was comprehensible and I finally shouted, "SHUT UP!"

They did and I went on, "I can't let you live. You know I tortured and murdered somebody and I broke in here, kidnapped you, and assaulted you. No. There is just way too much jail time on the line."

They started to babble again and shut up when I said, "But I am sorry."

Mr. Jarelski was almost in tears. "You can't be serious! You can trust us; we won't say a thing to anybody!"

Mrs. Jarelski joined in, "Right. Nothing, not a word!"

I laughed at them. "Sure. You say that now but that'll change. You'll change your minds once I'm gone. I've seen it happen."

I put the knife down and picked up the shotgun. "But I'm not a freak. I'll do it quick and painless, not with the knife."

They both just stared at me and I said again, "Who wants to go first?"

Mr. Jarelski swallowed and said very calmly, "What can we do to convince you we won't go to the cops?"

I sat down on the bench and rubbed the shotgun against my forehead in thought. It had taken them a while to reach this point and I wasn't sure how to take them the rest of the way to where I wanted them to be. I wanted them to take responsibility for the wrecked house and build a new one. I wanted them to clean up the rest of their properties and keep them clean.

"Hmmm."

In truth I was rationalizing, trying to convince myself these folks deserved what was happening to them. They had rented a house to drug dealers, apparently without a care in the world. They had accepted a very high rate of rent for that house, which should have tipped them off. And when the house had been destroyed, they hadn't fixed the problem.

Like Claire would say, they hadn't done their due diligence at any step of the way. They hadn't cared. They went through their whole business lives not caring.

I kept making the same noise, "Hmmmm."

The Jarelskis were both staring at me and both had forgotten to breathe, it was almost funny. Finally I said, "Okay. I'd want some kind of sign of your sincerity; I mean, I don't really have to kill you if I think you're honest …"

Mrs. Jarelski jumped on it. "Like money?"

I waved that off. "No. If it was money I'd have to meet you again to get the money and you don't want that. Right now you don't know who I am. If you did know who I was, then I'd kill you."

Mr. Jarelski was confused. "So what do you want?"

I shrugged. "I don't know. I'm here trying to avenge the fuckers who killed my brother. What the fuck do I know?"

Mr. Jarelski started to say something and his wife interrupted him, "Hold on. This is about your brother, right?"

"Yeah."

"So what if we made the house into a memorial to him?"

I scratched my head with the shotgun again. "I don't know … it's a pretty fucked-up house … it doesn't make much of a memorial."

Mr. Jarelski nodded frantically. "That's a great idea. We'll tear down the house and donate the land to the city; they can turn it into a park. We can name it after your brother."

I pointed the shotgun between his eyes and he blanched. A second later his bladder cut loose and I whispered, "You trying to find out my brother's name? You trying to find out who I am?"

They both babbled no again and Mrs. Jarelski spoke to me calmly, "No. We can dedicate the park to … the community, whatever. Would that be okay?"

"Sure. That would be … sure. That would be okay."

They both smiled and I smiled back under my mask. They were probably thinking they had me figured out and conned. They were probably thinking they could just string me along, call the cops, take a vacation somewhere warm while the cops hunted down all the leads and, eventually, caught me. They were probably thinking they had me beat.

People always thought the way they were taught. Businesspeople thought in terms of business games, for them every deal was a hand of poker. Cops thought in terms of cop games, for them every encounter was a game of checkers. Psychiatrists thought of the world in terms of chess.

But bad guys ... bad guys played it differently.

For them there were no rules. And I was still a bad guy enough to remember that essential truth. Sometimes I wondered if I would ever be able to forget it at all.

So I smiled at Mr. and Mrs. Jarelski and said, "Okay. But I want to leave you something to remember me by. Just so you're not tempted to go back on your promise."

They both stared at me stupidly as I cut the bindings on Mr. Jarelski and then taped his hands back together and ushered him upstairs. He told me where his car keys were and I picked them up and took him out to his garage, where a grey Lexus four-door sedan sat with heavily tinted windows. I put him in the back seat and taped him into immobility (including a couple of twists around his face), and only then did I fasten the seat belt securely around him.

He may have been thinking of fighting back but the shotgun in his belly kept him quiet.

After he was safely in the car I brought his wife up to keep him company. Then I went downstairs and returned the Sako rifle to the gun case, placing it inside along with all the ammunition and the gold coins before shutting the door as well as I could. After that I put the jewelry back and replaced the cash in the flour jar. The last think I did was pick up the barrels I'd cut off the shotguns and add those to the backpack along with the shotguns, which I disassembled into four pieces with a small screwdriver for easy disposal.

Then I went into the kitchen and found the cupboard where they kept their liquor. The Jarelskis had an excellent selection and I used bottles of 151-proof dark rum and vodka along with regular 80-proof rye and Scotch.

And no, I didn't drink any of it.

Although I really wanted to.

When I had the bottles arranged around the coffee maker, I set the automatic timer for 1:30 am and put a rag on the burner (under the pot). Then I tipped over the rum and vodka, soaked the rag, and let it drip and pool into the sink.

The coffee maker would ignite the spilled alcohol, which would run into the garbage pail, which would flare up and ignite the rest of the alcohol. I'd create a fuze with rags, and the fire would spread under the sink, where various chemicals were stored; those would add more heat to the fire, which would then travel into the wooden frame of the house and, voila.

An accidental fire.

A smart fire marshal or cop would probably have suspicions but it would be hard to prove much.

Instead I let the booze pool in the sink without the fuze. There it would smoke and score their granite countertops but do little more.

When I was done I joined the Jarelskis in their car and drove around the block and parked where we could see their kitchen between two houses. I turned in the seat and faced them. "I'm burning your house down."

Their eyes bulged and I went on, "Because I want you to remember me and I can't think of a better way. Every time you go into your home from now on I want you to think about it. I want you to think about how safe you are, about how much your home is your castle. You took that safety away from people you don't even know and you did it for money with your North End house."

Neither of them tried to say anything, they just stared and I went on, "So you can keep your money, but now I'm taking away your safety and security. Think about that, I can always come back. Or it will be someone like me. That'll happen if you don't start paying attention to what's happening in your houses."

They were both crying and after awhile a bright red light filled their kitchen and they both groaned into their gags and I left.

Blocks away I slowed down to a walk. The Jarelskis would get loose in time and then they could clean up their home and make their decisions. If they did what they promised, that would be great; my neighbourhood would get a new park. If they didn't then that would be fine too.

They'd probably be really careful about their business dealings for the rest of their lives.

#28

I changed my clothes back at the church and then I walked home on foot. The shotguns I left one piece at a time in garbage cans and storm drains scattered over a ten-block stretch.

The next morning Claire handed me a piece of paper. "Frank called."

"Good for him."

"Wants to know when he should schedule the Hunter's Safety Course."

I froze and admitted, "I'd forgotten."

"You forgot about wild boar?"

"I forgot on purpose. It was very hard."

"How do you forget about wild boars? I mean, they're not even that important to me and I can't forget about them."

She gave me the paper which had an address, 70 Stevenson Road and starting at 10:00 in the morning on Saturday. She had written underneath it that the class was near Red River

College, about an hour or so away by bus. While I was reading she breezed past me on her way to work and I yelled at her back. "It was damn hard to forget about those pigs. You try to forget about giant, blood rending ..."

Smiley came down from the bathroom, combing his hair with his fingers. "What, the kids are here already?"

"Very funny. Where you off to today?"

"No idea. Where do you go to find jobs?"

Good question. "An unemployment insurance office maybe? Check the yellow pages."

The doorbell rang and while Smiley was looking up the number and address I accepted Jacob from his cop mother and Rachel from her mom. By the time I'd gotten them settled Smiley had closed the book and put down the phone. "It's EI, not UI. Employment Insurance."

I was confused. "So they help you find a better job than the one you already have? That makes no sense."

"It's the government, what do you expect. Time to go."

In disgust I motioned for him to leave and he batted his eyelids. "Don't I deserve a kiss?"

"Oh, fuck off!"

Wanna guess the one word Jacob learned?

Claire was back at noon with a bulging briefcase, a travel mug of coffee, and a headache. She entered the house, stared blankly at Rachel, Fred, and Jacob who were (in order) looking at a comic book, colouring in a colouring book, and plotting something while looking adorable.

"Sanity."

Rushing to pull on shoes and jacket, I didn't answer and she kept talking. "I have clients who don't want anything I have but don't want to find another company because they like me. I have another client who feels he shouldn't have to pay rent this month because it's his birthday. And I have a gang who want to rent any one of our properties, any one at all, as long as it has an attached garage."

"Well, marijuana grow operations are a growth industry."

"Hardy-har-har. People who use puns should be shot." She took off her shoes, stretched upwards and yawned. "So this little bit of sanity will be nice. Plus I have some more ideas for Smiley."

"Okay, I'm off! But first, a kiss!"

With my last glance I saw that Rachel was now colouring in the comic book (who ever heard of Captain Carrot? I'd picked up a whole bunch of them for five dollars at a used book store, but who ever heard of a rabbit super hero? Bugs Bunny, sure, but that was it.) Fred was eating the colouring book, and Jacob had started to stuff one crayon up each nostril.

None of which was my problem. So I kissed Claire in a slightly more serious fashion and ran before the screams started.

At Buttes Frank was working on a bow, restringing it with the help of a huge, nasty machine that looked like it could tear a human in half.

"Stupid, god-damned …"

It was entertaining to watch but I interrupted him anyway. "Has the delivery come yet?"

"Huh? Oh, no. Can you do me a favour and help me with this stupid bow?"

I stared at the machine, the big rollers and weights, the clamps and vise grips. "No."

He glared at me. "What do you mean, no?"

"You don't pay me enough to work with that damn thing."

"Damn thing? You mean the 'Mangler'? Come on, it's harmless."

For a brief moment I hallucinated that the machine was grinning and then I gave in and helped Frank. A few minutes later he was putting a bandage around my right forefinger while I rubbed feeling back into my left wrist.

"I don't think you'll lose your nail."

"That's good; this is evidence that no machine called 'The Mangler' is ever safe."

The bell in the back rang, telling me that the delivery had arrived, so Frank finished and motioned me to work. "You shouldn't lose it; anyway, I don't think so. You better get to work."

I was heading for the back door. "As long as it doesn't involve wild boars."

"Hey, I almost forgot about that ..."

Groaning, I went to work with my injured paw and unloaded the partial pallet the trucking company had sent. My dealings with the driver, an obnoxious little freak, were always somewhat stressed. This time he stayed far out of my way and showed his contempt by peeing on the wall of the shop.

It was going to be a long, long day.

On the way home I stopped at Marie's and found a house full of people from Bangladesh. She introduced me and then shuffled me out the back with an envelope full of cash, part of my pay in installments, whispering, "It's working perfectly. No calls, no visits, nothing from Sam or anyone else. Frankly, there are no hitches at all so far. Knock on wood."

I left and headed east via two buses until I reached the Club Regent Casino. As I walked to it I started to hum the old Louis Armstrong tune "It's a Wonderful World." It didn't help, though, and a few seconds later I entered the giant space full of noise and light and people. And money, lots of money. Turning hard left I walked through a giant aquarium and found myself frozen in space watching a coral reef full of living jewels and beautiful monsters.

"Cool!"

The older couple behind me patted my back gently and agreed. I tore myself away with difficulty and only managed to do it by promising myself to bring Claire. I kept moving into a fake tropical nightmare.

"Yo-ho-ho."

Turning my head slowly, I saw a skeleton of a Chihuahua and a Spanish conquistador. I put my hand out towards the dog and, speaking deadpan, I repeated back to them, "Yo-ho-ho?"

"Hey, not my choice, I have a script here …"

The dog's head stopped moving and another voice came on.

"Yo-ho-ho. Don't pet the dog, he bites." This made me draw my hand back slowly and the voice went on, "Yo-ho-ho!"

Shaking my head gently I kept on, searching the main floor and finding the quarter-and-nickel slot machines. Many of them linked together with progressive jackpots. And scattered around were also table games with blackjack, roulette, paigow, mini-baccarat, keno, poker, and baccarat. Lots and lots of ways to lose your money.

Casinos have limits on how much money you can walk away with before they issue you a cheque, and in Manitoba that limit is $10,000. The casinos claim the limits are designed to stop terrorists or people like me from washing my ill-booten-gotty. However, that rule was fine, because what I really wanted was a nice, clean, easily traced cheque. And for that little piece of paper I was certainly willing to pay taxes.

I exchanged a hundred for a cup of loonie coins from a beautiful girl pushing a metal change cart around, and then I found a big impersonal machine with no one nearby and proceeded to drop the coins into the hopper. In five minutes I dropped all hundred and pulled the lever. I actually played three times, winning once and losing twice. Then I pressed the cash out button and received a slip for $99.75 and the first wash was done.

Wandering out of the main casino I did the same in another room and then once downstairs for $250 at a bank of keno machines for a total loss of $2.25. Then I went upstairs to the gaming tables. I passed by two blackjack tables and a baccarat table as being, respectively, too busy and not busy enough. Near the end of the ranks of tables there were roulette tables, American-style ones with a double zero pushing the odds seriously towards the house. Despite that I bought $300 worth of chips, lost a red five-dollar chip betting even, won betting odd, and then exchanged the chips for black hundreds and wandered away.

At a blackjack table limited for $25 to $500 I cashed in another $200 for green twenty-five-dollar pieces and lost twice before winning a blackjack. They were using the eternity deck, a constant six-deck mechanical shuffle that eliminated any kind of skill or treachery on the part of the players. Before I could leave a waitress came up and brought me a complimentary coffee, so I tipped her a dollar. I now had washed $950 and had gotten a free coffee for a total cost of $20.75. Not bad math for washing money, and a lot less than the average underworld accountant would charge.

I went back to the slot machines and dumped $450 before finishing up at a mini-baccarat table where the odds were, according to the croupier, about 50.5% in the favour of the house. So I dropped the rest of my money in chips, played four times, won three times, tied once, tipped the croupier five dollars and found the cashier's wicket with $2,003.25 in chips, blacks and greens, and slips of paper from the slot machines.

The cashier was a fairly pretty girl, albeit kind of dirty, although that may have been the light. Her voice was deadpan. "Good evening sir. How would you like to be paid?"

I felt a breath on my neck and turned to face a beautiful woman wearing a tight green dress cinched around her waist with an ornate belt made of black iron links. She smelled ... good. Rich, earthy, electric, and I was pretty sure she wasn't wearing much under the dress.

And I was pretty sure the smell wasn't perfume out of any kind of bottle.

"Sir?"

It was the cashier again and I turned back to her and then back to the woman behind me. She had large dark eyes with long, long lashes. Eyes I could lose myself in, eyes I wanted to lose myself in for forever and a day.

"Sir?" The cashier still didn't really seem to care but she was waiting. So was the woman behind me. But they were waiting for different things. I smiled brightly at the cashier. "A cheque, please."

The woman beside me sighed deeply and her whole body did interesting and hypnotic things. "Maybe next time ..."

It was a promise and she was gone, so I collected my money and fled home for a long, cold shower. Claire took the cheque and had me endorse it so she could deposit it in her account the next day.

At my house the chaos was reassuringly normal and comforting. Fred was asleep in his bed and the dog was asleep on our bed and Thor the mouse was looking through his food dish in his fastidious manner and throwing the black seeds away when he found them. Claire and I were sitting there to ambush Smiley when he came in at 9:00. He saw us and froze in the doorway, staring at the two of us sitting at the table in the living room. He was pushing a folding metal trolley loaded with boxes from a big-box electronics store.

"Is this an intervention?" He sounded wary.

"No," Claire answered.

"Thank God."

We all ignored the cargo and he sat down on the floor and gestured at the 3x5-inch cards stacked beside Claire's elbow. "What are those?"

"Job opportunities for you."

"Oh."

I felt obliged to add, "More like job possibilities."

"Right."

He braced himself visibly and said, "Go!"

Claire flipped over the first card. "Lion tamer."

His eyes lit up. "Are you kidding? That's an option?"

She kept her poker face. "Not really, just wanted to make sure I had your attention. These following jobs have been chosen to match your skills as a thug and general layabout."

"I could be a lion tamer."

"Sure you could." She put the card down and raised the next. "Call centre."

"What's that?"

I answered. "You call people during dinner and annoy them, selling them stuff or asking them to take a survey."

"Oh. How much does it pay?" Smiley was interested.

Claire had that one. "$9.25 an hour. Plus bonuses."

"Which is what in real money?"

"About $19,000 a year minus taxes, maybe fifteen you take home."

He stared at me. "Fuck you!"

My wife cocked her head to the side and smiled seraphically and Smiley finally absorbed the message. "I mean, fuck me."

He thought about it and went on, "That's one bank robbery with good planning. A small bank. A bad bank. The kind of bank an amateur with a note and a broken stick would do."

I nodded. "So that's a no."

Claire was nothing if not cheerful. "Right. Don't become discouraged. Don't worry so much about the money though; I'll help you with budgets and stuff. The first thing is to have a job you can stand."

"Right. I guess."

"Fine. Next up is retail clothing salesperson." Claire made it sound exciting.

"Would you like to buy these pants?" He said it straight faced and I had to laugh. Which made Claire hit me, so I flinched, which made Smiley say, "And two for flinching. No."

"All right. Delivery driver." If Claire was getting tired it wasn't showing.

Smiley mulled that over. "Do I need a licence?"

"Yes. Can you drive?" I knew he could but Claire didn't.

"Sure. I've just never had one legally. And I sure don't have a licence in my own name. Is it hard to get one?"

Claire listed things off on her fingers. "You need to pay money, take a test, pay more money and they give you a licence."

"I can do that." Smiley sounded confident.

Claire paused and then said slowly, "I just realized something. What ID do you have?"

He dug it out of his pocket. "My prison ID card."

I took it from him and looked it over with a sense of familiarity and trepidation. A small piece of paper, coated by an amateur in plastic, with a bad picture of Smiley grinning like an idiot in the left-hand corner. In the centre top was his name and beneath that was the information that this person was an inmate of the Correctional Service of Canada, with INMATE written in big letters. On the back it was gridded off with Smiley's name and the finger-print system number (FPS), which consisted of six digits and a numeral. There was also Smiley's date of birth, his weight in kilos, his height in inches, eye colour, complexion, and hair colour.

"Your name is Hershel Wiebe?"

Smiley became quietly belligerent and menacing. "You have a problem with that?"

"No, I guess not. I believe that is the kind of question that a Hershel would ask. Explains your enthusiastic acceptance of 'Smiley' as a nickname."

He just glared at me and my wife took the card gently between two fingers. "This won't do, not at all. It'll be hard to find a job if the only ID you have is a card certifying you're a federal inmate."

Smiley snorted. "You think?"

She ignored the question. "So you'll need a driver's licence, a social insurance number, a birth certificate, and a few others. Monty, that's your job."

"No problems."

Everyone leaned back and finally Claire broke the silence and asked, "Now, what's in the boxes?"

His face lit up. "Presents. A wide-screen LCD television with surround sound, a DVD player, and copies of some of the best westerns ever made."

He handed me a box and I looked through the titles: *Unforgiven, Billy the Kid vs. Dracula, The Treasure of the Sierra Madre, The Good, the Bad, and the Ugly, High Noon*—the list went on, about twenty in total, all westerns. Most of the films were second hand. I looked up at Smiley, speechless, and he just smiled.

"I love this town! I found a movie store in Osborne Village with everything here, all dirt cheap and ..." He leaned towards Claire and me. "The clerk was smart and pretty. I like that."

"Where did you get the money?" I made it sound casual.

He shrugged. "Some people got off their asses and sent it along."

When he looked at me his eyes were clear and smiling and I had nothing to say, so, while he was putting the system together, I took Claire upstairs. When I fell asleep I dreamt of beautiful women in green dresses while Smiley stood behind a counter asking if I wanted fries with that.

#29

Claire went jogging with Smiley the next morning. I was feeling physically sore and a little angry, not for any particular reason, just because. However, Fred managed to cheer me up by ramming his head repeatedly into the dog, who was begging for peanut-butter toast at the dining room table. The focus of both was inspiring, Renfield in his large-eyed begging technique and Fred in his determination to go through the dog. Finally he yelled, "Bad DOG!" and I gave in to the begging.

When Renfield had his toast I picked up Fred and bounced him on my knee. "And what makes you so angry today?"

He howled and glared at me. Toddler rage is something special, something different, very incoherent and diffused, very pure in its own way, and right now he was mad at me. So I tickled him until he was out of breath from laughing and then read him the first chapter of *Moby-Dick* while he piled blocks on top of each other. By the time Claire and Smiley were back I was in a fine mood. So was Fred, but both Claire and Smiley seemed preoccupied, and neither of them would tell me why. When they had both showered and were drinking coffee I asked, "Any plans for today?"

Claire answered. "Gonna go buy Smiley some clothes after dinner."

He nodded agreement and I asked, "How late will you be? There are a few things I need to do tonight."

They both looked at me suspiciously and then my wife answered. "We should be done by 9:30 at the latest ..."

She trailed off and gave me space to add information, space I ignored. After a long time she cleared her throat and asked me directly, "And what do you have planned for tonight?"

"Nothing at all; well, nothing much."

She looked at me suspiciously and they both went off, Claire to try to sell houses and apartments and Smiley to try to not be a criminal. And, before I was ready, Jacob and Rachel came, and I just tried to survive the experience of diapers, snacks, wrestling, story time, and utter chaos. When Smiley and Claire came back at 7:00 I took the time to admire their purchases: two sedate three-piece suits, shirts and two pairs of shoes. Also sundries like socks and underwear, and even ties.

"Very nice."

Smiley's face was bleak and unhappy. "This is not me, man. Not me at all."

Claire made sympathetic noises. "It's not what you were; it's what you're trying to become, which is something different."

He nodded and I headed out. Before I could reach the door, my wife said casually, "So, you off?"

"Yep. Things to do ..."

I spent the rest of the evening scouting around Samantha's houses very quietly and checking Marie's neighbours for anything suspicious. In both parts of town there was nothing strange going on at all.

Thursday morning started with another run with Smiley. We covered a lot of ground, on Main Street down to the Manitoba Museum and the Planetarium and then up to Salter and back home. On the way we passed the working poor, the dispossessed, the insane, gang members, whores, psychopaths, Jesus freaks, schizophrenics looking for their lost dope, coughers hacking out tuberculosis germs, junkies hunting their fixes, boozehounds looking for another fast drink to shovel the snakes and the shakes back underground.

When we arrived home we were both quietly depressed. Claire had some free time so she took the monsters while I went to wash some more cash. Dressed in my best clothes and carrying a briefcase, I caught the bus and walked to the New Balmoral Hotel on the corner of Balmoral Street and Notre Dame. They opened at 9:00 so I walked in and went to the machines in the back and to the right, changing twenty-five twenties into loonies as I went. Then I sat at a machine and dumped 'em all in, pulling the lever now and again.

When the waitress came by with her plump thighs under a stiff skirt, I admired her until she repeated the question. A few minutes later she brought a shot of vodka and a Coke with ice, and when she was gone the vodka went onto the floor and the Coke was drunk. In forty minutes I'd put all the loonies into the machine, bought three drinks, and lost six dollars the twenty-seven times I'd pulled the lever.

So I left. At the bar the bartender looked at the slip and said, "Congratulations."

"Thanks."

She looked at it some more and then nodded to herself. "We'll have to pay you by cheque."

She looked scared, like I was going to beat on her over getting paid by cheque. Eventually a manager came and gave me a cheque for $479 and I walked a long way to the McPhillips Street Casino, where I played around with the slots and the table games and washed another $1,133.25 by 2:00.

When I reached home, Claire had all the children sitting on the floor cross-legged with their hands on their knees, palms upraised.

"Ohhhhhhhhmmmmmmmmmmmm."

They all exhaled in unison and it was memorably scary.

"Oh Mani Padme Hum."

The ones who could barely speak squeaked it out, or something vaguely similar. Claire opened an eye and gestured with her head that I should go to the kitchen, where she joined me.

"That's creepy."

She kissed me. "A little. How goes?"

"Another $1,600 clean and clear. I have to go down and work on Smiley's licence and certificate. Is there anything I need to do?"

"Nope, I'm having a fine time here with the rug rats. Wanna go out tonight?"

I paused and thought about it and realized that it would be the first time in … a long time. "I'd love to … what about Fred?"

"Let him find his own date."

"I mean a babysitter. Smiley?"

"No." Her eyes were dead. "No. Anyone else you can think of?"

"Sure. Call Martinez-the-cop, she owes you."

"That's true."

"Where is Smiley?"

"Out." Her dead eyes didn't invite comment.

"'Kay, it's a date. We can wash some more cash."

She rolled her eyes and smacked me in the arm. "My husband, last of the romantics, doubles love and business and wonders why I'm thinking of taking lovers. And that's two for flinching."

"Are you?"

"What?"

"Thinking of taking lovers."

"Nope. Not thinking about it at all."

That didn't sound right but I went back out to try to make Smiley a real, live human citizen. I thought about bringing him with me and letting him help, but I knew from past experience that he wasn't good wheedling and conning. He was more of a gun-in-your-face kind of guy.

Which was just fine because I found myself really enjoying the whole process.

At an Internet café on Osborne Street I rented access and while I waited in line I thought my way through the problem. To be real in the Great White North you needed three pieces of ID, the holy trinity: Driver's Licence, Social Insurance Number, and a Birth Certificate. Those three let you build everything, bank records, credit rate, and anything else. I had done all that before for various other people for sums of money, and for myself in order to avoid prosecution.

So I needed to find him those three. But faster than that I should find him something he could show around town as soon as possible. Something other than the prison ID card he had. For that there were a number of possibilities. One was a cheque-cashing card at one of the cheque-cashing stores that charged ridiculous rates of interest. Another was a liquor ID card, one that indicated the bearer was old enough to buy booze, go into bars and such.

Out of the two the liquor card would be better; it was government approved; so I dialled up the Manitoba Liquor Control Commission on the Internet and found that the ID was pretty well protected. To receive one required three pieces of ID, tough ones, too, like a passport and birth certificate and health card. On the plus side the cost was a very reasonable seventeen dollars. However, the needed information put that card out of easy reach.

Then I checked the website of one of the bigger cheque-cashing companies. It had thirteen locations in the city, or was it fourteen? Anyhow, they had a lot of stores. Their ID card would cost $1.99, but I'd have to show a photo ID—well, Smiley would have to show a photo ID. I wondered what they'd say when he showed them the prison ID?

I noted the number and address on a scrap of paper. With that basic info in hand he would have the start of a paper ID. Next was the social insurance number, the laws were tight on that in the post-9-11 world.

Thinking about that made me pause. Something Claire had told me in 2001 still resonated in my head. I was on my way into prison for something I'd done to someone and we'd been on the phone to each other when the planes had smashed into skyscrapers and pentagons and the Pennsylvania countryside. And Claire had said that she could no longer look into the skies because "… they had turned planes into knives."

I'll never forget that.

So nineteen Saudi Arabians used box cutters to steal four

planes and killed thousands of people in three states, and the world shuddered.

And a few hundred miles to the north and a few thousand to the west, what happened? I ended up making fake ID at the time, as fast as I could, because I was on my way into prison at the time and needed to pay off as many debts as I could. So the governments of the world tightened up the laws and rules and regulations. And that meant that the value of what I was producing went through the roof and my profit increased.

Back to SIN's. Smiley would need an original of his birth certificate, I wondered briefly if he had one. Once he had the original certificate and ten dollars he could get his very own SIN after filling out a form or two. Which meant I needed to find him a birth certificate. I thought he had been born in Vancouver, which meant I had to deal with the Victoria-based BC Bureau of Vital Statistics. On the way into the site I was sidelined by a note that stating over 1000 birth, death, and marriage certificates had been stolen. Made me wonder who had gotten greedy. Also made me wonder how many imaginary people would be created from that one windfall.

Back at the site I double-checked that the cost was $27 with the required information, like where Smiley had been born, who his parents were, and other details. Then I went back and looked up the Manitoba Health system; that card would be useful for Smiley too. In order to have that he'd have to have lived in the province for three months. He'd also have to provide a social insurance number, a health card from somewhere else, his birth certificate, and his driver's licence.

So that went onto the back burner and I turned to getting him a driver's licence. For that he'd need to provide the Manitoba Public Insurance Corporation with a birth certificate and a social insurance card. And, of course, some money, like maybe $75 and voila, it would all be done and he'd be a real boy!

Going over my little pile of scraps I realized I had to start with the birth certificate. It was a joke, but seven years after 9-11 no one seemed to care that it had become even easier to acquire fake ID in the States. Give me an hour on the Internet and a week to make some phone calls and send letters and the ID would start flowing in. I could be from Texas, or New York, South Carolina, or California. Find a newspaper with its files on the Internet, find the name of a baby who died (and probably wasn't registered with the right authorities), use that info with the bureaucrats, and have the certificate issued.

All the work made me think fondly of going back into business, just a little. And that way lay madness. Suddenly my time on the computer was up and I had to leave and go find a place to take Claire for dinner. I made my way across town through chaos towards normalcy and away from temptation. To confirm my good intentions I phoned Marie and found out that everything was just fine on her end. Then she asked how I was and I had to hang up.

I had no idea, frankly, how to answer that.

#30

Saturday started very slowly at 7:00. I let Claire sleep while Fred and I played with the dog in the backyard. I raked leaves and the dog and boy destroyed the piles. Smiley woke up before Claire did, coming out into the backyard with his face completely slack and his eyes narrowed into slits against the dim light.

"Hesus Marimba."

"What does that mean?"

"No idea." He watched me work from the stoop.

I was mildly curious and asked, "Hangover?"

"No thanks, got one. Went out last night when your lovely wife told me you two were painting the town red …"

He was quiet and fished in his pocket for a cigarette. With trembling hands he lit it. "Met a nice little hard body. Sweet girl, wanted a nice architect for a husband, or maybe she wanted to do some modelling work or just luck into a really, really nice apartment. Or maybe she wanted to work with animals or little kids."

He paused and I encouraged him to go on. "And ..."

"Dumped her and found two trashy-ass semi-pro whores. Somewhere downtown. They were badass chicks, coke off the tip of the little knife one of them kept tucked down the front of her bra, straight shots of Courvoisier and Hpnotiq. Trick shit like that."

"And ..." Off to the side Fred and Renfield was wrestling. Fred was losing.

Smiley shrugged. "We had a party. I didn't touch any chemicals, swear to Christ, but they sure did."

Smiley looked at me with bloodshot eyes, waiting for me to judge. When I didn't he went on, "They used my money and bought coke and ecstasy and grass and crack and crank. VIP'd my ass into a big club somewhere, all red velour and black-patterned carpets ..."

I coughed loudly and Smiley's face lit up in pleasure. "You'd a loved it; you could hear the dope and whore money getting washed, scrub-scrub-scrub. There were only twenty people there and most of them on the payroll. So we ended up in a private room."

He motioned for me to come closer. "I was hitting the bottle hard ... I was hitting it pretty hard and couldn't get it up, limp-dick city ..."

I interrupted gently. "You don't have to tell me this, man."

His face flushed red with anger. "Sure I do. So they started making out with each other ... to help me out, I guess, they weren't getting off on it ... and I didn't feel a thing."

"So what happened?"

"Took off. Ran away. Paid the bills first and then ran."

Fred tried to bury the dog in leaves and got mad when I started to stuff them into the garbage bag. I gave him that to fight and turned back to Smiley. "It ain't gonna be easy, man.

Stay away from chicks like that. Don't put yourself in the way of that."

"All I want … all I really want is …"

"What?"

His face was rigidly anguished. "I don't fucking know!"

"'S alright. It'll pass. Get a shower. Clean yourself up. Then we'll go running. Changing the subject. Wanna meet a nice girl?"

He stood up. "What the fuck is that?"

"You'll see. It might help."

"Might." He ground the cigarette out on his belt buckle and dropped the butt into his pocket. "Might be nice. I want to tell you something and ask you something."

I waited.

"One, I finally understand what Ol' Doc Holliday meant at the end, you know when he said, 'This is funny.'"

That went past me and I shook off what I was actually thinking. "And?"

"Never mind. Hey, do you get laid when you date nice girls?"

I hadn't seen Claire coming up behind Smiley, but she heard him and said, "Don't be crude."

He looked embarrassed and she went on, "And Monty is not the right person to ask. He doesn't know any nice girls. Ask me."

Smiley turned to me. "Is this true?"

"Yep. I only know Claire."

She looked at me suspiciously and Smiley turned back to her. "So, do you get laid when you date nice girls?" She nodded primly.

"Sure. But it'll never happen when and where and why you expect it."

Smiley turned back to me. "True?"

"So I've heard."

Energy and joy were creeping back into him and his pleasure was growing along with the bruise on his cheek. "Sounds great. Let's go."

"Shower first."

When he had headed into the house Claire sat down in the exact same spot Smiley had occupied and held the peas tight to her forehead. "Christ, do I have a hangover."

"Poor girl. Could be worse."

She looked at me suspiciously. "How could it be worse?"

I grabbed Fred before he managed to crawl entirely into an open bag of leaves and suffocate. "It could be me suffering from a hangover instead of you."

If looks could kill.

The two of them agreed to go out that night and find nice girls, and that started them off making phone calls and plans. I was too busy getting ready to go to the Hunter Safety Course, which started at 10:00 and lasted until 6:00, a truly dim way to spend a Saturday. When I arrived home at 7:00, Claire and Smiley were both dressed in new clothes. They looked happy, clean, and gleeful. My wife kissed me and let me sit down in the bedroom for a minute or two before leaving. "So how was school, dear?"

I glared at her and suspected a pun before clearing my throat. "Hunting is a natural endeavour of the human animal and it's nothing that the hunter should be embarrassed about. There are rifles and shotguns suitable for hunting." She motioned for me to go on. "And bows, ha-ha-ha. The whole class laughed until I held up my hand and told them I was using a bow. Then the teacher went on. Do not hunt within 100 metres of the road. Do not shoot unless you know what you are shooting at. And do not shoot anything wearing Day-Glo orange. Unless you're a cannibal."

I changed my socks. "More laughter, followed by an amusing anecdote about an RCMP constable who was arrested for shooting a Styrofoam decoy deer put out by the game wardens. After which he was given a large case of Styrofoam cutlets by his butcher. More class laughter. Followed by a quote from a man I've never heard of before, José Ortega Y Gasset, who said, 'One does not hunt in order to kill; on the contrary, one kills in order to have hunted.'"

Claire looked at her watch. "You know, this is interesting but ..."

"Wait. You started this with your wild boar rant, and the rant about how much I owed Frank, and you should hear the end of it. Did you know that wild game has less fat than chicken? Or that hunting is an activity that is much safer than swimming or bicycling? Then a lecture on muzzle-loading muskets, the advances of the percussion system, magazine-fed versus single-shot weapons, orange safety vests, primers, and safeties. This went on for awhile."

"So did you pass?"

"I did."

"So can I leave?"

"You may."

And she and Smiley went off to look for nice girls. I dug out the books I'd picked up from the library during the lunch break at the training centre. *Gunfighters of the Wild West, Gunfight at the OK Corral, Encyclopedia of Western Gunfighters, The Range Wars*, and others. Names like Doc Holliday, Sam Bass, William Bonney, Tom Horn, William Brooks, John Wesley Hardin, Patrick Garrett, and Black Bart.

Fred played quietly with his blocks while the dog snored. We'd brought Thor's aquarium out into the middle of the room so it could feel it belonged to the family and vice versa. While I read I drank a cup of coffee and thought some long and dark thoughts.

You can tell a lot about a man by his heroes, and Smiley's made for interesting reading.

Black Bart, my favourite. Born in 1829, last seen in 1888, and liked Wells, Fargo and Co. stagecoaches in California, of which he robbed twenty-eight. Caught and served four years in San Quentin and then vanished upon release. Left poetry behind after the robberies, including the ditty:

I've labored long and hard for bread
For honor and for riches
But on my corns too long you've tread
You fine haired sons of Bitches.

Sam Bass robbed the Deadwood Stage four times. An inept and unlucky, thief he died at the age of twenty-seven after being shot in the groin. His sister put up a tombstone that read, "A brave man reposes in death here. Why was he not true?"

In later years the tombstone was chipped away by scavenger hunters until it vanished.

William Bonney, dead at twenty-one, accused of having shot either twenty-one or no men. His first crime was stealing butter at the age of twenty-one. He was shot to death by his friend Pat Garrett. His last words were, "Quien es?"

Doc Holliday died at the age of thirty-six from tuberculosis, described by Wyatt Earp as the most dangerous man in Tombstone when Tombstone was a dangerous town. Walking to the gunfight at the OK Corral the three Earp brothers wore frowns and dressed in black while Doc wore a natty grey suit and whistled.

Like I said before, you can tell a lot about a man by his heroes. The coffee had grown cold and Fred had fallen asleep so I moved very quietly as I refilled my mug and thought deep thoughts. The phone ringing made me jump. It was Marie calling me from a pay phone to tell me they were running a Yugoslavian family across the lake that night. I had told her to give me the occasional call and keep me in the loop in case they needed an enforcer. She didn't this time. I wished her luck and she hung up.

And I went back to wondering who the hell my heroes were. When that stopped bothering me I wondered about the heroes Smiley had acquired. Not one of them was a good guy, not really, not seeing them from this place in time. So why would he ever go straight?

And that question bothered me even more. I thought about the hunter safety course and then I rephrased the philosophy of "One does not hunt in order to kill; on the contrary, one kills in order to have hunted" into something more appropriate for thieves. It became "One does not steal in order to make money; on the contrary, one makes money in order to have stolen."

When I slept I dreamed and when I woke up I remembered something very important about being a bad guy, about living on reflex and momentum and that there were NO coincidences.

Not ever.

#31

I woke up Smiley early the next day and told him all about Marie and the smuggling operation she was running. I told him about the money I was making, I told him about the potential of the route, and I told him about Samantha.

In biblical terms I took him up on the mountain and showed him all the kingdoms of the world.

And he listened and I waited and I saw greed spark deep in his eyes.

I talked about drugs. "We can pick up crack cocaine in Minneapolis for cheap and move it across the border and then straight up north to the mining towns, where it sells at a premium ... "

He became more and more excited and added his own words. "We can run loads of hydroponic weed from up here straight down to Chicago ..."

He was pumped now and I kept talking. "We can pick up top-of-the-line Glock semi-autos for $400 in Macon, Georgia and sell them for $1500 to Japanese sailors in Churchill ..."

He was so excited he made mistakes. Like I said, there are no coincidences when dealing with bad guys.

Smiley was transcendent. "We can take away the route from Marie and her crew; she's only got two guys ..."

I'd never mentioned the size of Marie's crew.

Ever.

A few minutes later he proposed cutting Samantha out of the picture permanently and taking over her business.

"We can take her out. Shoot her down or wire her van to go *boom* ..."

I'd never mentioned Samantha had a van and he knew one hell of a lot about what she did and how she did it.

I agreed, agreed, and agreed, and let Smiley tell me, "Let me set it up, man, it'll be great ..." He grinned, ear to ear.

"I knew you weren't straight. I knew you were conning everyone."

He looked abashed and then challenging. "You knew Sam hired me, right? This honest shit—that was just a con, right?"

I nodded and the final words from both our mouths were, "It'll be just like old times."

From him it sounded like a promise, from me it was full of sorrow.

Then he went out to, in his words, take care of everything.

#32

After supper Smiley called. "Monty? Can you come down to a bar? It's in the McDiamond hotel? I've found Samantha."

"Sure. When? What's the bar called?"

"It's called Hell. I don't know the address."

"I have a phone book. Don't worry. When?"

"Make it 7:30. I'll be in the bar."

He hung up and I told Claire what was going on.

"He's going to betray you?"

"Probably. Or he's going to betray Samantha, if he's working for her."

Claire had been working on a large pile of paperwork and she tapped her teeth meditatively with a pencil and spoke slowly. "What do you think?"

"I think I don't know."

She smiled and stood up and kissed me and I went on, "I think I'm operating in the dark here."

Claire wiggled her eyebrows. "You do some of your best

work in the dark. Remember what you told me: instinct, re-flex, and momentum."

I'd told her about my dream and she agreed. She'd prom-ised to skin me alive if I fucked up but she'd agreed that it was the best way to deal with all the problems at once. Have one problem deal with the other.

I kissed her and said, "Right." Then I went upstairs and changed clothes. A plastic cup to protect my testicles. Jeans with reinforced knees and butt. A tight black T-shirt in case someone tried to grab me. Steel-toed shoes in case I had to kick someone. Lastly I pulled on a black denim jacket I'd had custom made years before by an understanding tailor. It had extra pockets sewn into the reinforced inner lining, steel chain mail around the left arm for dogs and knives, and a hidden pocket in the back with a single-edged razor blade as a last-ditch weapon. At the dresser I selected some ID and tucked it away in my front pocket along with four twenty-dollar bills and a roll of quarters in case I had to punch someone. Then I was ready to dance. On my way out Claire called again and then repeated, "Instinct, reflex, and momentum."

Her smile was sweet and she went on, "And if Smiley comes back alone I will kill him. It's a promise."

It took thirty minutes on the bus heading west and north to reach near to where I wanted to be. Had I walked I could have been there in about the same time. East/west travel in the North End really had a way to go.

Hell had been built into the front of a hotel with a beer vendor around back, rooms on the second and third floors, and parking space in lots on either side of the hotel so no one had to park on the busy street. Some effort had been made to grow trees and bushes along the outer edges of the parking lot and there were two planters right in front of the doors full of juniper bushes that you could smell a block away. The windows of the bar were painted black and the noise shook me as I neared. Heavy country rap about saving a horse, with the bass turned up so high the sidewalk itself seemed to vibrate. I paused between the junipers and looked down at a ground littered with spent cigarette butts and a brick wall covered in burn marks where people had butted out.

The sharp brick corners of the entryway were covered in sheets of stainless steel, marred by deep scratches. The steel was there to stop the brick from crumbling away if hit by fists or skull or whatever. Up close I could see that some of the scratches were words, but not good ones, not the happy graffiti that I occasionally saw in the city. No, I LOVE YOU! and IT'LL GET BETTER or (my favourite) YOU'RE A GOOD PERSON AND YOU DESERVE TO HAVE GOOD THINGS HAPPEN TO YOU! Instead there were words and ideas of pain and rebellion and hate. RAHOWA, for racial holy war, a white supremacist credo, anti-Jew, anti-black, anti everyone who didn't have "blood in the face," by which the racists meant people who could blush. There was also 88, the eighth letter times two, or HH for HEIL HITLER, and 198 for SH or SIEG HEIL, and of course the infamous 13 for marijuana. Some song lyrics flashed into my head about a guy wanting ink done and getting 31 instead of 13. So I was smiling when I walked into the place, which was a mistake.

"What the fuck you smiling for?"

There was a big guy, six eight and 300 pounds at least, not much of it fat, standing just inside the door, holding a wall up. It was very dark and he didn't sound angry, just someone doing their business, which was to be intimidating.

"I'm just a happy man."

He didn't believe me but accepted my three-dollar cover

charge. I walked into a big room full of noise with pool tables, lots of battered tables for customers, and a crooked bar along one wall.

The whole place was a dance. People at the tables stood up and went to talk closely to other people at other tables, slot-machine players raised their hands for more change, pool players shot the balls, won and lost, and moved away or towards another table.

A pool player missed a shot and slammed his cue down and stalked away to a table in the corner where a young white girl curled her hands protectively around something blue in a tall glass. In the States they passed a law requiring that manufacturers start putting blue dye in Rohypnol, the date-rape drug of choice. The result was an increase in sales of blue lagoons and blue Hawaii's and blue daiquiris in a certain kind of nightclub.

It was that kind of nightclub.

A drunken guy came out of the bathroom energized and headed into the music. A girl in a bright red silk shirt ran her nails up the jean-covered thigh of a balding man whose leather vest advertised the United States 101st Airborne Division. From where I was I could see her other hand was making small loving circles in the lap of the man's middle-aged female companion. Everyone was smiling.

"… you … "

A loser at a pool table reached for the white ball and I could see a band of tension crease his forehead as the brown bouncer stepped behind him and put his arm neatly around his neck. Slowly the ball was lowered to the table and the man apologized and walked away.

"… arrested DWI …"

There was laughter from a nearby table where two thickset

middle-aged white guys and two equally beefy brown-skinned men sat. DWI, driving while Indian. Or DWI, driving while in-toxicated. One of the brown men snorted and said loudly, "It wouldn't have been fucking funny if it happened to you."

Which meant he'd been Driving While Indian.

Out of curiosity I went into the men's bathroom and washed my hands. There were no mirrors, only a sheet of pol-ished steel along three walls. There were also no urinals, just a porcelain lead to a trough in the floor. No one was using the facilities, so I popped into a stall and saw that the toilet tank's top was covered in sheets of sandpaper glued into place. That stopped people from cutting lines of cocaine but wasn't quite as extreme as some bars I'd been to, where the owners would spray surfaces with WD-40, which turned coke into unusable slush.

The sandpaper also stopped casual bathroom quickies quickly and painfully. The WD-40 stopped the same quickies but in a funnier fashion.

Back outside there were signs behind the bar so I walked over to read them. NO GANG COLOURS ALLOWED, WE WILL NOT SERVE ANYONE WHO APPEARS INTOXICATED, and NO WEAPONS ALLOWED.

As I watched, a tightly wound redheaded guy walked up and ordered a pitcher of draft. He wore a red bandanna like a dew rag on his forehead, which would have meant he was a member of the Crips street gang in East LA. He also had MM embroidered on his jacket above his heart, which in prison might mean Mexican mafia. It also had a line through it and three red drops falling down.

Which meant what? A wannabe? A been there? Or maybe he was an active member in diametrically opposed organization?

He went back to his table, where he sat by himself and

drank the beer directly from the pitcher. I could see his high-topped runners and a bit of brown leather that showed when he seated himself. This satisfied me because it meant he had to be an undercover cop. No one else carried a pistol in an ankle holster.

I turned back to the signs and a vacant-faced blond girl came up and ordered two rye and gingers. When she paid I could see into her purse, where the bright red plastic handles of two carpet-cutter razors rested on top of her wallet. When she saw me looking she closed the oversized purse and went back to her table with her drinks.

"Gonna order something?"

The bartender brought me a coffee and accepted the payment and tip with bland indifference. Idly I looked at the bouncer on the stool and found he was very busy talking to a girl in a pink blouse and black leather skirt who looked underage. His hand was busy up her skirt and his face was flushed, which made the tattoos on his neck stand out even more. He had two on the left and two on the right, under his ears. Black lightning bolts, a Gestapo collar they were called, a bad tattoo, unless you were a bad dude. His hand kept busy and the girl squealed. I leaned back against the bar and watched and waited.

#33

At a quarter to eight Smiley came in from the hotel entrance.

"Waiting long?"

"No. Nice place."

He looked around and then back at me with a blank expression. "Are we looking at the same thing?"

"It's honest. Not many places can say that. It's crude, vicious, and alive. But honest."

"I suppose." He swayed back and forth and belched.

"Are you drunk?"

"No, I'm just tired." He ordered a rye and ginger at the bar and then shook his hands to loosen the muscles. "This is where we're at ..."

The bouncer moved between us and forced us apart with his bulk. He didn't have to do it but he did it anyway, his way of showing everyone he was in charge. In a strangely high voice he ordered a pink torpedo on his tab and handed it to the girl. Still the place was loud enough that no one could hear Smiley when he started to talk to me, quietly and with minimum lip movement, which is the second thing you learn in jail.

"Like I was saying, Samantha's upstairs in a room. She has two guys with her; one's a boyfriend and one's muscle. I've asked around and I think that both are semi-pro. Sam'll be carrying a gun and she's good. The guys might be carrying."

He said it without passion, without caring, and I knew it didn't matter to him. I asked, "How do you want to handle this?"

"We go in and kick ass. Are you heavy?"

"No."

"Me neither. So we bluff. However, I sure do wish your lovely wife had left me a gun. Or anything."

He didn't look nervous and I didn't feel nervous, and when he finished his drink I gestured. "Let's go ..."

I wondered when he was going to betray me and then I wondered if he was going to betray me.

I followed as he went through the doors to the hotel. Once the door was shut behind me the noise level dropped by more than half. The lobby was small and cramped, with industrial carpet a painful shade of blue, and real hanging ivies and spider plants festooning the ceiling. Beside the front desk was a staircase. Smiley went up it without hesitating and I followed.

My hands were loose at my sides, fingers open and spread. Strangely enough I was calm, relaxed, and ready. The situation hadn't begun to cause me fear or stress and the adrenaline hadn't kicked in. I was ready to kick, bite, punch, whatever was needed, but I wasn't looking forward to any of it. At the top of the stairs Smiley turned right. As we moved down the scrubby hallway the noise of the bar beneath our feet became louder and more strident. At the end of the hallway was a fire door with a large sign stating an alarm would ring if it opened. We were about three metres away when I whispered to Smiley, "So, will the alarm ring?"

"Nope. Fixed it."

He knelt down to tighten the laces of one of his expensive running shoes and kept talking. "The door will open fine. Head down to the first floor and there's an exit to the parking lot. I've jammed that door. Instead head towards the middle of the building and pop the sealed door into the hallway between the vendor, the lobby, and the bar. Then you can go out the bar front, the lobby back, or the vendor side. Whatever works best."

"You've done your homework."

He stood up and brushed some dust off the back of his right hand. "Yeah, about an hour ago when I came through the place, just to make sure. Let's do this."

He knocked on the last door, which opened immediately, and a thick-bodied man I'd never seen before waved us into a small room full of furniture. From where we stood I saw two double beds, a dresser with TV, a small table with a coffee pot, two chairs, and two bed tables. On the wall were three big pieces of art, crude paintings of twisted trees and rocks, clear water, and bright leaves. One whole wall was blocked with a lime green drape; behind it I supposed was a window. There were also three people: Samantha lying on the bed farthest from the door, a man standing right beside the TV, indeed his hand rested on the box; and lastly the guy who'd let us in; he'd stepped back into the bathroom to let us pass.

"Smiley! And I recognize Mr. Haaviko behind you."

Samantha was up on one elbow facing us, with one hand under her pillow, and I focused on her. Women were always more dangerous than men; ask any soldier, any cop; for both groups it was a rule, a mantra: shoot the women first. Women didn't have second thoughts or fears once they'd decided on what to do. Women succeeded more often in suicide than men, and women were much more likely to shoot if they had a gun. They were less likely to panic and make mistakes. And in the back of my mind was a poem Claire had recited to me once by Rudyard Kipling; a poem about what happened to wounded British soldiers when the Afghan women came out.

Smiley grinned from ear to ear. "We're here to talk."

He paused for two heartbeats and I closed the door behind me. The noise from the bar beneath us reverberated in the room. I was keenly aware of where everyone was in the room and what they were doing.

I was keenly aware of momentum and instinct and reflex. I was keenly aware of the dark. I was keenly aware of the potentials in the room.

The two men were nothing special and no one I recognized; maybe Sam was trying to show me how many people she had on salary or maybe she was using disposable guys or maybe this was her A-team.

I still wasn't impressed.

The guy in the bathroom looked like a hockey tough; the other guy looked like an amateur bodybuilder but nothing really scary. Neither of them had enough scars. I could feel the tension building and the adrenaline started to move. Sam said, "You gents carrying?"

"What do you think?"

Smiley was still smiling. The guy beside me in the bathroom doorway inhaled and exhaled while the guy by the TV took his hand off it and brought it down to his belt. I noticed that he was wearing a badly fitting suede sports jacket over his blue shirt and that his hand trembled a lot. Sam nodded and gestured, "That's fine. Let's talk."

That was the signal. I was watching Sam and Smiley, focusing on them. I caught a brief look of surprise on her face when he started to move forward.

Apparently that was not part of the plan.

Sam was fastest, drawing a long-barrelled pistol from under her pillow and sweeping it towards me, trying to avoid Smiley.

While she was doing that the guy by the TV squatted a bit with his legs wide apart, a shooting stance he'd seen on some cop show. He flipped his coat open with his right hand and pulled out a darkly blued pistol from the small of his back. And the guy in the bathroom suddenly had a knife in his right hand as he adjusted his feet and lunged.

But by then it was all too late.

Smiley jumped over the bed towards Sam, moving slightly to the left so she had to reverse the track of her pistol as she tried to target him.

She didn't want to pull the trigger until she was sure and while she was making sure I took one step forward and kicked the guy with the pistol square in his testicles. The crack of my steel toe slamming into his pelvis made me wince but I was already spinning back towards the guy in the bathroom who was slashing at me with the edge of the knife.

I feinted with my right foot and he turned a little in response. When the knife was pointed away from me I stepped forward and the presence of the grotesque blade made my stomach clench and sped me up.

The knife was right there in front of me, a kind I hadn't seen in years, a copy of the dumb bowie-style survival knife used by Rambo in that interminable film series. It had a blade maybe thirty centimetres long and ten wide, with razor-sharp edges along the front and top third of the rear edge, plus a whole whack of saw-edged teeth.

A real toe-stabber, or was it toad-stabber?

I offered my left forearm and the hockey player took the opportunity to slash at it with the blade. He was surprised when the armour in the sleeve did what it was supposed to do and the blade grated down and off. While he was adjusting his grip on the hilt, I reached out and took hold of his wrist. I could have levered him down from there and disarmed him, or used the axis to throw him, but I didn't. I was hurrying and I twisted his wrist with both of my hands, away from me and then back, like I was wringing out a dishcloth. Both the ulna and radius bone shattered and splintered and his fingers opened and the knife fell. I changed the grip on his arm and his left fist cracked into my temple, enough to give me tunnel vision, but then the guy squeaked loudly and his second punch landed like an aunt's kiss.

I grabbed his elbow and separated the unbroken top half of his ulna and radula from his humerus and then his eyes went blank and he started to fall. Before he'd hit the ground I was moving towards the bed where Smiley and Sam were still struggling. I was surprised there was no shooting—maybe Sam was a real pro and didn't shoot unless there was a target?

As I moved forward Smiley took hold of the pistol and wrestled it to the side and she let it go. He was straddling her as she pulled a thin-bladed filleting knife from somewhere and rammed it straight up at his throat.

"Nope."

Smiley sounded happy as he brought the gun back and caught the blade on the barrel to deflect it. Before she could adjust her aim he slammed the receiver down into her forehead and she was driven into unconsciousness. The guy behind me groaned and I turned to find him slumped over in the fetal position, still unconscious but with both hands touching the handle of the knife, which had fallen blade first to pin his foot to the floor. I paused and then wrenched the knife out and wrapped his foot in a towel.

"You are a cruel man, Monty."

Smiley had walked over to the guy I'd kicked and poked him with the barrel of the pistol. The guy was curled up and covered in a great deal of vomit.

He went on cheerfully, "Yes sir, a cruel, cruel man."

Without hurrying I picked up the man's pistol. It was a Colt Woodsman with a silencer brazed onto the barrel. I clicked the safety off and then worked the action to seat a round.

He stared at the bullet I'd ejected from the port and then looked down at the gun in his hand before I said, "I am not cruel. They rushed me."

"Uh-huh."

"It's not like I planned it. Really."

"Uh-huh."

He stared at me for a few more seconds and then he tossed his pistol onto the bed, flipped Sam over, and tied her hands cruelly tight with shoelaces he pulled from his pocket. Then he did her feet and finally stuffed a wad of cloth into her mouth and tied it into place with another lace. The last one he held up towards me. "Need this?"

"Nope."

I kept the Colt in my belt while I tied another towel around the hockey player's foot to stop the bleeding before dumping him into the bathtub. When I picked up his friend he squeaked ultrasonically and I felt his legs shift unnaturally under my arm. For a second the pain woke him up but then his eyes closed and I put him carefully down on the bathroom floor. I gathered their wallets and threw them to Smiley.

"All done."

Smiley was sitting on the second bed with the pistol in his lap and a handful of money. I tossed the knife onto the bed as well and he looked up when I said, "Here you go."

He marvelled at something as he examined the gun. "Look at this; a Charter Arms Explorer pistol. I've never seen one of these before. The magazine goes in front of the trigger like on those old German pistols and there's a spare one in the butt."

I glanced at the pistol and then at mine and realized they both had home-made silencers attached permanently to the barrels.

Sam was planning on killing someone in this room. Silencers are unreliable and unwieldy, there's no other reason to use them. And she'd brought two silenced guns and a knife into the room when a shotgun would have been much safer.

The question was, was Smiley in on it. I looked at him and said, "What now?"

"We wait for Sam to wake up."

"Right," I said conversationally. "I don't want to clean this up, do you?"

"Not really."

"I mean, she started it."

He nodded in thought; he'd picked up the pistol and dumped the magazine and worked the slide to clear it.

"It's a nice piece. Ever use one?"

I didn't take it but I looked it over when he held it out. "Nope."

He put the pistol back on the bed and we both waited for a little while before I spoke. "I guess no one noticed the fight?"

"I guess. It's kind of loud downstairs, though."

"Well, I thought so. Here, you do that pistol and I'll do this one."

"Do what?"

He looked quizzical as I filled the small garbage pail from the bathroom with water and brought it in. And he opened his mouth in protest when I swept all the ammo in.

"Hey!"

I stared at him. "Right now the cops walk in and they find us with guns and we each end up with six years in stir. Give us five minutes to wreck the trigger mechanisms and all we can be caught with is toys."

"Right." He started to work on the gun and borrowed the knife from me for the fine work of gouging and smashing the internal sears. As he worked I went on. "We just went from assault and attempted murder with prohibited weapons down to assault and attempted murder. We just shaved three years off both our sentences. If the cops walk in."

Smiley did his job. When he was done we counted the money and found we had sixty bucks and some change from the pockets of Sam and the guy with the sore pelvis, and 500 bucks from the pockets of the guy with the knife. Smiley separated the money into two piles and offered me one. "Here you go." He held a bundle of bills in one hand. "Two hundred and eighty bucks and change."

I took the money.

Sam was waking up and I went over to take her gag out. Unconscious people often throw up. If they have a gag in place they suffocate, and that would have made me a murderer. I didn't want her to die, so I took the gag out and splashed a glass of cold water in her face. "Rise and shine, sunshine."

She looked blearily around. Getting knocked out in real life is not like in the movies; you don't wake up spry. You lose memories, you lose the ability to rationally plan, you get, pardon the expression, fucked up.

"Oh, my head." Her voice was small, weak, trembling, until Smiley leaned down into her face.

"Remember me, hon?"

She inhaled massive quantities of air but before she could scream I punched her hard in the belly and all the air came out along with a lot of spit and a bit of her last meal. I hated hitting a woman, even one who had tried to kill me—scratch that, I didn't really like hitting anyone. But I wanted her to know I was serious.

"No yelling." I said it mildly and her eyes went from me to Smiley and some kind of alertness came into her eyes and she asked in a hoarse voice, "What do you want?"

Smiley's voice was cold. "Your biz. Now, and this is the big question, what do *you* want?"

Her eyes narrowed and her breathing became faster. "To live."

Smiley had picked up the big-ass Rambo knife and ran a finger along the edge and winced. "Not very sharp." He said it conversationally and then smiled back at Sam, "You can live. Keep your mouth shut, drop everything and walk away."

She exhaled and smiled. "Okay, I drop all this, never think of you again, and forget all this shit. I can do that. For me this is all over."

"Great. Then I don't have to kill you. One more thing though …"

"What?"

"You have to clean all this up. It's your penalty."

She winced but I didn't react at all and he kept on, "Your friends are in the bathroom and need a lot of medical help. I don't want to have this come back to me, do you understand?

223

If it does then I'll feel obliged to come back for you, with, what's the term, oh yeah, malicious intentions. And then there will be hair on the walls and blood on the floor. So are we cool, hon?"

"Sure."

"Good. And my friend here," Smiley gestured at me, "he's with me. Do you understand?"

"Sure, sure."

"I'm not really believing you but you think about it, hon. There is no place you can go where I can't find you. If I want to find you. So whatever happened before, that doesn't matter now. Our deal is off."

He cut the shoelaces around her wrists and ankles and stood up. He held the knife in one hand and the sheath in the other and bounced them up and down idly, weighing them, and finally he sheathed the knife and tossed it on the floor where Sam could reach it. She watched him and lay there practising deep breathing while Smiley stared at her as though daring her to say something, anything.

And then we walked out the door and locked it behind us.

#34

Outside we walked far away through residential areas and industrial parks until we found another hotel. There we got the front desk to order us a cab. While we were waiting for the cab, I turned to Smiley. "You were conning me?"

"Yes."

I thought about it. "Sam hired you to blindside me?"

"Yes. For cash and a cut, her description of the route told me it would be plenty."

"But now there's enough on the table for you to take her out?"

"Yes. I'd rather work with you. I trust you."

I ignored that. "So you never had any intention of going straight?"

"Maybe a little. I wanted to see."

"'Kay. Don't tell Claire."

His face split in a grin. "Did I have you fooled at all?"

"Yep. You did."

Back home Smiley went into his room without saying a

word and I went upstairs to Claire. On the way I turned on the monitors on the stairs and at each window. She had lit several candles and made the bed, alerted, I supposed, by the dog.

"Rough day at the office?"

She was beautiful, wearing a black flannel bathrobe. I'd mocked her for the fabric when I'd bought it years before but she'd stuck to her guns, insisting that flannel was the fabric of love, warm and comforting. Claire came over and helped me take off my clothes but I kept my mouth shut.

She whispered, "How was it?"

"Bad." I leaned into her. "You were right—Smiley's conning us. Sorry."

She pushed me onto the bed and stood there fingering the tear in my jacket sleeve where the knife had missed my flesh and cut the fabric.

She said loudly, "I see."

She collapsed slowly and gracefully onto her knees beside me and touched my fingers and forehead. "Looks painful."

She kissed me and then straddled me. "Don't move."

The robe slipped off her shoulders and fell onto my legs, and she began to move, slowly and carefully. Even though I was tired, bone tired, what she was doing worked and in time, in time everything fell away and vanished.

She whispered into my ear, "Wake up."

I whispered back, "I was not asleep, I was thinking. Sometimes I snore when I think."

She kissed me again and adjusted her weight until she covered the whole right side of my body. The candles had made the room warm and she had made it sweet and that was enough.

"No sleeping yet. I want to talk."

By rolling my head a little to the side I could talk into her cheek, no way Smiley could hear, and I said, "You mean talk 'bout your feelings?"

"No ..."

"Because I have the book ready ..."

It was an imaginary book I'd written with her help. titled *The Big Book of Relationships*. Very popular with imaginary couples all around the unreal world, a necessity, one might say.

"Page 32: No, of course I still respect you."

She giggled and there is something very special about a beautiful woman's giggle. If you hear it, you know you are doing something right.

"Page 53: And how do you feel about that?"

She leaned up on one elbow and for a moment Sam popped into my head, fearless and mean. But Claire wasn't Sam and the resemblance was fleeting and lame at best.

"Can you be serious?"

"Page 89: No one's ever made me feel that way before. All done, the book is closed."

"Cool. Funny. I'll give you an E for effort. I want to talk about our house guest."

"'Kay."

"What happened?"

"He set me up with Sam and her crew and then betrayed them. He was supposed to lure me into a small room and then they'd take me down. Either that or maybe he's SISO."

Claire didn't smile at the word. A cousin of hers had once gotten into bad company down in Los Angeles and we'd gone down to support the family while everything worked its way through the system. At one point her cousin had read the parole officer's report backwards and thought they'd said SISO in brackets by her name. It had taken me three days to track down that they'd written 5150. This was police and health code for "dangerous and disturbed." Which she had been, but we'd finally managed to sort everything out and had left the city of angels with nothing permanent but a few scars and a new word for our dictionary.

I kept talking and thinking. "I think he just took Sam off the board."

She stood up and put the robe back on before drinking from a bottle of tap water she'd left by the window. "Good. Where does that leave us?"

"Worried. It leaves us worried."

"Okay."

"Smiley said he kind of tried to go straight. I've never seen him unsure, it's like he's not sure how to play it. It's like he's keeping everything as an option."

She made a guess that sounded right. "Maybe he saw what you have and wants it. Cons like structure, they pretend they don't but they do."

"Even me?"

She ankled over and kissed me before going back to the window. "Even you. You replaced the chaos of crime and the order of jail with this." She gestured. "All this and me and Fred and Renfield and Thor. Maybe he wants something like this."

Then she said wonderingly, "So, where does that leave us?"

I moved over and kissed her neck. "In a room, all alone, almost naked."

She was mischievous. "Wanna get completely naked?"

"Yes. Yes I would. That would be nice."

Claire was outraged. "Nice?"

"Nice. Yes, nice, that's the right word, nice."

"I'll show you nice!"

And it was. And she did.

#35

The next night Claire took Smiley out to paint the town red. Her intention was to keep him busy and develop her own reading of what he was and what he wanted. She proposed that he come with her and then she'd introduce him to nice girls. I asked him why he wanted to meet nice girls and he looked lost before finally answering, "I guess because I've never known any. Does that make sense?"

I told him it didn't make any sense. Both of them asked if I wanted to come but I turned them down. I told them I wanted to stay home and wait.

And search Smiley's room.

I had told Claire about my plans. She had agreed and patted my head. "So I get to be the Judas goat?"

"What's that?"

She explained, "That's the goat you stake out to distract the tiger before you shoot it."

"Aha. Okay, yep. Practise bleating."

"Baaaaa."

"Actually, that's kind of sexy."

"You are a sick man. Later."

They left, and after mouse and dog and son were all tucked away in their beds I took a coffee upstairs and thought some more, sitting on the futon on the floor in the dark and waiting. One thing being a bad guy teaches you is patience; you spend a lot of time waiting for things to start or for conditions to be right. You wait for banks to open, for jewelry stores to unload their vaults, for meth to cook, for grass to ripen, for boats and planes and couriers to arrive. And when things go wrong you wait for the cops and for security guards, you wait for lawyers and judges, you wait for doctors and nurses, you wait for cell doors to open and close.

You wait in the quiet of hotel rooms, and in the reek of alleys. You wait in loud bars and in windswept forests. You wait by rivers and by freeways. You wait with guns in your pockets and knives taped to your extremities. You wait with cold cash, or hot credit cards, or jewelry, or drugs. You wait in the sun and in the dark and in all the seasons, spring, summer, fall, winter, and the extra season, jail, which only cons know, the non-season season. So you either become good at the waiting or you quit the biz and go legit.

Claire had agreed to come back in four hours. I could wait while Claire and Smiley looked for nice girls. I could do it standing on my head. With an arm tied behind my back. With a grin.

I called Marie but she told me she had seen nothing and that everything was still going fine, just fine. And that made me a little nervous. Was Sam actually keeping her word?

After I'd hung up I listened to the night around me through the open window. The sounds of night birds, pigeons and such, cars passing, fast far away and slowly near by. I heard sirens in the distance getting closer, then farther, laughter and dogs barking, conversations and arguments. Wind in the trees, and, once or twice, the sounds of cats fighting or making little cats.

I breathed the night air and smelled all sorts of interesting things. Car exhaust and the perfumed hot air from someone's nearby dryer. I smelled dust and a vague tang from grass recently cut, and even the richness of dog shit and damp, turned earth. In time I smelled cigarette smoke and woodsmoke from a fireplace or one of those outdoor firepits I lusted after secretly. These were the smells that came to me as I waited.

After a long time I went downstairs and tossed Smiley's room.

In the closet a floorboard had been pulled up and the nails cut flat so it looked normal, and in the space underneath I found an old-fashioned English Enfield revolver in .38 calibre with a one-inch barrel. Beside the gun was an ancient cardboard box with forty-four soft lead-nosed bullets; the other six rounds were in the gun itself.

There was also a Ziploc baggie holding an assortment of pills. I held them up to the light and catalogued them: 2-mg Rohypnol pills marked ROCHE, crystals of crack cocaine that looked like macadamia nuts, even some old-style yellow jacket and Dexedrine amphetamines.

I smiled to myself and took the bullets into the kitchen, where I used a pair of needle-nosed pliers wrapped with duct tape to empty each cartridge of its grey-and-black load of powder down the drain. When I was done I re-seated the bullets in the cases and twisted the hammer spring a little until it would never work again. Then I put everything back where it belonged.

Eventually I fell asleep. Claire and Smiley coming home

didn't wake me at all, which shows how honest I was getting. I just slept and dreamt complicated dreams of cowboys and river gamblers, six-guns and dynamite, gold coins and paper money. I dreamt of horses and mesas and half-naked men and women drinking beer and listening to fast music in wooden houses with a wind blowing outside and keening through cracks in the planks. There were thieves in my dreams and bankers, whores and dudes, sheriffs and marshalls, red-coated Mounties and blue-coated cavalry, bad guys and good guys, Indians wearing feather headdresses and Chinese workers in pig tails and straw hats.

And then it all segued into another kind of dream, full of forests and rivers, plains and fields. The whole dream was full of animals, deer and rabbits and squirrels and prairie chickens and wolves and bears and wild pigs. But as the dream went on I realized that I was either hunting them or they were hunting me. And in either case it was all perfectly fine by us all. When I woke up all the dream animals and men stayed with me for a surprisingly long time.

The next morning the memories of my dream kept me in a fine mood for dealing with my wife and our guest discussing the women they had met the night before. Claire's acting was impressive. "... she was the one with the open shirt so you could see her belly, do you think?"

Smiley snorted. "Sure. And she was a real blonde too."

They laughed and made coffee and toast and eggs while I sat on the floor and kept an eye on Fred, who was under the kitchen table rattling pots.

Claire asked, "How many of what kind of eggs?"

When I realized the question was aimed at me I answered that two sunny side up would be good and went back to watching the baby under the table. He was becoming more ... intelligent? Not quite the right word, he was becoming more ... capable of planning. I rescued the pots and let Fred wrestle with the dog while I ate, sitting there under the table and watching Claire and Smiley. It was a strange sensation, that, to be reduced to the size of a child and watch the adults do their adult things.

"So, do you think she'll call?"

"Nope. But I've been wrong before."

There was flippancy, an intimacy that hadn't been there before. I felt jealous so I asked, "Did you meet anyone nice?"

Smiley grinned. "They were all nice. Some liked the way I looked and others liked my history."

"You told them the truth?"

"Yep. A couple of them were turned off and walked away but most thought it was cool." Claire nodded and added, "I kept him away from the nasty ladies. He met secretaries and office workers."

"And how did he do?"

She answered, "The boy ended up with a pocketful of seven-digit combinations."

"In English?"

"Phone numbers. They thought he was cool and hot, he danced, he laughed, he bought drinks and he was so not a player."

I had to ask, "What's a player?"

Smiley wrinkled his brow and answered, "A guy who just wants the notch. Not the girl, just what she's sitting on."

They both laughed and I finished my food. "So you're trying to say you don't want the notch?"

They helped me to my feet and he slapped me on the back. "I want the whole damn thing. I always do."

#36

I went to clean Fred's room and the bathroom. When I was finished Claire told me that Smiley had already left and that he had been in a good mood. While she was getting ready to go to work and I was getting ready for the arrival of the kids, she asked me about what I'd found in his room and I told her.

She nodded. "What now?"

I just shook my head. "I'm not sure."

Neither of us was satisfied but we both walked away. Claire went to sell houses and I watched children and thought about crime. After supper we read and listened to the radio, alternating between an old rock-and-roll station on AM and CBC's FM's stellar *The World at Six*. Claire was still deeply engrossed in *Buying Homes for Canadian Dummies* while I was trying to chew through *Of Mice and Men*, which she had conned me into by priming me with *Tortilla Flats* and *Cannery Row*.

"You know, this isn't funny at all. Not even remotely. You're sure it's the same author?"

"Uh-huh." She put a finger in her book and looked at me.

235

"Did you know that Steinbeck wrote a really bad propaganda novel at the behest of William Randolph Hearst called *The Moon is Down*?"

"No, should I?"

"And that William Randolph Hearst is the grandfather of Patty Hearst, kidnapped by the Symbionese Liberation Army?"

"Didn't know that either."

She flipped the page of her book to look at a diagram and went on. "Anyhow, before Patty started robbing banks the SLA demanded that the Hearst Department Stores start handing out free food for the poor and downtrodden. At that point Ronald Reagan, who was the governor of California, said that it would be good time for an outbreak of botulism."

"Hmmm. Cruel with a touch of crazy. What was his nickname again?"

"The Great Communicator."

"And the point of all this is what?"

She smiled, which made my heart flutter. "No point. No point at all. But it was under Reagan as president that the war on drugs started to heat up in the States, which jacked the price and popularity of the stuff to astronomical heights. It was also under him that many, many handguns were produced."

"Aha. Which truth profited me greatly just a few years later as the trend trickled down to the poor and up to the north. Interesting."

"Maybe. But like I said; there's no real point, no point at all to this whole discussion. The next question I have is: how can you relax while the Smiley problem is still with us? And why aren't you worried about Smiley's current absence?" Claire was genuinely curious.

"Those are easy questions. If I let the stress get to me I

might make mistakes. I can't afford those so I have to relax. Necessity requires it. Now, a question for you. If Reagan heated up the war on drugs, who started it?"

She perked up. "Finally, something you don't know! Tricky Dick Nixon started it."

"Aha." That made sense. Nixon had had trouble dealing with everyone, especially hippies. Maybe he had associated the two in his mind. "As for Smiley, I know he'll come back."

"Aha again."

"Although I do admit that relaxing is not easy. Without you it would be impossible."

"You flatterer, you." She went back to her book and I went back to trying to relax and working through the book, which seemed to be leading unstoppably to a dismal ending. While I was doing that Smiley came back. He was wearing his party clothes: black pants and blue shirt and a really nice black leather duster jacket that ended at his ankles. It had probably cost a grand and a half.

"Hi Mom, hi Dad!"

Claire looked at him and snorted. "You're drunk."

"Nope. Never. Well, maybe a little."

I looked him over and spoke mildly. "So where have you been, what have you been up to, you drunken bastard?"

He sat down on the sofa and picked Fred up. For a few minutes they played together and then he offered, "Went out with Tracey, to whom your lovely wife introduced me. She's a sweetheart."

"What does she do, he asked, somewhat fearing the answer?"

"Guess."

"Dancer-waitress-bartender-card dealer-hairstylist-student …"

237

He started to laugh. "Nope. She's a secretary at a law firm. Beautiful girl, with a great big ..."

Claire cleared her throat and Smiley caught himself. "... sense of humour. A very firm and hefty sense of humour. And long, elegant vowels. Two of them, just beautifully formed. Yep, a stone-cold beautiful person."

"So where did you go?"

"First for coffee and then to her place. She has a nice apartment by the Convention Centre. She introduced me to her roommate."

"Sounds like a *Penthouse* letter, *I never believed it could happen to me* ..."

"Naw. Her roommate's a guy named Louis; he's a bodybuilder and a bartender."

"Okay, sounds like a *Hustler* letter, *I never believed it could happen to me* ..."

Claire glanced at me and winced before asking, "So, are they an item?"

"Nope. Just buddies."

Smiley went to bed and Claire and I looked at each other and she said slowly, "Beautiful women don't normally room with beautiful men."

I agreed and wondered why Smiley wasn't doing anything about the route, nothing at all. And I wondered wishfully if maybe he had changed his mind again about going straight. But I knew that was bullshit and I settled back to wait some more. He would act eventually; he was built that way. He had already betrayed me once to Sam.

All I had to do was wait, patiently or impatiently, it didn't matter.

Eventually he'd act.

#37

The next day was tortuous for me but uneventful. Late that night Smiley came home. Claire and I were at the dining-room table, playing a desultory game of crib and waiting for him to show. He opened the door with the key we'd given him on his first day and then stepped inside. When he saw us he froze and slowly put down the plastic bag he was holding.

"Is there a problem?"

"No."

"Did I do something wrong?"

"Uh, not that I know of."

He took off his shoes and padded forward and I could see he was wearing some of his new clothes, but they looked a little unkempt. His tie was loose, his shirt had the buttons done up wrong, and there was a deep furrow between his eyes.

"So Tracey didn't call?"

"No."

Claire smiled and shuffled the cards. "Should she have?"

"Who the fuck knows?"

He put the bag down on the table and drew a medium-sized bottle of Southern Comfort liqueur out of it and bit his lower lip until a thin trickle of blood started.

"I want to get drunk."

Claire smiled again. "You're a grown up. Do what you want."

He looked at me and I told him, "It's your choice."

"Do you, either of you," the words seemed to stick in his throat, "… want some?"

Claire nodded and brought glasses from the kitchen, one for her and one for him, and he filled them to the brim with the thick, sweet liquor. He drained his glass and my wife from sipped hers and silence spread through the room.

"So …," Smiley started, "… were you guys waiting up for me?"

I looked at Claire. We silently agreed to keep our mouths shut and that's what I told him. "No, everything's fine. What's wrong?"

"Nothing. Everything. I had a date with Tracey."

"And?"

He refilled his glass. "I went to her place. She didn't want to go for drinks, or dinner, or see a movie … she just wanted to screw. So we did."

My wife shrugged. "It happens."

"Yeah. Sure. Sometimes. But she kept getting louder and louder as we did it. You know sometimes women fake it, right?"

I agreed, "Sure, sometimes men do too."

Claire stuck her tongue out at me. "And why would they do that?"

I listed reasons on my fingers. "First if they're tired and

can't. Second if they're just not in the mood. Third if the girl is a real dead lay. Fourth is if the guy can hear the husband walking up the stairs. And fifth is to have it over and done with."

"I may punch you."

Smiley interrupted. "Yeah, anyway, back to me. I think she was faking it. Loudly. Over and over again. And her roommate was in the next room. He started to pound on the wall, telling us to shut up."

It was hard to imagine that, and I tried to figure what Smiley would've done, but he kept talking.

"I wanted to go over and punch him out, make him shut up. Whatever. And she wouldn't let me. Just kept doing things and making noise and telling me to keep doing things we weren't doing. It was embarrassing."

Claire flinched and filled her glass again and let him keep talking.

"You know, put it in … don't stop … harder, harder … stuff like that. And throughout it the roommate's pounding on the wall. It was fucked up." He said it mildly.

"Anyhow so we finished and she goes over to the door and pulls it open, you know, *bang*, like that."

Nope, still couldn't imagine it.

"And there's the roommate standing there. And she's yelling all sorts of shit at him. And she's buck-ass naked and she's holding this condom she pulled off me in her hand and she throws it at him!"

Claire let out a bray of startled laughter and Smiley just nodded. "No, it's cool. It was funny. So she steps out and shuts the door and starts to talk to him and I'm left in the room and I don't know what to do. So I pull on some clothes and wait there, feeling like a dick. Pardon the expression."

He drank some more and I realized that the two of them

had almost polished off a forty-ounce bottle, with 90 percent going down Smiley's throat and neither of them was showing any effects.

"Anyhow. The door opens and the guy comes in, this big fucking bodybuilder wearing pajama bottoms, and Tracey's in the doorway wearing his robe and sniffling. He sits down beside me and puts his hand on my knee."

He stared off into space and then shook his head. "First I thought he was coming on to me and then that maybe this was some kind of three-way hustle. But no. He starts talking that him and Tracey were an item and had some problems but now everything was cool between them and maybe I should take off."

I realized I was waiting for the punchline, but there was none, and he kept right on.

"I didn't know what to do." He said it wonderingly. "And I look at him and say that I need to hear it from her. And before I'm finished saying it, well, Tracey is opening her hole and says that I took advantage of her at a difficult time and that we shouldn't see each other again. And the guy's nodding and the chick's nodding and I can see past her head to this light fixture in the middle of the living room and the condom she pulled off me is stuck to it. And I swear it's smoking and stinking from the heat off the bulb."

I couldn't help myself, I had to smile. He saw me and his face flushed with rage, and something snapped as he stood up and said, "Fuck you, Monty."

I stared at him and he blew out hard through his nose before getting control of himself and calming down. Then he went on with a strange edge to his voice. "Let's do it now. Let's dump Marie. Let's take the route. Let's make some real money. Let's have some fun. Let's see some action. I'm tired of this half-straight shit—it's not for me. It's not for you either. Fuck it. Shit or get off the pot."

I shook my head and I could see a creeping look of pity coming into Claire's eyes, and then I said softly, "No, man, no."

His anger flared. "You're doing nothing. Let's get started. Let's do this." I didn't say anything and he went on in a more conciliatory tone, trying to con me. "Let's go. Your family's slowing you down, you have to realize that."

He stared at me hard and I shook my head. "No."

I had set him up. His eyes widened and he realized that I had never intended to go into the biz with him again. "You fucking bastard, you chickenshit coward ... you betrayed me!"

The words hung there.

#38

Words, they were only words, and I let them rush over me. "I'm not your enemy. I didn't betray you. You were the one who took Sam's contract to set me up."

I took a deep breath, swallowed some words, and finally came out with, "I'm not your enemy. You are."

His rage was like a fire in a forest, leaping from tree to tree, boiling creeks dry, and cracking rocks. "Aren't you? Aren't you the one with the fucking clean slate? Aren't you the one with the fan-dam-ly? Aren't you the one who said, 'just let it go.' Maybe you can. You and your fucking family. You owe me. I did you a favour. I could've handed your ass to Sam."

He exhaled and went on. "I didn't because we have connections, because we have a history."

His voice was calm, silky now but his face was still red and his whole body was taut with something. Claire looked back and forth between us and the anger started to burn in me but when I spoke my voice was just as silky as his, just as smooth and unyielding and slick. "Leave my family out of it."

His rage flared again. "I don't want this. I don't want any of it. You can FUCK your normal citizens and you can FUCK the honest people and you can FUCK YOURSELF AND YOUR FUCKING BITCH AND BRAT TOO!"

That was apparently my limit.

He was out of breath there and I hit him in the upper belly with the tips of my fingers and his eyes widened as he folded in with the blow. Then I was out of my chair and looking for a new target. Claire stood up too and backed up a little to circle behind Smiley.

For a heartbeat Smiley was shocked and for another heartbeat he was betrayed and then he pushed back hard to move away from a hammer blow I'd aimed to break his collarbone and end it.

"FUCKER!"

He wheezed but I said nothing.

Claire came in while he was distracted and aimed a kick from behind at his balls. Smiley twisted slightly and used the motion to scoop her leg up high.

The sound of Claire hitting the floor back first was loud and I feinted a combo to drive him back and then I followed him into the living room. Out of the corner of my eye I saw Claire catching her breath and then she palmed one of Fred's wooden blocks and pitched it at Smiley's face.

He ducked it easily but when he raised his head I was ready and moving and my kick took him square in the chest and drove him right through the front window onto the lawn. The rage inside me bubbled over, the feeling of having been controlled and manipulated, of his having put my family in danger and I took it all out on the man in front of me.

Outside I moved; left foot, right foot, weight centred over my hips ready to kick or punch. Watching for a knife or a club or a gun, wanting to take him out with the rage red and bright in my face and feeling that friendly coldness start somewhere deep inside, that happy glorying in pain.

"Fucker!"

He had his breath back and straightened up flipping his jacket into one hand. There are two theories to words in a fight. The first one is that if you use the right ones you'll make the other guy mad and he'll make mistakes.

The second theory is to save your breath.

In this case I saved my breath.

A fight is never one move. It's never one kick or one punch. In a real fight each blow leads to another and to another and every defence has an offensive component and every offensive move has a defensive component. Until the other person is on the ground and you can heel stomp their throat flat and kill them.

Smiley punched with his right hand and I directed it away from me with my left forearm. And when he was open I tried to use the heel of my right hand to flatten his nose or break his jaw, either would have been fine. But he was very close and turned his head away and used his left elbow coming up to hit my chin and blur my vision.

Before I could recover, his jacket was somehow around my throat and he was behind me taking my weight on his back. If he'd finished the throw I would have landed with the jacket still in place and my neck and back broken or dislocated.

"That's two for flinching!" I broke my own rule and muttered. Then I slammed an elbow into his kidneys, first on one side and then on the other. The pain was enough to make him drop the jacket and turn to face me as Claire yelled from the house that she was calling the police. Smiley just grinned at me and kept coming, "Bitch. Fucker. Chickenshit."

He whispered it all, lunged for my forearm, and took a

grip on my wrist. From there he could do many different bad things, but I turned my hand quickly towards the gap between his thumb and index fingers. Then I pulled my hand towards my chest and slammed an open-palm strike roundhouse into his ear. While he was still reeling, I put the flat of my foot back into the middle of his chest and drove him back to give me room. Before I could do anything more, though, he kicked at me himself and buried the tip of his toe in my gut. While I was backpedalling, he used a right-armed horizontal elbow blow across his body aimed at my throat.

Had it connected he would have crushed my larynx and killed me, but I leaned backwards and the blow missed.

Remember what I said about a fight never being one move? When I leaned back to avoid the throat shot he took the second shot and brought the same hand in from the side to clip me hard in the soft tissue below the base of my skull. In his perfect world it would have dislocated my neck but it didn't and instead swept me down to his left knee, which rammed all the rest of the air out of my belly.

And I went down. The whole fight had taken maybe ten seconds ... maybe less. And I was down on the ground and he was over me raising his heel just like he'd learned in the same schools I'd attended. Heel comes down with all the weight on the throat and the victim suffocates fairly soon.

It takes about two minutes to die that way.

Two minutes to think about everything you haven't done in life and everything you wanted to do. Above me Smiley's face was ... ecstatic, and I'm not sure he could recognize or even see me. And then the sirens roared again, this time from much closer, like at the end of the block. He had to look, and while he was doing that, Claire reached the dining-room window and screamed "FIRE!" as she threw a box of toys to clatter and shatter in the grass all around us, which made him flinch.

At the same time I realized he was standing on his own jacket and that I had a sleeve in my hand. So I grabbed it tight to my chest and rolled away and he went up and down onto the grass and screamed as his ass smashed onto a solid steel Tonka dump truck. Which gave me a chance to reach my feet and gesture at Smiley, "Come on."

He stood there with Claire screaming "FIRE!" and Fred screaming, the dog barking, and the neighbours yelling at us to please shut up! Smiley was frozen in indecision and confusion at the chaos that was filling the air around him.

And then he ran.

#39

The cops came two hours later, but I refused to press charges, which pissed them off. Six of them stood around for awhile and tried to figure out what to charge me with. They wanted to search the house and we told them to show us a search warrant because you never, ever let cops into your home unless they're holding a gun on you. That made them even angrier. Finally they left, telling us over and over again to call if he came back, to be careful, that it was really our fault all this happened because we let him into our home in the first place.

When they were gone Claire put ice on this and that and we cleaned up the toys in the yard. The Tonka truck had taken a beating, though, and had to be pitched, and a few other things were broken, but in total the damage wasn't that bad. When the doors and windows were all locked and nailed shut with scraps of lumber and alarmed with glassware gimmicked precariously at the entryways to give us warning, we went to bed. Fred was tucked in between us, a dresser was in front of the door, Claire had the bayonet and I had the crowbar.

She looked at me. "He's gone now?" It wasn't a question.

"Yep."

"Do you think he was ever really trying to go straight?"

I shook my head. "Maybe a little. Probably not. And it doesn't matter shit."

I locked the house down and we went to sleep and I cancelled babysitting for the immediate future. After a few days I got Claire to lock down the house and divided my time between Marie's operation and home, but I couldn't find Smiley anywhere.

I didn't tell Marie about Smiley. I didn't want to worry her. Maybe I was just being selfish or maybe I was using her as a lure for Smiley. I just told her to be extra careful. After a day I got both Claire and her to hole up with the doors locked while I expanded my search to every dive in the city. But I could find not the least trace of Smiley and I started to hope he'd run off.

And then the shit started again.

The scene was played over and over on the television, both locally and nationally, eventually even making it onto the cheesier hardcore news channels in the States. Finally I saw it. Three days after Smiley had left I was in the kitchen, doing laundry in the sink, watching Smiley's TV picking up bad reception.

The film came from a grainy camera in the basement garage of the Health Sciences Centre. It showed an elevator door opening and a couple coming out. A medium-sized brown-or blond-haired woman was limping a bit and pushing her boyfriend in front of her in a wheelchair. He had a cast on his pelvis and a cell phone in his hand.

His phone call was recorded by fluke, a conversation with

his mother about when he'd be home. "On my way now, Ma, no I'm fine ..." The conversation was picked up and recorded by a strange little man in Winnipeg's West End who played with scanners and listened to all sorts of things. When the news came out he realized what he had and gave a copy of his recording to the police and a second one to the CBC.

As the two figures approached, the door to the parkade itself opened automatically. A medium-sized man in black with a wide-brimmed cowboy hat, trench coat and gloves came into view. About ten feet away he raised his arm. There was something silver and white in his right hand, and the woman reached for something in her purse, but she was too slow.

"No, no, no!"

The curiously dead popping of small-calibre gunfire filled the cell phone. The narrator counted down: six shots into the couple; four into the woman who was pushed back away from the wheelchair and two into the man who slouched forward, bowing to the impacts.

"Charlie? Charlie? What was that?"

The figure, his back still to the camera, held the gun up, barrel to the ceiling, and fiddled with the extractor until the cylinder opened to the left. Then he shook out the brass and you could hear it on the cell phone, a cheerful tinkling sound over the panting breaths of the man and woman. The figure reloaded the cylinder one chamber at a time as he walked forward. When he was right in front of the wheelchair, he brought the gun forward again and squeezed two shots into the forehead of the man. Then he stepped to the side and put two more into the face of the woman.

The shooter never showed his face and the pictures of the couple coming out of the hospital were so grainy as to make them unrecognizable. But the voice ... that I recognized. On the recorded cell phone call you could hear his voice, calm and disinterested: "And that's two for flinching."

I watched it to the end and then left running to find Claire, leaving behind a sink full of half-washed clothes.

#40

Claire listened without interrupting.

"Smiley hunted down Sam and her boyfriend as they were coming out of the hospital."

"Dead?"

"Dead."

"Oh." Claire swayed and for a moment I thought she'd fall. "I thought he might make it. Even after everything."

"I hoped too."

She picked up Fred and we both went to his room and started to pack, first for him and then for her. When that was done I handed her the bayonet and helped her tape it to her arm for a quick draw. Then I called for a cab and we finished packing. The last thing I did was pull on my thief's coat and, on top of that, a grey-lined windbreaker.

"What happens now?"

I wondered about what to do with the dog. Claire saw me and offered, "I'll take him with us. What do we do now?"

"We get you safe. Then I find Smiley and deal him out."

"Okay."

"He's after Marie's route and that's what I'm being paid to protect. And I'm a threat to him so he'll have to take me out. And he's my responsibility."

She said sweetly, "I never should have given you that book."

I just stood there and chewed my lip and repeated, "He's my responsibility."

Claire snorted, "Fuck that. You just want to deal with him yourself."

I couldn't argue.

We were heading out the front door with the dog on a leash and Fred in his stroller and got into the cab. I was ready for it to be Smiley but it wasn't; instead it was a fat South American who drove carefully and precisely downtown. While we were travelling I kept an eye on our trail but saw nothing. Her comment finally sank in.

"What book?"

"*Of Mice and Men.*"

"What are you talking about?"

"The moral of the story."

I was genuinely confused as we exited the cab and went inside an office building. I'd wandered most of the downtown and knew that it was possible to move across whole blocks without ever crossing a street. We kept our heads down and scuttled from a hotel to an office building and then via walkway into the Convention Centre. There Claire withdrew $500 from the bank machine and handed me the card and two of the casino cheques worth $2342.25. I could cash those at a payroll company if I needed the money. Other than that I had about sixty dollars saved from babysitting and a Swiss Army knife in my pocket, so I was ready.

Finally I asked Claire, "What moral? Don't make friends with big, slow people who like rabbits?"

"Oh shut up. Hmmm. Bus, train, or plane?"

"Bus, it has flexibility. We can lie about the ID on a bus. We can buy you tickets to Regina and then reroute you to wherever you want to go at the last minute. Call your folks."

"Are you sure?"

"Yeah."

We bought peanuts, bottled water, and chocolate from a Morden's chocolate shop that advertised the best chocolate in four provinces and eighteen states. Then Claire went to the nearest phone and started to dump quarters. While she was distracted I repeated the question about the moral of the stupid book while watching for anything suspicious. Finally she answered me.

"Oh, that moral? The moral is that you have to shoot your own dog. You can't farm it out, it's unethical."

"Oh. Really? Is that true?"

"Probably. It's a moral, maybe not the only one ... Hi, Dad!" Her voice suddenly became much more chipper. "No, I'm still in Winnipeg ... no, I'm still with Monty ... no, everyone's fine ... no, he's not in prison again ... no, everything's still fine ... it's all fine, Dad. We were thinking maybe Fred and I could come visit you in Banff. Spend some time around your grandson."

There was a long pause and then she went on. "No. Monty can't make it. He can't exactly take the time off work right now. He's kind of busy. It'll just be me and Fred and a dog and a mouse ..."

Strange watching your wife turn into someone else's daughter. A minute later she hung up and we went out the main doors of the Convention Centre and into a fresh cab.

Ten minutes later we had navigated the confused series of one-way streets to the nearest pet shop, where we bought a carrier for the stupid dog and another for the stupider mouse (whom I had been carrying in a half-empty margarine container with air holes punched in the top).

Ten minutes after that we reached the bus station. While Claire went in to buy tickets she was in a room with about thirty people, including three cops. I took a chance and went to a sporting goods store on Portage Avenue. There I bought a pair of cheap leather gloves, two big canisters of pepper spray (advertised as dog repellent), four highway flares (a most excellent and underused hand-to-hand weapon), a cheap backpack, a whetstone, and a Cold Steel Spike knife. The clerk was distracted, so I pocketed a pair of Simmons mini-binoculars from one display and a cased set of three steel-tipped tungsten Nodor darts from another. After I paid she looked me carefully in the eye.

"Is that everything?"

In clerk that meant she'd seen me steal the darts and the binoculars. I looked her in the eye and answered, "No."

I reached over to her side of the counter and picked up a twine cutter she'd been using, a viciously hooked razor about an inch long worn on a ring and used to open packages quickly.

"That's not for sale."

I handed her a twenty. She pocketed it and stared at me while I made the cutter vanish into my pocket. It would make a fine last-ditch weapon and I needed every edge and gimmick I could beg, borrow or steal. I looked the woman over and waited for her to make a decision. Was she willing to accuse me of stealing? She was a lot smaller than me. I was feeling kind of mean. And it wasn't her money.

Finally she rang up the bill minus the darts and binoculars and let me go without comment.

At the bus station I gave Claire one of the cans of pepper spray and two of the highway flares to put into her purse. She gave me half of the peanuts and water and I put that into the backpack. Then I kissed her.

"And if I see Smiley?"

I took a deep breath.

"Use the pepper spray to make sure you have his attention, then set fire to him with the flare. While he's burning use the bayonet and stab him in the belly, chest, and groin. Twist the blade as you withdraw it to speed bleeding. Bury the body at the crossroads and hammer a stake through his heart. As you leave, salt the earth."

Claire didn't smile. "Right."

"When you get to Banff, is there a computer you can use, one with Internet access?"

"Why?"

I thought quickly. "I'll e-mail you every day, but if there's anything important I'll phone you."

"Okay. I can think of one or two I could use."

"Computers that can't be traced back to you?"

She seemed insulted. "Of course."

"Okay. I'll open an e-mail account with the address—what would you remember?"

"How about ... inthebeginning?"

"That works but it's probably in use by some Christian group somewhere. What if I preface it with a prime number, if the first is in use, then the next one?"

"Like 1-2-3-5-7 ..."

I asked, "Two is a prime number?"

"You bet."

"Really?" I was positive she was pulling my leg.

"Really."

"You're so smart."

Claire nodded. "That's why you married me."

I corrected her, "No, that's one of six reasons I married you."

"Six?"

"Uh-huh."

Her brow was furrowed. "Which six?"

The bus was already there so I kissed her and helped her to a seat in the middle and on the right side with Fred between her and the window. From there she had the greatest number of options if Smiley found her and got on.

"Hey, wait a minute, what six? You never told me."

I kissed her again. "I'll tell you later."

And then Claire, Fred, Renfield, and Thor were off on their way to Banff.

Which left me to shoot my own dog.

#41

In the bus station bathroom I locked myself into a stall and dressed for work.

The Spike knife was a fighting knife reduced to its essentials, with a ten-centimetre blade and a handle wrapped in cord for a good grip. It was very light, less than 200 grams, and came with a plastic sheath that held the thick, narrow blade. It had a beaded metal lanyard that allowed me to hang it under my shirt where it rested with the handle pointed down.

Like all of Cold Steel's products, it was well made and pre-sharpened; despite that I spit on the whetstone and sharpened it some more. Then I tucked it away and put away the rest of my purchases, pepper spray in this pocket, flares here and there and the twine cutter around my neck on a bit of string in case of emergency. Last I tucked the darts in my right-hand jacket pocket where I could easily reach them. Although they look silly they are actually a very effective concealed weapon and could be quite dangerous if aimed properly. And the darts would work until I found a gun.

Thinking that made me pause. I was actually thinking that I would be getting a gun. Not *if* I had a gun, but *when* I had a gun. The violence was escalating fast. Which sobered me, so I headed to the Millennium Library to think some more.

Smiley knew I went there sometimes, but if he showed up I'd be ready for him.

Or at least that's what I hoped.

At the library I dug out some books, found a desk on the big glassed-in side, and sat there blankly. An ex-con in a library is both perfectly ridiculous and perfectly reasonable.

It's like an anti-drug president fighting for freedom although he has problems with cocaine and suppresses freedom (because it is so precious it must be doled out in small amounts).

It's like a prime minister fighting for Canadian jobs by having his shipping company registered in Panama and staffed by Philippine sailors. Or like another who leads the country but who once described it as a European welfare state.

Maybe an ex-con in a library made sense.

And in terms of defensive position it was pretty good. From where I was I could head up the stairs or down or across onto the second floor. From there I could kick my way through a couple of shitty security doors onto the hamster trail walkways that linked the city. And I had lots of lines of sight to see Smiley coming.

Until then I could think and consider and wait, with myself as bait. Had Doc Holliday in the books maybe been made into Smiley in the real world?

Did that make sense?

Around me students studied, old men played chess, young boys tried to con the Internet into showing porn, tired mothers shepherded rude children, and small groups of visitors swarmed mindlessly. It was a good place to feel safe and to think.

Cops are concerned with many things, truth amongst them, in theory. They worry about how things are done, why they are done, who they are done too, where they are done, and when they are done. I am a thief, though (okay, an ex-thief), and am more concerned with specifics.

Because the devil is always in the details.

Smiley had always told me that Doc Holliday was his hero so I considered that gunfighter. His apex was at the OK Corral, that made his reputation, but that wasn't the end of it for him, his life went on after and had gone on before. At the OK Corral he brought a shotgun to a gunfight when everyone else brought pistols.

This meant he was a realist, a pragmatist, and more than that, an absolutist.

He carried either a sawed-down 10-gauge WW Greener or Meteor shotgun, carried a bowie knife, carried a Colt Single action .45 revolver, carried a Colt .41 with a short barrel, carried a Colt Thunderer and carried a short-barrelled unknown Colt in .44. And he died at about ten o'clock in the morning of November 8 in 1887 as Doctor John Henry Holliday at the Hotel Glenwood in Glenwood Springs, Colorado. Cause of death was listed as military tuberculosis, which made me wonder if there was such a thing as civilian tuberculosis.

One hundred and thirteen years later history recorded what guns he carried and when. Unanswered was the question of why he carried them. Was he perhaps caught in a cycle of the truth that he carried guns because people tried to shoot him and people tried to shoot him because he shot people, and he shot people because he had guns?

Doc gambled with cards and dice, shot people for vengeance

and convenience and to save his own life. He was a dentist no one wanted to frequent because he had tuberculosis and kept coughing in their faces. He was a drinker of bourbon and laudanum (that marvellous mixture of opium distilled into brandy). He wore a grey jacket and whistled and he had a gold stickpin in his possession on his deathbed, which had in it a diamond inherited from his father. And he sold the diamond to pay for his deathbed stay.

In later life his friend Wyatt Earp wrote the following: "I found him a loyal friend and good company. He was a dentist whom necessity had made a gambler; a gentleman whom disease had made a vagabond; a philosopher whom life had made a caustic wit; a long, lean blond fellow nearly dead with consumption and at the same time the most skillful gambler and nerviest, speediest, deadliest man with a six-gun I ever knew."

Was that Smiley? Was that how he saw himself, and if so, was he my friend?

The fact he had betrayed me meant nothing—the little criminal voice in my head told me that. Betrayals happened, they just happened, like rain. It was nothing in the grand scheme of things; it was just something to deal with and move past.

And if Doc Holliday was Smiley's hero and he was basing himself on that ideal, then what would he do next? And did I really want to know?

When the library closed I headed home cautiously, getting off the bus many blocks away and moving through backyards and down alleys. Upon arrival, I found a letter in the mailbox, hand-delivered. In the envelope was a single sheet of paper that read, "I would never have hurt you or your family."

Without thinking I dropped the paper and ran, around the corner of the house and away.

#42

I spent the night and most of the next day in a room of the seventh floor of a fleabag motel near the airport eating peanuts and drinking bottled water. I had a chest of drawers across the door and the knife and darts ready for use. I'd pre-gimmicked the window to open and had at hand a length of Edelrid Sky Pilot rope I'd bought at the downtown Mountain Equipment Co-op store. That would give me quick and pain-ful access to the ground if things got really bad. I say painful because I had the mountain-climbing and rappelling skills of a large, irregular stone with palsy.

When it was dark I visited the offices of Ultra Realty and stole their office gun, the Polish Radom semi-automatic pistol with its heavy leather holster, twin eight-round box magazines and the extra eleven rounds. I also took the cleaning rod and a small tube of gun oil.

In the dim light of my flashlight I stripped the gun and oiled it, popped all the shells out and polished them, and then reloaded them. The holster went on my belt on my right side, covered by my jacket but easy to reach. I went into the basement and used a black marker to make a one-inch dot on one concrete wall, then stood with my back against the other, about twenty feet away. I clicked the safety off, aimed for the centre of the dot, and squeezed the trigger against a three-pound resistance.

Bang.

A sharp, authoritative noise and a big chip of virgin white concrete appeared two inches below my dot while shards of metal and stone whizzed around the basement and broke something glass in the far corner. I waited but no one reacted, so I assumed no one heard anything or recognized it as gunfire. I adjusted my aim up and squeezed twice more. The dot vanished and more stone and metal shards broke more things around me. Then I reloaded the magazine, gathered up my spent brass, and left.

Outside in the alley I dumped the empty cartridges into a storm drain and kept walking.

It had taken me a while to figure out where Smiley could have gone. He had told me that Winnipeg was new to him, and he had killed off Sam, his main contact. Since it was a new city he would be cut off from most of his friends; he would have no one he could use as cover. It would also cut him off from anyone who could betray him. But Winnipeg was also a new city to Claire and me, that was one of the reasons we had come, to make a new start.

So I thought about the problem from Smiley's point of view and that led me downtown to the big apartment building where Tracey and her boyfriend lived.

In the building I could see when I got close that the door to the suite had been jimmied with a sharp knife or chisel, I paused and pulled on gloves. The job on the door had been done carefully and you had to look hard to see it. Maybe Smiley was still there, so I held my breath and slowly pushed on the knob with every sense alert, listening and feeling for clicks or snaps or anything else that would mean a booby trap or someone pointing a gun at the door, but nothing happened, and I slid into the suite low to the ground.

Silence hung heavy in the room and my hands tightened around the stolen pistol. My right finger rested hard on the outside of the guard, a half inch from the trigger. In my mind I went through the positive visualization of shooting many bullets into Smiley's main body mass and then the rest into his head.

Simple and direct.

I went through the apartment room by room, checking every place where a person could hide. I checked the closet, living room, kitchenette, bathroom, little bedroom, closet, big bedroom, and the closet there. And it was there that I found the bodies, two of them, a well-built male and a well-built female, both naked and wrapped carefully in a plastic cocoon of transparent wrap and duct tape. Their cocoon had swollen with the gases of putrefaction which meant they had been dead for awhile.

I examined the bodies as closely as I could through the plastic and thought I saw blunt trauma on the man's head and face and more marks on the woman's neck. I also saw that their hands and feet had been taped into immobility with more of the ubiquitous grey duct tape. And my mind twisted again to thoughts of *Possum Lodge* and the *Red Green Show* fixing everything with duct tape while George W. was telling everyone to seal themselves into their homes real tight.

Sitting there gave me the time to reconstruct it. Smiley comes in fast, hits the boyfriend, immobilizes the girl, and puts the two of them into two separate rooms. Then he asks them questions, which was the only reason to keep them alive; maybe he rapes the girl. Maybe not.

Then, with his questions answered, he beats the guy to death with some heavy, round object. Something like the barrel of a gun. I stood there in the silence and my mind raced through trivia. Never believe the shows on TV where someone hits someone else with the butt of the gun. In a semi-automatic pistol that's a delicate bit of hardware that holds the ammunition, and in a revolver the butt plates break off easily. No, the cowboys of the old West knew better and used the barrel. They called it pistol whipping and it still works just fine. Now if you have a rifle or a shotgun with a wooden butt, that's a completely different story.

So Smiley had a gun when he got to the apartment, but getting a gun was never hard, so big deal. It wouldn't be the Enfield revolver I'd ruined though. He would have checked that out and thrown it away or repaired it. And the barrel would have been too short for the damage he had done to the man's body.

Smiley kills Louis and then Tracey, strangling her with his hands, and then wraps them in plastic and stows them. I wondered where he got the plastic and couldn't come up with anything. Why kill the two though? To use the apartment, was the simplest answer, so I went back into the smaller bedroom and saw for the first time that there was the imprint of a body on top of the sheets about Smiley's size. And a couple of dozen cigarettes, Marlboro and Benson & Hedges, had been butted out on a china plate on the dresser. Flipping the pillow over showed me an oily outline the size and shape of a gun where it

266

had lain on the cover as Smiley had slept and dreamt whatever dreams he had.

Back in the kitchenette I saw that there were several dirty dishes out, with the unmistakable traces of peanut butter and toast and black coffee with sugar. In the fridge were deli packages growing old, a few bottles of Dos Equis beer, and a bottle of non-vintage champagne. Above the sink were four bottles of red wine on their sides, a half-filled bottle of single-malt Scotch and a full bottle of butter-ripple schnapps. And all that meant that Smiley wasn't drinking, which was bad, because it meant he was still in control.

So I searched the rest of the apartment. Wallets and purses empty of all the ID and cards, no keys anywhere, and an empty antique gun case under the bed in the small bedroom. I checked the case out, a wooden hinged box lined with red fabric and the owner's manual still in place for a Smith & Wesson Model .22/.32 Target revolver with heavy frame. With absent curiosity I read the manual. The gun fired .22 longs, had a twenty-centimetre barrel with adjustable sights, and was made in 1911.

A very accurate gun indeed, though not very powerful, capable of putting all six shots in a one-centimetre circle at fifteen metres if the shooter was accurate.

I kept looking. In the freezer there was an empty plastic pork chop, sold by security stores to yuppies to hide valuables. In the closet of the small bedroom there was a crudely built secret compartment on the shelf which held a small baggie of grass, three bottles of oral Turinabol (chlordehydromethyltestosterone steroids in pill form), and a carefully assembled spike-and-spoon setup for shooting up intravenous/intramuscular drugs. And in the big bedroom a very cheap jewelry case had been rifled, with some badly made amateur and costume jewelry left behind.

Eventually I left, pulling the door closed behind me. Smiley had at least one gun, he had cash, he was in control of himself, and he had assorted credit cards and identification which might help him. And he probably had a car, whatever Tracey or Louis drove when they were still breathing.

In the elevator heading to the garage downstairs I thought about dropping a dime, actually two quarters these days. One phone call would put the cops into the apartment. That would lead them to Smiley if he'd made even the smallest mistake. But if I called too soon, someone from the building might describe me, which would put heat on my trail too. Balancing the two things out made me decide to keep my mouth shut. I went through the garage and cut the wire to the fire alarm before I walked out through an emergency door.

#43

Smiley was loose in the city and had nailed Samantha and boyfriend plus Tracey and Louis. And he could have done all that for lots of reasons, the standards for murder being jealousy, revenge, and money, the unholy three. There was also the possibility that he had been delivering a preemptive strike, but that was close enough to revenge to make it an unnecessary addition.

Like an appendix, or a conscience.

I believed his motive would lead me to him.

While trying to figure his motive out I decided to check out my house, just to make sure. I wondered if Smiley could be in the house, waiting for me with a gun, or he could have a partner of some type, waiting for me with a gun, or the house could be clean and empty, or he could have booby-trapped the place. If I had to bet I'd put money on booby-trapping because it would mean he wouldn't have to be there and risk anyone. It would also be what I would do if I was in his place.

This all led me back to the house. On the way I found

an Internet cafe and rented a computer for long enough to open the e-mail account Claire and I had agreed on. I was lucky, managing to create it within ten minutes, and then I kept moving.

In the North End I circled my house a few blocks out and then moved in slowly. On the way I passed where the drug house had been and found a backhoe chopping the place down while a small sign on the edge of police tape read that this would soon be a local park dedicated to "The Residents of the Neighbourhood." It would be tiny, but it would be a green place for children and adults.

And it was better than a drug house.

That meant that the Jarelskis were behaving themselves, which meant I didn't have to go and burn their house down after I'd dealt with Smiley.

As I walked towards my house I thought about booby traps—I know them inside and out. I know the low-tech ones and the high-tech ones, the ones that are long term and the ones that are short term. I'm comfortable with the lethal ones and the ones you use to warn or wound. Take a grenade, put a rubber band around the lever, pull the pin, put it in a fireplace, and walk away. Or drop it into a gasoline tank where the gas degrades the rubber and *boom* with the grenade becoming the detonator and the gas becoming the primary explosive. Or give me three minutes with a rat trap, a length of pipe, and a rifle cartridge, and you'd have a detonator for a bigger bomb.

Make a few changes and you end up with a neat way to blow off someone's foot or face.

During the war in Vietnam a friend who had been a member of the Vietcong told me they used to wire up motorcycles with stolen C-4 and leave them where Americans would find them. *Hey Johnny, look at me, I'm a rebel without a cause …*

Later they watched the GI's kick soda cans down the road, so they used those as triggers to buried grenades and left them in handy places.

And bad guys had borrowed from the military and come up with their own variations. I'd been at marijuana grow ops where the entryways had explosives buried under the doors. Open the door and *boom*. Others had pits set up on the approaches full of wooden spikes (to fool metal detectors), some pointing up and some pointing down from the side in case a boot was worn with a reinforced sole. At another farm the trees around a clearing were booby-trapped with explosives to take down any helicopter that came a-visiting.

I'd seen guys set daisy chains that were booby traps linked in series to channel the targets and to eliminate them with maximum loss. I'd seen homemade crossbows and shotguns set up on trip wires to fire down a path at knee height to generate crippling wounds. I'd seen snares, barbed fish hooks hung on fishing line at face level in case anyone came knocking, and I'd seen varieties of leg-hold traps modified for people.

And you can booby-trap anything. With practice you can gimmick a body, a book, a door, clothes, condoms, a whistle, pets, beer, windows, and plates. You can do cigarettes, lighters, stoves, bathrooms, cars, and letters.

You can even booby-trap a vagina.

I knew the triggers. Pressure could be a trigger, cutting a wire could work too, opening a door could pull a pin, walking into a room could set off a cheap radar security device, and the heat sensor used to control lighting in a room could set off anything you could imagine. A trap could be set to detonate when an electrical current was interrupted, or on pressure, or on the absence of pressure. You could use a handyman's level to make a motion-sensitive trigger and you could make a command detonator with a garage door opener, or a cell phone, or a pager. It was even possible, I'd heard, to set up a trigger that would go off when someone breathed.

And what I knew, Smiley could know, which made coming home … a little nerve wracking. Because I would have wired the place in a serious way.

Which meant he would have done exactly the same thing.

Trick to avoiding booby traps and ambushes number one is: don't go in by the normal entry way. Instead I went next door to the Kilpatricks' and knocked politely. The wife answered, "Oh, hi Montgomery."

She's the only person still alive who uses my full name. My grandmother, gone and buried, did it but she's not around any more.

"Hi. Can I borrow a ladder and your upstairs window?"

She stared at me. Not too long ago she and her husband had tried to run Claire and me out of town by leaving threatening notes and such. When I'd found out I'd hurt her husband fairly badly and scared both of them quite a lot and now I was babysitting their grandchild.

Go figure.

"Ummm. Sure?"

The ladder was in their garage. I picked it up and carried it through the house, carefully while Mrs. Kilpatrick ran ahead of me and kept offering me coffee or maybe a beer and would I like a cookie?

"No. Thank you but no."

Upstairs I found a window in the main bedroom that faced my bedroom in our house with maybe eleven or twelve feet between us. Carefully opening the window first I laid the ladder down until it reached the sill. I adjusted it twice until I was sure.

"You know, I changed my mind about that cookie."

"Oh, sure." And off she bustled. While I was waiting I checked my bag and made sure the tools and gun were in place. When she brought the cookie (one of those soft-on-the-inside chocolate chip ones) and I'd eaten it I climbed onto the ladder and started to crawl across to my own window with the backpack strapped to my belly where I could easily reach it.

"Thanks, and can you pull the ladder back when the window's open?"

"Sure. May I ask what you're doing?"

"You probably don't want to know."

"Oh, I do. Really."

"It's called mouse-holing. It's a way of moving from one house to another by soldiers without leaving the house and exposing themselves to enemy fire. This is one way; another is to use explosives to blow through the walls of adjoining buildings."

"Oh. Well. Yes. Right."

And off I went. At my window I drew the Swiss Army knife and puzzled briefly over the blades. My in-laws had given it to me while I was in prison with the little file extended and CAKE TO FOLLOW engraved on the handle. It had, of course, been immediately confiscated, but one of the screws had shown it to me through a pane of bullet-proof glass before it had ended up in storage. The whole thing still rankled, but I now found the thinnest blade on the knife and went to work on the sill, sliding the knife past the layers of paint and dirt and using it to slowly push the hook out of the way.

While I did that I watched the room carefully but saw nothing that leaped out as wrong. I did, however, note that the shades were open, whereas Claire and I always drew them, and that the door was shut, whereas I always left it open to promote air circulation.

When I had the window up I put my legs over the sill and gestured for Mrs. Kilpatrick to pull the ladder in while mouthing, "Thanks!"

With my back to the window I kept my legs up and used the time to really examine the floor but there was nothing out of place. No wires, no devices, nothing other than the open curtains and the closed door to tell me that anyone had even been here since Claire and I had fled. There were also no noises in the house, no sounds of someone running up the stairs with a gun or something like that.

I did not want to step onto the floor so I sat there and thought and stared and thought some more. The term *booby trap* is a relatively old one. Originally it comes from the term *balbus*; the Latin word for stammering, which the Romans thought meant the speaker was stupid. A little later on the English used the term *booby* to describe really stupid seabirds which were easy to catch and kill. From there it became used for all sorts of descriptions, culminating by the middle of the eighteen hundreds when it was used to describe a trap used to catch an idiot, because they, whoever "they" were, would have to trigger it themselves.

And because I have a dirty mind I also once looked up the earthier meaning of *boob*. Apparently it had never meant that breasts were stupid but instead came from the Elizabethan English term *bubbies* which meant any alcoholic drink. This probably came from the Latin term *bibere*, to drink.

Which makes me, personally, feel much better. I'd hate

to think that breasts were stupid. Mostly I was in favour of them.

After all that raced through my brain I found myself still waiting. Because I did not want to touch the floor.

#44

Finally I lowered myself down, closed the window, and drew the blinds. Only then did I pull the pistol from its holster and take the safety off. The noise was horribly loud but nothing went *boom*. Then I exhaled and, inch by inch, I went over the cold, cold room, starting at the window, then the futon, the closet, the door, the dresser, the bookcase. Then I opened the door and did every inch of the hallway and the bathroom and the tub, the sink, the toilet, and the linen closet. And then I looked over Fred's room, the crib, his closet, his dresser, the change table. Ad infinitum, and what did I find?

Under my pillow on the futon was an oldie but goodie that took me a few minutes to identify. Back from the USSR, folks, an old Soviet Russian F-1 fragmentation grenade, originally produced way back in the days when the Nazis were knocking on Stalin's gates.

I stared at the damn thing and sweated despite the cold, and for a moment I distracted myself by wondering why it was so cold. Then I had to think about the grenade again. There are two kinds of grenades, defensive and offensive. Offensive grenades are to be used by your glorious troops as they charge forward against their inhuman enemies, so they contain relatively little explosive, and produce relatively little shrapnel. Then there are defensive grenades, which are designed to be used against your inhuman enemies as they charge the defences occupied by your glorious troops. They have a big charge of explosive and produce a lot of shrapnel.

The F-1 was a defensive grenade that dumps sharp bits of metal at high rates of speed out to twenty or thirty meters. The pin had been pulled and was held in place by the weight of the grenade on the spoon. Lie on the pillow and the grenade moves, the spoon flies off, and three to four seconds later those little bits of shrapnel go flying off in all directions. I wondered where Smiley had gotten the grenade and then I taped the spoon into immobility with duct tape and moved on. Only now I was moving even more slowly if that was possible.

Why was it so cold? I almost turned the thermostat up but then I stopped and decided to check out the whole house, and that was a good thing. Here and there were hidden big Remington .44 magnum hollow points and twelve-gauge double-ought buckshot rounds set up with spring triggers to make real toe poppers. Not enough to kill if you stepped on them, just enough to blow your foot into hamburger. And they were set in door jambs and under overturned shoes and under carefully loosened floorboards.

And there were two more of the Soviet grenades, one balanced over a doorway and one tucked behind a book on its shelf. So the next time I needed to read *Joy of Cooking*, like to find out how to boil water, *boom*. There were also a couple of surgical rubber bands stretched back here and there and ending in blades taken from carpet-cutting utility knives, all hung at eye level.

And every light bulb in the whole house had been drilled and tapped and filled with black powder and copper BB's or gasoline and laundry soap. Turn on the light and *bang*, instant napalm or instant shrapnel.

In the umbrella holder by the front door Smiley had gotten cute, and it took me twenty minutes just to figure out what I was looking at. Finally I identified them and used some tape to make them harmless: a pair of cyanide dispensers, used in the States to kill coyotes and wolves. Push down on here and powdered cyanide would come shooting out over there, *poof*, a cloud of dust. And if it worked on wolves it would work on a person.

The pièce de résistance was in the basement, and I almost missed it. I was exhausted by the time I reached the basement but I couldn't stop.

If you ignored the trip wire at the top of the stairs and the gasoline-filled liquor bottles packed around the water heater, the basement was clear. The water heater was an old trick, when the boob(y) comes home, he turns on the hot water (which he will do at some point), which lowers the amount of water in the tank, which makes the tank fill, and the heater turn on. And when the heater turns on the flames touch the wicks you've set up and *boom*.

I was feeling insulted that Smiley had tried that on me when I knelt down and noticed the furnace itself, sitting there, untouched. Why untouched? It would be the only thing in the house that hadn't been gimmicked.

With trembling hands I took the cover off the furnace and looked down into the pan that was not part of any furnace ever built.

"Shit."

He had rigged the furnace to kill everything in my house. Everything, Fred and Claire and me. It would have killed Renfield and Thor and every insect and spider that dwelled in the dark corners of the basement and every mouse in the wainscoting. And then it would kill anyone who came to check on the bodies. And those who were not killed would suffer from permanent and irreversible brain and neurological damage.

I thought very hard and realized that all the rest of the traps were designed to distract from the main one. And I felt a little bit of awe about Smiley's work ethic.

"Shit."

Hate is sometimes a mild word.

It made me wonder about Marie, about whether Smiley was stalking her right now, setting her up.

#45

I loaded the backpack with the stuff Smiley had left for me, the grenades and the razors, the cartridges and the other implements of destruction, and when it was full I found a suitcase and filled that too. In the basement I picked up the Bionic Ear and a few useful tools and packed them away as well and left, this time by the front door.

I had the backpack and shoulder bag slung and the suitcase in my left hand. In my right hand was one of Smiley's hand grenades with the tape removed and only my fingers holding the spoon down. So if he showed up and shot me I would drop the bomb and *boom*. Or if he showed up and tried to talk to me I could lob it at him and *boom*. And then I could pull the gun and shoot the shit out of whatever was left. Three blocks from home I stopped at a phone booth and called for a cab. When it arrived I climbed in and re-taped the bomb in my pocket without taking it out. We headed downtown to Osborne Village, where I would wait until dark to climb under the bridge and dump the various bad things in the Assiniboine River.

When the time came I threw everything else away except for the three hand grenades. Smiley had taken the pins with him, so I used steel finishing nails as replacements, bending them into place for security. Then I re-taped the grenades with more duct tape and those went into the shoulder bag. I found a bench in that gloriously bohemian part of town and sat there to think some more. So far I wasn't doing too well on that front, but maybe I'd be lucky.

Where was Smiley and what was he doing right now? And what were his future plans?

My brain was turning up nothing so I went back to basics. Advice drilled into me over an entire career as a criminal: first you wait and watch. And if that doesn't work, make a plan and follow it. And if that doesn't work, do something, anything. Because another rule is that it's better to do something than nothing. The coordinator of a prison-run anger management course had put it thusly: when in danger, or in doubt, run in circles, scream and shout. It had been ten years since I'd taken the course and I wondered if he knew to what use his advice was being put.

So it was back to basics and thinking about what Smiley had done that I knew about. He had shot Tracey and Louis and Samantha and her boyfriend.

Again, why?

With criminals one rule of understanding their behaviour is to follow the money. Always follow the money. Where was the profit here? My brain hummed along and said no idea.

A friendly woman with short hair and glasses wearing a chef's uniform (including the hat) walked by on Wellington Crescent in front of me and when she saw me she stopped and asked, "Are you okay?"

"I'm fine. Beautiful night, isn't it?"

She looked around and smiled broadly, "Stunning!"

And she walked on and I felt better; a pretty, happy girl is a kind of medicine. However, I was still thinking about Smiley shooting Sam. I needed more information, which meant I needed to find someone who knew something.

My brain thought about all that and agreed with me.

This led me to … the hockey player whom Sam had used as muscle. I should really talk to him, sooner rather then later. So, with a plan, although one I had no idea how to implement, I wandered off to find someplace to sleep. After a brief internal debate I decided that it was unlikely that the lady who thought the night was stunning would let me stay over at her place, which meant a hotel and a cheap one.

The nearest hotel was cheap and loud and wonderful. It even advertised an amateur wet T-shirt night with cash prizes. And the front desk clerk didn't blink when I paid in cash and asked for a room in the quiet half of the hotel, away from the bar. When I'd rigged the window with the rope for a quick escape down from the fourth floor to the back alley, I stashed the knife and grenades and pepper spray in useful places. The gun I kept in my belt, ready to use, not the safest place but the only place I had without wearing the damn holster.

With everything set up I realized I was starving so I ordered from a Papa George's restaurant down the street. The desk clerk had recommended them for Italian-slash-Greek food and he'd also mentioned a Japanese restaurant called Wasabi if I wanted sushi. Actually I wanted both, so I ordered a Greek salad, large meat pizza and a dozen cans of diet Coke from Papa George's and thirty-six pieces of California roll and another dozen cans of ginger ale from Wasabi, because I have a strong and deep and abiding lust for avocado and crab—even fake crab.

It took forty minutes until the delivery guys came and when they did I paid them (and tipped them well—crooks, even ex-crooks, are good tippers; why, I do not know) with my right hand under a towel and the gun therein. But no Smiley. I dragged over the bureau to cover the door and rigged a Bible and some light bulbs to fall on the floor if anyone tried to force the door itself. Then I took off my underwear and socks and rinsed them in the bathroom sink before hanging them on the shower curtain to dry.

I drank the ginger ale with my food and turned on the television and watched a few minutes each of a series of very strange shows. Some of them were supposed to be real, but weren't, and others were supposed to be staged, but didn't seem to have hired real actors. And the whole television universe seemed to be full of hyper-sexed, hyper-beautiful, plastic people with beautiful cars and beautiful houses and no apparent means of support whatsoever. As I watched I felt my mind melt, so finally I panicked and started to flip the channel until I could find a nature documentary. Then I watched David Attenborough narrate *The Blue Planet* about penguins and leopard seals and relaxed as much as I was able. A little later I turned off the lights, including the TV, and rigged some blankets and stuff to look like a body in the bed. A cheap gimmick, but it should attract fire if Smiley decided to become a sniper. Then I crashed on the floor and slept.

The next morning I drank diet Coke (all the caffeine as regular Coke and the chemical sweetener didn't block the uptake of the drug like sugar did) and ate the rest of the sushi liberally dosed with soya sauce and Japanese horseradish. Leaving the bathroom door open I showered and brushed my teeth with a packet of salt from Papa George's.

With that done I reached the point of greatest danger and

cleaned the gun, emptying the magazine of its copper shells while wearing a pair of gloves. I kept one of the Soviet grenades right by my hip, ready to throw. Then I reloaded the gun, put a shell into the chamber, put the pin back into the grenade and turned the TV back on, this time hunting for local news reports, since I had another two hours before I had to check out.

I was not surprised to find out that the shooting of Sam and boyfriend still topped the news. While I was considering what to do next, the solution to the earlier problem, how to find the hockey player, came to me. I packed up the remainder of the food and the weaponry, put the room back together, and then checked out, buying a brand new baseball hat in the hotel gift shop as a disguise on the way out.

#46

There was an Internet cafe down on Corydon, within walking distance, so I kept to residential streets and watched for Smiley or anyone else I recognized. I had the two bags and I kept my right hand loose at my side ready to pull the gun.

I was ready for Smiley to pop out and start shooting. I was also ready for a car to drive over across the sidewalk and slam through me. Frankly, I was ready for just about anything I could imagine and a few other things as well.

When I found the right address I walked up to the second floor and rented access to the Internet for the princely sum of one dollar for ten minutes. I figured I was fairly safe; whenever Smiley had heard of me using the Net, it had been at a library, which might make him focus his attentions there. When I checked my new e-mail address I found a note from sexy&beatch147@ that read "Here. Missing you."

Made me feel good to know someone gave a rat's ass whether I was dead or alive. "Hi Hon." I typed slowly with two fingers. "Give me a sign that means something so I know you are you."

Then I went to work on another database and twenty minutes later I had the address and phone number of Smiley's Vancouver lawyer. I copied that down along with the numbers of Winnipeg's Crime Stoppers and the number of Mildred Pennyworth, one of Winnipeg's dumbest television reporters. Who, by the way, had truly fantastic breasts, which had nothing to do with why the cops liked to talk with her. And it was definitely not the reason thousands of Winnipeggers liked to watch her bobbling along every night at 6:00 and 11:00.

Back on Corydon I pulled on a pair of gloves and found a telephone booth far from any bank, convenience store, or indeed any place that might have a camera that might be surveilling me, if that was a word. Then phone call number one went to the local Crime Stoppers, known amongst cons throughout the country as one-eight-hundred-squeal. When a man answered I pretended I was James T. Kirk and made. Every. Word. Its. Own. Sentence. In the best *Star Trek* tradition.

"Hi! Can I report a crime here?"

The voice came back immediately, smooth, professional, a little suspicious and absolutely untrustworthy.

"If you have a crime to report you should call the 911 emergency line."

"Can I do that and then phone you guys and ask for a reward?"

The voice was silenced while he ran his mind over what I'd said. Crime Stoppers was supposed to involve the public in fighting crime, and towards that end they had a policy of anonymity. You called, gave your information, they gave you a number, and when a conviction was obtained then you received your payment. The money came from donations to the charity; however, the size of the reward was at the discretion of the board governing the organization. But if they were informed before a crime was reported to the police, what could they do? What would they do? Would telling them something like that make them accessories after the fact? I suddenly realized that I didn't know the answers; perhaps I was committing a crime right now by calling them before the crime was reported to the police.

The guy on the phone said, "Ahhhh?"

I may have backed myself into some kind of corner, so instead I said, "Never mind." And hung up. "Crap."

Picking up my bags I went downtown looking for another phone. When I found a good one I phoned Mildred Pennyworth's station and asked to talk to her assistant. After a brief wait I was connected with a young woman who talked very fast indeed.

"Yes? Yes? Yes?"

"Hi! I want to give a tip about a double murder to Mildred."

"What? We're not the police, you know? We're not that crime dog, you know?"

"You mean Scruff McGruff and that's a US thing—the whole Let's Take a Bite Out of Crime. Did I mention that what I wanted to tell you is an exclusive?"

"What? What? What?"

"The police don't know about it yet. No one does."

Her voice dropped to a low intimate buzz, "Did you do it?"

I dropped my voice too. "No. Anyhow, in the following apartment you will find the bodies of ..."

I gave her the details and hung up, walking around the corner and changing to a new baseball hat before going to find a new phone booth. On the way I bought some more hats and a very cheap blue windbreaker two sizes too large so I could wear it over my own jacket. When I finally did find a pay phone with no cameras around I was way downtown near the Red River, which made me nervous because the river cut off my retreat and limited my options. A worst-case scenario was that I called Smiley's lawyer, who had a direct line to the cops, who proceeded to surround the area I was calling from with many, many cops. And then I'd end up arrested with a gun and three hand grenades in my backpack, which all would translate into me going away into a small place for a long, long time. I thought it through, took the chance, made my call, and talked to a professional voice.

"Chang and McQuaid. How may we help you?"

"My name is Smiley, shit, Hershel. I need to talk to my lawyer. It's an emergency."

I tried to make my voice hoarse and coarsen it. It didn't have to sound like Smiley; it just had to not sound like me.

"Your lawyer?"

"McQuaid."

There was a brief pause and then a man's voice came on, "Smiley! Nicetohearfromyou." He ran the words together fast and then said slowly, "Where's my money?"

"Coming. I need you to give me the address you gave me last time."

"Can't do it."

"Why not?"

There were the sounds of a computer keyboard being lightly manipulated and then, "Because she's dead. Shot a lot. Would you like to talk to me about something?"

Translation from lawyerese was, would I like to turn myself in so the plea-bargaining could start?

"I had nothing to do with that ..."

"Uh-huh." Flat, unbelieving.

"... but I need her address. I lost my copy."

"No. Not that I ever gave you that in the past. And not that I'm admitting I ever had it in the first place." Smart lawyer was he, playing the game for whatever listening and recording device might be attached. I figured he would have Samantha's address; Smiley had mentioned that his lawyer was bent when he'd first shown up on my doorstep. Most bad guys don't automatically know other bad guys. We have to have lines of communication and bent lawyers are great lines of communication because they can hide behind client confidentiality.

And I was betting that maybe the lawyer had been the person to connect Sam with Smiley. Which meant he would probably know where Sam had lived before her untimely death.

"I need the address. Now. And of course you never gave it to me before."

That should please him if anyone was recording it.

"No can do."

Stubborn prick and I was getting tired. "In North Korea today they have a simple method of interrogation. First they ask you a question. Then they use crazy glue to hold YOUR ..." I said it loud "... hand flat on a wooden cutting board and then use a ball-peen hammer to crush the first joint on YOUR ..." loud again "... little finger, the one nearest the nail. Then they wait five minutes, timed by a clock on the table in front of you, and then they use the same hammer to crush the first joint on YOUR ring finger. And so on. Then they move on to the next joint further down and do it again."

"Are you ..."

I cut him off, "There are fifteen joints on each hand ..."

"... THREATENING me!"

He roared into the phone and I went on, "... and no one's made it past four joints on the first hand that I've heard of. They all cooperate before the thumb is reached."

"You piece-of-shit ..."

"Wanna see how long you last? You wanna break the record? Now should I stop and visit a hardware store before I come to your home? Or should I stop at a bank?"

"I see. You're threatening me."

"Yes. So tell me what I want to know, before this moves to a place neither of us wants to go."

McQuaid thought about it for a long time. And then he gave me the address and slammed the phone down as though he was punishing me. I hung the phone up and listened to the echoes and wondered if the lawyer would phone the cops right away and then decided no. He could always plead he'd been frightened of me and that coloured his decision. Frankly, he struck me as the kind of guy who'd take the safe way every time.

#47

Ah, burglary! It was ten o'clock at night and I was right back at it for the second (or was it third?) time in a couple of days after years, positively years, of abstinence.

I thought about it and realized I was lying to myself. I had broken into several locations when Walsh had been busting my ass that spring. Which meant it had been months since I'd broken into anywhere and now I was breaking into Samantha's house, a simple bungalow right near the edge of town along Lagimodiere Avenue in the east end of the city. I stared at the place and weighed options as I walked up the sidewalk and tried to work out some basic assumptions. First, the house would be purchased and not rented. Second, the bungalow would not be located anywhere near where Sam was working. Third, there would be something interesting in the house that the cops had missed.

And I could make these assumptions because Samantha was a career criminal and a good one. She would buy and not rent because cops could always pressure the owner of a house (if she was renting) to allow them access without having to deal with those pesky search warrants. "After all, Your Honour, we had the permission of the owner of the house and therefore could look." The second thing she would do is live far away from where she worked because you do not want to live right beside where you work, it is too dangerous. See the rule of crooks and hustlers titled "Thou shalt not shit in thine own nest." And the third assumption was actually supplied by my own ego and superego; I believed Sam would hide things in her house, hopefully including the hockey player's address. And I also believed that the cops would not have found them because they weren't bad guys and didn't think like bad guys.

Check out the bible, "Set a thief to catch a thief." Or something like that.

I used the Bionic Ear, standing in front of the house and fumbling in my bag while the machine did its job of amplifying noise. I didn't hear anything so I put the machine back in the bag and then walked up to the front door and in. Sam had had a good lock, but the cops had used a portable ram to knock the door entirely off its steel frame, so all I had to do was pry loose the padlock they'd used to secure the place. And then I was inside in the silence and the dark with my fingers resting lightly on the butt of the pistol.

Living room, bedroom, kitchen, pantry, dining nook, and bathroom on the first floor. Recreation room, spare room, laundry room, and bathroom in the basement. Attached garage off the kitchen. Concrete pad patio off the dining nook.

Nobody inside, but many signs of a search, including emptied drawers and papers strewn about. I closed all the drapes, turned on the lights, and started going over everything millimetre by millimetre.

In the basement bathroom I found one hiding place concealed behind a very large medicine cabinet in the perfectly finished bathroom. What attracted my attention was the realization that the cabinet did not match the one that was installed in the upstairs bathroom; it was a lot bigger and newer. Using a screwdriver to remove the screws allowed me to pull the whole unit up and put it in the shower stall. Behind the cabinet was the hole that had held the original cabinet cut between the two-by-four frames of the wall itself.

There was nothing there, just a thin layer of dust and smears of grease. That probably meant that someone had gotten there first, probably Smiley, and he had found the cache and cleaned it out. Which might explain the hand grenades, if Sam had been keeping them for a rainy day. I considered the cache and liked it; if the cops brought in metal detectors, the steel frame of the cabinet and the steel nails in the walls would mess up their readings. All in all it was a great hiding place.

With that found I kept looking; odds were that Sam wouldn't stop with one cache, just in case the first was discovered. But I found nothing until I reached the backyard, which was surrounded by a wooden fence almost two metres high. It was there that I found six cast-iron flower pots along the edge of the lawn and the porch, each pot of the same design as the ones in the house. Which meant what, that Sam and boyfriend rotated their plants from the inside to the outside? Nothing suspicious there, but an interesting idea I decided to remember to use when Claire and I were back in our house.

Just to be thorough, I picked up the first pot and found that there was a metre-and-a-half-long sealed length of PVC pipe twenty centimetres in diameter pushed down into a round hole. So the pot was there to distract any metal detectors, and the pipe was the cache. With a little elbow grease I managed to pull the pipes out one at a time and unscrew the tops to gain access.

Packed inside the first PVC pipe driven into the ground was a heavily greased Chinese SKS rifle and a bandolier of thirty rounds of military hardball ammunition, each with its primer carefully covered in a dab of grease. The SKS was a good choice for an emergency rifle, cheap, reliable, powerful, small, light, and, most importantly, it fell into the non-restricted weapon category of the Canadian Criminal Code, not the restricted or prohibited weapon category which translates into longer jail time.

The next four pipes were full of freeze-dried-food packages, a water purification kit, a Second Chance Deep Cover bullet-resistant vest that looked like a T-shirt, a big first-aid kit, an assortment of tools and other odds and ends that your average paranoid thief might need. And the last pipe held a rolled-up fisherman's vest with many pockets. I pulled it out and patted it down to find an even thousand dollars in mixed Canadian and US currency along with five dollars in quarters. Also driver's licences and social insurance cards for Sam and Charles, her boyfriend. Then a big ring of keys, granola bars and beef jerky, tubes of vitamins, Aspirin, Demerol, and a vial of cocaine. Then some band-aids, antibiotic gel, a good quality Leatherman multi tool (which looked like my Swiss Army knife on steroids). And the pièce de résistance, a Ziploc baggie with a small address book and pencil.

I was impressed; the pipe was a great cache. You could buy them in varying sizes and lengths at any hardware store along with the tools to cut them, the glue to seal them, and the end caps. You could also buy a posthole digger, which made installing them relatively easy, and the pipes were pretty much impervious to the weather. And if you stored your illegal stuff outside your home, it made the prosecutor's job that much harder, as long as you didn't leave fingerprints.

"Your Honour, I had no idea those things were hidden near my house because they certainly were not in my house ..."

Right? Wonder if the judge would buy it.

I kept the bullet-resistant vest, the money, the Leatherman knife (which I had lusted after in the past), and a plastic jar of dry roasted peanuts. With difficulty I left the cocaine and Demerol, although the monkey on my back felt it would be a great idea to take that with me.

I might need it.

I might want it.

It might be a clue.

I took the rifle and bandolier into the basement, where Sam and her boyfriend had kept their tools, found a hacksaw and a heavy-duty file, and took twenty minutes to saw off a chunk of the barrel and the buttstock. That left me with a seventy-centimetre-long, fundamentally inaccurate monstrosity that I could tuck into my backpack. Fully loaded, the gun held ten 7.62x39 mm rounds of ammo, all solid military bullets that would go through an engine block without slowing.

Then I left, walking the six blocks south until I found a bus stop, and headed back downtown on the last bus running. On the bus I went through the little notebook and found a long list of names, phone numbers, e-mail addresses, and even a few physical addresses. Most of them, however, were area codes from Toronto, Montreal, and Vancouver; only two were in Winnipeg.

After another lousy night in a new lousy hotel I was ready to check out my addresses. The first one was the hotel where Smiley and I had braced Sam and company. The second address was in a run-down housing development downtown, rows of brick houses built side by side and maintained by the Manitoba Housing Authority. I looked at it curiously and went off to find a different library where I could use the Internet. In the e-mail box was a brief note: "Six reasons you never told me about." Smiling, I typed "Wild pig." Then I typed some more: "Our friend came back and gimmicked our crib, trashed it, could've hurt the next person in. It's fixed now. Stay loose but stay away from it."

After I closed the computer down I went back to the Housing Authority and walked past the address I was interested in. In the parking space right in front of the brick building was a big, ugly purple T-bird car, so I wandered a hundred metres away and found a bench in a tiny, decrepit park. No one was there, so I took out the binoculars I'd gotten from the surplus store and watched to see what would happen next.

At a little past noon the hockey player came out of the front door and carefully locked the door behind him. He had his right arm in a cast, from the tip of his fingers all the way to his shoulder and then across to the other shoulder, with a brace on his neck as well. He also had his left foot bandaged and walked with an aluminum cane as he moved down the sidewalk towards the T-bird. I still didn't know his name, but I was up and moving, weighed down with my packs but moving pretty fast on adrenaline and anger.

"Hey!"

He turned slowly to see me coming across the parking lot and sputtered, "You!"

His left hand reached into his jacket and pulled out something. Before it had cleared his pocket, though, I opened the jacket and showed him the butt of the pistol. His fingers opened slowly and whatever it was fell to the ground with a clank.

"Now don't move."

I moved over to him carefully, watching his hands and his feet and his eyes for any hints of ill intention. The casts didn't impress me; Ted Bundy had worn a fake cast to elicit help and sympathy from the women he was going to rape and murder, and many true crime writers had written about that, so maybe the casts were real and maybe they weren't. Up close the hockey player stank with the reek of old sweat, unwashed dirt, reefer smoke, and stale beer. He hadn't shaved for a long time, either, and his fingers trembled as he swayed from side to side.

"Drop the cane, too."

"I need it to walk."

I shrugged; time to be a bad guy. "If you don't drop the fucking cane, I assure you you'll never walk anywhere again. If I need you to walk, I'll give it back. Drop the cane."

He dropped it and I risked glancing at the object he'd dropped. It was a short-barrelled cop's flashlight; good for beating someone's head in or shining light. Either/or.

"We need to talk."

"Fuck you."

He said it mildly and without passion, and his eyes glanced all around the parking lot looking for someone to help him. But there was no one. I tried the carrot. "I'll give you a thousand dollars."

"What?"

"A thousand dollars for you to talk to me, right now."

"Cash?" He didn't trust me.

"Cash."

"That's not a lot."

That was bullshit on his part. A grand was a lot of money to a penny-ante bad guy, so I showed him the wad of money I'd pulled out of Samantha's yard. "A grand. Half in US funds, half in Canadian. Nothing bigger than a twenty. Nothing marked and nothing funny."

He looked at it and swallowed. "What do you want to know about?"

"Smiley. What he's doing right now."

His face soured and then he nodded and reached for his cane without asking. Had I been a little less trusting I would have shot him but he never even realized that.

"Okay. But not for a grand." And now, the bargaining. "I want two grand."

If I paid him that I'd only have about eight hundred left. Which really didn't matter to me, because if I ran low I could always find more. There's too much money in the world, they print more every day, and that was always a comfort to me when I thought of my eventual old age.

"Sure. Give me the keys, I'll drive. We'll go someplace quiet."

He did and I dropped my bags in the tiny luggage area behind the seats. Then I drove us just out of town heading west to the Assiniboia Downs race track, which was closed for the season. When we were in the parking lot I gave him the money. He licked his lips, and I could see anger and sneakiness at war in his eyes.

"And the gun ... I want the gun ... I don't trust you. If I'm holding the gun, that means you don't have any plans to turn on me."

So I handed him the gun and sat there, turned in the seat to face him with my right hand on the steering wheel and my left in my jacket pocket. The hockey player checked that the chamber was loaded, although it was hard to do with only one hand. Then he rested it on his knee and pointed it at the centre of my stomach. I inhaled involuntarily.

He gloated, "You dumb fuck."

"Uh-huh."

"You cockless bastard." He was enjoying this.

"Sure."

"You ignorant, spineless freak."

"Sure. Now about Smiley ..."

"I'm not telling you anything ... after what you did to me I'm gonna pop a cap in you. I'm gonna cash you out."

Rappers. Love their influence and deep reach into culture. "Okay. You've got me. Why don't you tell me about Smiley first, you know, to torment me with all the knowledge you have. Show me you're way ahead of me."

"I'm just going to kill you ..."

This was getting boring. "No, you're not."

He looked a little confused, "I'm not?"

"Right. Because of this ..." I pulled my hand out of my coat pocket and showed him the hand grenade I was holding. "See? No pin. You shoot me and the bomb goes *boom*."

He still looked puzzled so I went on, " ... and I'm wearing a bulletproof vest, so the gun won't work."

The hockey player's hand twitched a little and I went on, " ... and if you try to point it at my face I'll drop the grenade anyway and take my chances. Bet ya everything you own, will own, and have owned, that I can move faster than you can. Considering you're in an assortment of casts."

Very carefully he put the gun on my calf and withdrew his hand while smiling like a beaten dog. When his hand was in his lap I let go of the steering wheel and reached under my left arm.

"Hey!"

The Cold Steel knife slid out of its sheath easily and I brought it up and down fast. His scream filled the empty parking lot as the knife punched through the meat of his hand and pinned his left hand through the back of his hand to his left thigh. There was surprisingly little blood and I waited a moment before pulling the knife out. I wiped it carefully on the lapel of his leather jacket and put it away before picking up the pistol. When he stopped screaming I shook my head: "Now, don't do it again."

"You bastard …"

"Shut. Up." He shut up and I went on. "Now talk to me about Smiley."

"Fuck you!"

"Or I'll hurt you some more. And take the money back. And then you'll talk to me anyway."

He swore at me for awhile and then finally thought it through and decided to talk.

#48

The hockey player's story.

"Okay. Okay. Smiley tracked me down at the hospital and told me that he was taking over from Sam."

"Was this before or after Sam was killed?"

He paused for a second and touched the tip of his tongue to his upper lip. "After."

"Bullshit. Try again."

He looked at me and opened and closed his mouth, "How did you ...?"

"Simple. He wouldn't kill Sam until he had everything set up."

"Oh. It was before. He just showed in my hospital room before I was released and gave me some money ..."

The hockey player froze for a second while he tried to figure out whether to lie about the money on the plus side or on the minus.

"Don't bother lying. Just go on."

"... anyhow he gave me $5000 cash and told me Sam was

out and he was in. Then he said he could either shoot me in the face or I could work with him, then he showed me a gun and told me to choose. So I made my choice."

"Fine. What did he want you to do?"

The hockey player tried to shrug but he'd forgotten about his injuries and screamed briefly before starting to whimper. At his insistence I opened the bottle of Tylenol 3's he had in his jacket pocket. He took six dry and choked them down with difficulty. As I watched, his pupils became really big and he started talking faster and faster.

"The same thing as before, nothing changed. I was going to boss the Saint Boniface house, he was going to set up new routes to the States, and everyone would make a mint."

The hockey player was stoned and maybe in shock, too, from the knife in the thigh. He took more pills and I waited for them to kick in before gesturing for him to continue. "What kind of route?"

"He was talking about a new one in the eastern corner of the province. Run by some do-gooders."

I didn't want to ask any more questions. He might put something together and then contact Smiley.

"Okay, that's it then."

The hockey player had big eyes. "I won't talk to anyone."

Right. Once a guy started to betray people, it was hard to stop. Something to do with a self-fulfilling prophecy about how bad and worthless they were maybe, or that's what some cops thought. Most cons just had the opinion that you never trusted a rat, never, ever, not once you found out what they were. And that was why the prisons had things like protective custody, jail within jail, to keep the rats from getting shanked, burned, or turned. Shanked meaning stabbed, burned meaning Molotov cocktail, and turned meaning rape and prostitution.

"I know, man. You won't talk to anyone. You won't say a word."

He looked at me with hope and fear and I thought about Smiley and my booby-trapped house. And I thought about the right decision, which would be to kill the hockey player and dump his body in the river with a couple of hundred kilos of iron weights wired in useful spots and some punctures to vent the gas build-up. And then I thought about how hard it would be if Smiley knew that I knew about the route he had inherited.

"Yeah. Ask anyone. I know how to keep my mouth shut."

I laughed hard at that and used the barrel of the pistol to shatter his lower jaw into pebbles.

I dumped the hockey player out on the sidewalk by the Children's Emergency door of the Health Sciences Centre on William Street. I wasn't a complete prick, though; I left the two grand in his wallet just to keep him honest and focused on his end of the deal. Five minutes later I sprayed the inside of his car down with a bottle of industrial cleaner I picked up at a 7-11 and left it parked, unlocked, in a handicapped spot in front of a restaurant. From whence it would soon be towed away to the nearest impound lot to further screw up any kind of forensics. With that done I walked away.

The next morning, after another night in another cheap hotel, I woke up with a vague disquiet in the back of my mind. After half an hour I remembered that this was the earliest day that the Province of British Columbia might be sending Smiley his birth certificate. That thought made me feel a little guilty and also rekindled my rage, which stayed with me as I ate a very toxic breakfast at the diner attached to the hotel. Then I took a cab to the Cabelas sporting goods store in St. James and bought an olive green duffle bag, a cheap compass, and a Beeman break-open air rifle with an already installed 4x32 power scope. Since it fired tiny 4.5-millimetre pellets at speeds under 150 metres per second I didn't need a firearms licence, it went into a cheap plastic gun case which also held a tin of 500 lead pellets. As an afterthought I also bought a ridiculously expensive sleeping bag, just in case I had to make a night of it. From that store I went to a Government of Canada office to buy a full-sized 1:50,000-scale map of the border. As I did so the guy behind the counter joked, "Smuggling, huh?"

"Yep. Is that illegal?"

"I don't think so, not anymore. Laws change every day."

I remembered a shirt a friend had bought out of the back of a *National Lampoon* magazine years ago. It had a drawing of a clipper ship crewed by topless women and surrounded by floating bales of grass and the caption read, "Smuggling! It's more than a job, it's an adventure!" I told the counter guy that and we both laughed.

Outside I looked the map over. It was detailed enough to show houses and barns in some locations and it was recent, only two years old. Then I was back at another downtown hotel for some packing. With careful work I managed to empty both bags and store everything I'd been carrying in the new bag. And those bags, which someone might be remembering if I was unlucky, went into the garbage bin behind the hotel. With that done I unpacked the sleeping bag and glared at it. It had cost over $180 with tax and theoretically it was rated as good to down to minus thirty degrees. I had cheated and bought some chemical heaters as well, the kind you twist to activate and then they keep your hands warm for an hour or two. Mostly I had bought those because I did not trust the sleeping bag.

Also they were cool.

When it was all I packed away I ordered some fast food chicken and went to sleep while watching another documentary, this one about skyscrapers in Singapore.

#49

It's an important rule, if you want to be a criminal: don't be one at night; it's too obvious. That was a rule I broke a lot. However, don't be one at night if you can avoid it. Instead do as I do and commit your felonies at ten in the morning. Which theory forced me into the driver's seat of a stolen Jeep Cherokee parked across the street from the Saint Boniface drug house Smiley had probably inherited from the dead Sam at ten in the morning. My luggage was all back at the hotel, except for the fully loaded sks carbine, which sat on the floor of the truck, covered by a copy of the *Winnipeg Sun*. I waited for a school bus to pass and then pressed the electronic window controls, lowering the passenger's side window, and pointed the carbine out, braced with my gloved hand around the top of the receiver to absorb the kick.

Boom!

First shot through the front door but way high. I adjusted and fired three more shots. Then two through the small window on the right and four more through the one on the left.

And then I drove away as the neighbours, cell phones in hand, were still rushing out and phoning 911 as fast as they could.

When the cops arrived they'd go through the house automatically to check it out and they'd be sure to find something incriminating. Drugs or weapons or something else. That would give Smiley a couple of extra headaches and, maybe, result in the arrest of some of his new crew. Either that or they'd run off and hide somewhere quiet.

I could dream, right?

The Jeep I left in a side street two blocks away with the gun back under the newspaper.

As for me, I took a bus back to the hotel to collect my things and went to visit Marie.

When I climbed off the bus near Marie's house I made a quick call and she answered on the first ring. "Marie? This is Monty. How are things?"

"Things are great. Just great."

There was a long pause and then I asked how her work was going.

"The work is going great."

She didn't sound right. She didn't ask how Claire was. She didn't ask about Fred. She didn't want to tell me in detail about what was happening.

Finally she said reluctantly, "Maybe you should go out to the cabin. See how Don and Al are getting along."

I said sure and there was another long pause and then I said good-bye and hung up. Two minutes later I was outside her house in the back alley with the Bionic Ear pointed at her kitchen window. The blinds and curtains all served to dampen the sound, but I could hear the conversation fairly well because it practically involved screaming. In French. First Marie and then Eloise. After a few moments I heard the name Smiley repeated twice and then a new voice spoke quite calmly, this one a cultured, somewhat upper-class English male voice. "I don't understand. Why can't you tell your friend about that animal?"

Marie spoke and I could barely hear her, "Because he'll kill Don and Al."

"So you'll let him walk into a … "

The voices became more indistinct as they left the room but that was fine with me. I could fill in the last word myself and it was "trap."

With option number one cancelled I went downtown and walked two blocks to a drop-in centre for maladjusted teens, where I borrowed a computer and wrote Claire and told her that I loved her.

When I was done I typed the word *love* and realized how ineffective it looked. There were all kinds of love: a man loves a cigar, a woman loves her shoes, a dog loves his bone, the politician loves to argue, and a barfly loves to fight. There was Agape and Eros, spirit and sex. There was the Christian god who loved man so much he sacrificed his only begotten son and there was the Indian Shiva who loved the dance. And then there were the other kinds of love …

I had to leave. Another block away was a food store cunningly hidden in the basement of the Hudson's Bay. After stocking up on bottled water, crackers, corned beef, batteries, and toilet paper, I was ready to party. As a final treat I ate a big meal of steak and eggs at a nearby hotel and then started looking for a new ride, which I found down towards the river where the big, expensive condominiums grew like mushrooms in shit. Most of the inhabitants were at work, earning the lu-cre to pay for their condos, and I slipped into the garages eas-ily, waiting for the drivers to leave and then entering as the doors shut. In the third garage I found what I was looking for on the second level down, where a rack of motorcycles were arrayed, wrapped in tarps and waiting for better weather. And all of them racked neatly far away from the nearest security camera.

I could pick and choose and finally selected a BMW K1200S bike, a big monster with legs, enough to outrun most cops if I had to do so. The bike could pull 275 kph on a good road. BMW made great bikes, and the one I picked had a multigear transmission like a car, not the chain assembly that most bikes had. That meant that the bike was a lot quieter than normal bikes. It was silver in colour with all sorts of options, most of which I was uninterested in, but it also had an antitheft device that puzzled me for six minutes and a huge pannier in the back which was locked and took me eight seconds to open.

Inside the pannier the owner had thankfully left a helmet (kind of him or her), a map of Manitoba, and a spare set of keys, because people are stupid like that sometimes. With the tarp tucked away I fired the beast up and backed out slowly. The nineteen-litre gas tank was almost empty but there was enough to take me away from downtown if I could make it out of the garage.

So I parked the bike and broke into the next car. It was easy enough because the owner had forgotten to close the passenger's window completely and had left the access card tucked into the sun visor, so I borrowed that, closed the win-dow, locked the door, and left. Five minutes later I pulled up to a decrepit gas station in Saint Boniface, an older one not owned by any of the big companies. A few minutes later the tank was full and I was gone, blowing down the highway with the duffle bag strapped across the back of the bike and the helmet firmly in place over my face.

#50

Twice on my way I stopped at rest stops and examined my map. On the reserve, north of the fishing camp (as far as I could tell), was an access road that led to a burned-out homestead, which was my target. From there it was about three klicks to the camp. When I reached the homestead I found the burned-out ruins of a farmhouse and two barns, with the ground packed flat by tires and feet over the years. As I drove through the yard I saw lots of empty beer cans, used condoms, and cigarette butts, the signs of young love. I passed a pair of underwear knotted together, a pair of Fruit of the Loom Y-fronts, very small, and a battered pair of lavender panties in size extra large, both baked into the mud.

I tried not to think too much about whatever story they told.

It took five minutes to wheel the bike behind the farmhouse and down a matted trail that led to a collapsed outhouse, where I left it; a present to whomever. Two big steps took me into heavy, cold brush. I waited and listened and looked but heard nothing. After an hour I ate some food, drank some water, and left the duffle bag with most of my stuff still in it under a fallen pine tree.

Before I went I patted myself down. I had the Bionic Ear and extra batteries which might, might, give me an edge. I also had the compass and the map, in case. The bulletproof vest was on under my dark thief's jacket and I had two grenades (with the spoons taped down to prevent accidents) in my jacket pockets. I had the pistol, locked and loaded, in its holster on my hip with the flap buttoned down so I wouldn't lose it, and beside it was the Leatherman tool with its assortment of blades. I had the Cold Steel knife strapped to my right arm, the twine cutter on my finger, a can of pepper spray in my back pocket, and two highway flares in my right-hand coat pocket.

And if none of that worked on Smiley, I could call him names.

I slung on the air rifle and I was ready to go. Grenades and pistol ready and the Bionic Ear pointed ahead, I moved very slowly and carefully through the fallen trees and underbrush.

Every few minutes I stopped, and when I didn't move at all, life came back to the spaces around me. Gradually the animals returned. There were red-winged blackbirds in the bushes, grey squirrels in the trees, prairie chickens moving through assorted low vegetation and bushes, and other things rustling and moving carefully. Once there was even a deer who looked offended I had gotten so close.

But no Smiley and no anyone else, and I kept crawling along.

When I stopped to eat in a clearing a tiny prairie chicken came out of a wild rose bush about three feet from me and stared at me blankly. Then it looked down and ate a fleck of corned-beef gristle I'd spat out onto my pants leg and cocked its head in silence, observing me with a black-on-black eye. After a long time it turned and vanished and I was alone again.

Six hours later I reached the edge of the forest and could see the fishing camp about 100 metres away across the water. With that established on my map I crawled back into the forest a bit and started heading west, towards the base of the peninsula. When I got there I circled around to the edge of the road just out of range of the alarm sensors. While I caught my breath I unslung the air rifle and loaded it, jacking the barrel down to open the breech and sliding in the single bright lead pellet.

It was early in the afternoon and the scope made everything nice and clear. It only took two minutes to find one of the motion sensors I had installed. The air rifle was accurate but not that powerful, so it took five shots to reduce the first sensor to shards of plastic and I moved up underneath it (avoiding the trip wires) to start scanning for the next sensor. That one took longer to find but I did eventually and shot it to pieces as well, each shot being heralded by an almost silent click of the air being released from the reservoir. As I moved I used the Bionic Ear constantly to check what was going on around me, and it took me almost until dusk before I was through to the edge of the camp itself.

From where I was I could see a small black sedan parked in the lot in front of the cabin and two of the camera mounts covering the space. Five shots into each camera took care of both of them and the Bionic Ear finally started to pick up movement and words in the nearest cabin:

Smiley: "Where the fuck is he?"

Don: "Why don't you go out and see?"

Al: "Or you could always go fuck yourself. That's an option."

Sounds of a blow—waiting had to be stressing Smiley. Or else he wouldn't have lost his temper. He knew I was coming, it was what he would do and he knew I would be somewhere outside working and waiting.

And inside he would be seeing his cameras go out one at a time and there was also a good chance one of Sam's crew would have called him from the city after I'd shot up the house in Saint Boniface.

He had to know I was outside.

I looked at the second cabin, which was maybe fifteen metres away from me, and thought like Smiley for a minute: he would keep all his bargaining chips in one place, there would be no hostages in the other cabin, they'd be useless there.

Actually they'd be useless no matter what he did; having Don or Al there would not stop me.

I laid the air rifle down and turned the Bionic Ear off first. Then I took one of the grenades out of my pocket, unrolled the tape from the spoon, pulled the pin (which made the spoon flip off somewhere), and then pitched it through the porch of the second cabin.

About three seconds later it blew up, scattering splinters for about thirty metres in all directions.

"Shit!" Smiley yelled from the first cabin. I turned the Bionic Ear on in time to hear the rear door slam shut and then I was moving around the cabin. I found Smiley standing in a patch of dandelions and weeds, all sere with the approaching winter.

He was about seven metres away from me and smiling.

#51

S miley ..."

"Monty. Can't say I'm surprised." He sounded calm, almost relaxed. There was time and experience holding us together and apart at the same time. I said his name again and he cocked his head to the side and answered, "That's me."

"How much do you know?"

"Everything. I planted a GPS on Marie's truck and her van. I wired her house for sound. I followed her and you and her two hick sidekicks when they came to town. I know everything so don't try to tell me you have one key piece of knowledge I have to know."

"I wouldn't do that but ..."

He spat and spoke again. "Go ahead, say it."

"Smiley ... what the hell are you wearing?"

His mouth twisted in a grin but his hands didn't move from where they were on his belt and jacket lapel.

"This? It's a rattlesnake-hide necktie. Like it?"

There was a moment of clarity and I could see the scales of

the leather from where I stood and the diamondback design on the short, fat tie. It sat in the middle of his chest framed by a black vest and a dove-grey duster, all leather and all expensive.

"It's certainly memorable."

He shrugged at the compliment and continued in a monotone. "Found a company in the States that made me a replica of Holliday's shoulder holster. Want to see it?"

"No."

"Found me a beauty of a gun too, a Smith & Wesson target revolver. Accurate as all get out."

"Nice to hear."

"A nice piece. Not anything like what Holliday carried but so it goes."

I exhaled through my nose, "You took it out of a dead woman's apartment. After you killed her and her boyfriend."

He ignored that. "I also bought me a genuine Bowie knife. An antique, holds an edge like you wouldn't believe."

"I believe and I don't want to see that either."

A few tiny, tentative flecks of snow fell out of the darkening sky and he kept talking, "I went back to the river. Went swimming and fuck was it cold. Finally found my shotgun, cleaned it up, still works like a charm."

"I believe you. Trust me, I believe you."

He spat moistly. "That's good. I loaded one barrel with a magnesium round, shoots out a lick of fire like a flame thrower, and sets fire to whatever's in front of it while dumping a full load of double-ought buckshot at the same time. The other barrel holds flechettes, military-issue shit, know what those are?"

I knew. Flechettes were tiny heavy metal arrows that would slice right through Kevlar armour and out the other side.

Leaving little bleeding holes behind as they bored through meat and bone. But Smiley was going on. "Of course you do. Not that Holliday had shit like that but if he was around today then he would have."

The wind started to blow and he said something I couldn't hear.

"What?"

"I said, did you like what I did to your house?"

I measured him with my eyes, the way he was standing, the way he held himself, the tension he was under. And it all matched the pressure I was feeling inside, the pressure and the hate. "Yeah, it was great."

Two heartbeats passed and I was in control of the hate again. "I have to say this. Smiley, it's not too late."

"Not too late?"

"Yes. You can put down the guns, walk away."

"You're kidding, right?"

"No."

He stood there and for a minute I thought he was going to go for it, I thought he was going to give it a chance.

"Fuck that! I can't go straight, neither can you, this is what we are."

There was nothing to say to that, but he repeated himself after a moment, as though his answer was a revelation to him, "So fuck that."

"That's not an option."

He laughed but his hands never wavered at his sides and his eyes never moved from mine. "You going to stop me? I'm better than you."

The truth hung between us and he went on. "It's just us right here and now and I'm better than you so you'll be dead if you make me shoot you. And that's where we're at."

I said the words. "So draw. Or you'll be picking daisies, that's what Doc said, right?"

"What did you say?"

"I said, draw."

I kept my hands motionless at my belt until he moved and then I did too.

His left hand flashed across his chest and drew his pistol. His right hand flipped his coat tail back and grabbed the butt of the sawn-down shotgun and pushed it towards me as he thumbed back the hammer.

And while all that was happening the Radom pistol slipped into my right hand and my thumb clicked the safety to off. The gun was coming up and out as Smiley filled the sights and blocked out the reticule. He became the sight and the bullet and the target and I became my index finger squeezing very gently and the trigger started its journey, a third of an inch against about three pounds of pressure.

But I was too late.

The shotgun boomed and his little pistol chirped and my bigger pistol barked and barked and barked as I jumped and fell to the left. Dragon breath blew copper balls into my chest.

The fucker had always been too good for me.

#52

The gunfire echoed away and died and I was on the ground and Smiley was still standing.

"How do you like me now?"

His words were slurred, full of phlegm and blood, laced with pain, but his hands were graceful as he moved towards me, the shotgun falling back under his arm on its string while his fingers manipulated the revolver. Cylinder open, bright brass cartridges tumbling to the ground, lead-headed new bullets sliding into place, clickety-click. I tried to breathe through broken ribs and reached for a new magazine. Smiley's face split wide with a smile through his own pain.

My gun was in my hand and I dumped the magazine and fumbled for a second one out of my jacket pocket. His thumb seated the last bullet and gently closed the cylinder as I was still slapping the new magazine into place. Before I could work the slide Smiley fired twice and my calf exploded into pain and the pistol flew from my hand and landed somewhere behind me. I grabbed my right leg and felt blood well under my fingers as Smiley fired twice more, but I could barely feel the impact.

"Wearing a vest, huh?"

He didn't sound angry, just curious. He gestured with the gun like a magician with a wand and put another round into my left shin. Splinters of bone slicked with more blood showed through my jeans and I grabbed at that wound. He was maybe three metres away and I could see gaping flowers of wounds in his chest and right arm. Blood oozed out and stained his fine clothes, but not enough to stop him.

Smiley winced as he knelt down with ponderous grace and his gun forced me back down until he could kneel on my chest. The noise of my ribs cracking some more was loud and more flakes of snow started to fall out of the sky.

"Any last words? For Claire? Anything I should tell her? When I see her, I mean? Because I do intend to visit her. I do intend to spend some time with her, yes indeed I do."

He leaned back on his heel to brace himself and pressed the long barrel of the pistol into my left eye.

"'Bye."

I could feel the eye being pressed back, almost crushed by the force, and I reached very gently and slowly for his gun hand with my left hand. It was so gentle that Smiley didn't react as my fingers brushed against it. He started to laugh, but it turned into an indrawn hiss when the twine cutter on my middle finger stroked through the meat on the back of his left hand.

With a moist noise the tendons parted. Pinky finger, ring finger, middle finger, forefinger, a long narrow wound greased and lubricated with blood. Without strength his fingers opened and the gun fell onto my face as Smiley leaned forward to scrabble for it with his injured right arm. He was focused on the revolver and didn't notice as my fingertips touched the hilt of the Spike knife on my right wrist. He grabbed the butt of his pistol and I grabbed the barrel with my left hand while I tightened my grip on the knife. For a second we wrestled over the gun and then I drove the knife roundhouse into the side of his neck just above his fine silk collar and that stupid rattlesnake tie.

Smiley's eyes bugged out and he stood up swaying above me and started to die.

But not fast enough.

Never fast enough.

Spasmodically he threw the pistol away and lurched about, fumbling awkwardly for the hilt of the knife in his throat with one hand while the other, the slashed one, pawed at the shotgun under his arm. Blood bubbled from his nose and mouth and almost covered the sound of his thumb cocking the hammers back.

"Asshole."

My voice sounded very far away and I rolled onto my right side and pushed my left leg out through the pain and then rolled and swung back and up as hard as I could. The side of my foot connected with the hilt of the knife and drove it all the way through his neck until the hilt vanished entirely into the flesh under Smiley's ear.

For a second Smiley stood there and then he fell straight back.

"Asshole," I repeated. "Bringing a gun to a knife fight ..."

I crawled over and wrenched the shotgun away from him, sat up on one hip and opened the gun. There was one unfired shell in the left barrel and a spent one in the right barrel. With the point of the twine cutter I extracted the bright red spent shell and dropped it. Then I closed the shotgun and propped it up under his chin. If he had been telling me the truth, that shell was loaded with nineteen flechettes, razor-sharp steel arrows about an inch long.

"'Bye."

The shot erased his face and his mind and I crawled towards the cabin.

Epilogue

I untied Al and Don and they took me to Marie's place and she took me in and filled me with guilt and recriminations. I ignored her and called Claire, who arrived two days later, although I didn't notice at the time because I was drifting, awash in a sea of agony. I was feverish and dreaming the whole mess over and over again, trying to make it come out differently.

Claire sewed the holes in my body together with undyed silk thread and heavy-gauge needles. She used a pair of needle-nosed pliers to push the needle through the astonishing thickness of my skin as I screamed into a rolled-up towel. We salted the wounds with diluted iodine to stop infection. We could have used fresh urine but we agreed that would have been gross.

We were terrified of infection and of doctors both. Infection would have killed me ugly, and doctors would have led to cops, who would have led to jail and a different kind of ending. The wounds went sour quickly, turning septic, and Claire drained them over and over and washed them clean with more iodine and distilled water.

When I could walk without too much pain I started to take the children again, using Marie's house while I figured out what to do with my own booby-trapped home. And when I was fairly steady and the fever itself broke, I was sent off to deposit the money I'd earned from Marie. My first honest pay, carefully washed in casinos, earned by helping to smuggle and by theft and assault and assorted violence.

But still the first really large sum of honest money I'd ever made, and I took it to the local bank to deposit it just like a real citizen.

That is where the bank robbery happened. Where I started this, and, you know what?

When I think about it honestly, it was all entirely my fault.

Acknowledgements

I'd like to acknowledge the support and aid of the Manitoba Arts Council and the Canada Council for the Arts. I'd like to thank Turnstone Press for their superb editing, advice and support. More thanks goes out to David N., William, Lois, Alison, Sēanin, Morgan and Erik for putting up with me. Even more thanks goes out to Robert and T, Kathryn L., Pat S., Rick R., Bill and Joan M., Ron and Carol, Chad and Wendy, Paul and Holly, Wayne T., Joan, Charlene, Mary Lou, Karen, Perry, Tavia and Cameron M. along with others too numerous to mention.

And, as always, my thanks to those in the shadows. Quis ipsos . . .

Michael Van Rooy was born in Kamloops, BC and raised in Winnipeg. His first book, *An Ordinary Decent Criminal*, won the 2006 Eileen McTavish Sykes Award for Best First Book by a Manitoba Writer, and Van Rooy was a finalist for the John Hirsch Award for Most Promising Manitoba Writer. He lives with his family in Winnipeg.